VEILED VIXEN

HAREM STATION

NEW YORK TIMES BESTSELLING AUTHOR, JA HUSS, WRITING AS

KC ROSS

VEILED VIXEN

NEW YORK TIMES BESTSELLING AUTHOR, JA HUSS WRITING AS

KC CROSS

Edited by RJ Locksley
Cover Photo: Sara Eirew
Cover Design by JA Huss

ABOUT THE BOOK

KC Cross is the not-so-secret naughty pen name of New York Times bestselling author, JA Huss (who normally writes filthy romantic suspense).

Valor only wants one thing for his fated princess, Veila.

Death.

But it's kind of hard to kill someone when they have total control over your body. He only has one weapon in his arsenal – the soulmate bond.

Valor has to make Veila believe that their bond is true, that his feelings are real, and that he is willing to sell out his brothers, take over Harem Station, and leave his old life behind to help her win the final war with ALCOR and become the ruling queen.

But it's never going to happen. Valor will never love

Veila. Ever. He'd rather die trying to kill her than spend one moment as her puppet king.

There's just one problem.

The soulmate bond goes both ways.

Veiled Vixen is book six in the Harem Station series and features an army of pissed-off princesses, five brothers facing their past, a station filled with angry ruthless outlaws, and a lesson in what matters. It's a love story about revenge, and hate, and regrets – but also forgiveness, loyalty, family, and having the courage to see the truth behind the veil.

PART ONE

CHAPTER ONE

Alone in darkness.

That's the only way to describe what the exit from cryosleep feels like. You are nothing and no one and then… boom, you're something else.

It's different than coming out of regular sleep in two ways:

One, waking up from regular sleep, for me, always starts in a dreamlike state. You kinda know where you're at—the place where you fell asleep—and you kinda know you were just dreaming—damn, that was a weird one, right? Why was I doing that? And then you open your eyes and you're like… *Yeah, new day. OK. Let's do this.*

Waking up from cryosleep isn't like that at all. It's like being born. There is nothingness, blackness, and a sense of nonexistence and then boom! You are in the dark. Not awake, not asleep, not dreaming, but not lucid either. A sense of otherworldness.

And you stay there for a long time. It's like being utterly lost. It's creepy, and scary, and there is this building panic inside you that you will never find your way out.

Two, when you do finally come out of it there is an utter and complete sense of dislocation. You are almost never in the last place you remember. Obviously. Unless you're on some inter-galaxy cruise ship and you went to sleep on purpose because you're one of those people who likes to travel to distant places that are lifetimes away, you don't wake up where you went down.

I've only been in and out seven times total, including this one, so maybe this isn't typical. I'm not into galaxy-wide traveling. When I go into a cryopod it's because Luck and I had some bad luck, no pun intended, and I got hurt severely enough to warrant a cryopod to save my life until we could get to a proper medical facility.

That sense of lostness is done on purpose, I think. I'm no expert on this shit but it happens to everyone and I'm pretty sure someone told me at one time or another that this is part of the wake-up protocol. It's a chance to come to terms with your sense of self because let's face it, cryosleep isn't normal. It fucks with your head. And I've heard that if you do it enough you lose parts of yourself each time you wake.

Which I can totally see happening.

Seven is going to be my limit. There are no long trips in my future that require cryosleep, that's for sure. I'm done. I don't like it because each of the times I've been woken up, I've come out screaming.

Including this one.

"You're OK," Crux says, his hands on my shoulders, gripping and shaking me slightly. "You're OK, Valor. Just calm down and look at me. OK? Look

at me, brother. You're home. You're fine. You're…
you're gonna be fine."

But here's another thing I hate about waking up
from cryosleep. You can hear them talking to you. You
can hear yourself screaming, you can think clearly, and
you can rationalize and understand these words.

But you cannot *stop* the screaming. You have no
control over your body, or your innate instincts, or
your reactions. So you just keep screaming.

It scares me. I'm not too manly to admit that. And
I do know that how I come out isn't the same as how
anyone else comes out. The screaming, that is. Because
Luck doesn't come out screaming, he comes out
swinging.

This makes me smile. Internally, of course.
Because I'm still screaming like an out-of-control freak
and have no control over my body yet. But I smile
inside because that last time Luck came out of cryo he
hit me in the eye. Fucking fist of his is like a sundamned
piece of steel and my eye swelled up and needed anti-
inflammatory injections so I could see that day.

But there is also something else unusual about
how I wake up. I have this sense of having *been
somewhere*.

It's not a dream. It's really not like that at all. It's
more like… a possibility. Like I might've been there.
Or like I *could've* been there.

Which is different in a very subtle way. Might've
been there, as in maybe I was in a place and maybe I
wasn't. But *could've been there* is more like I *was somewhere*
and it could be this place, or that place, or no place at
all.

It's very confusing.

11

I've asked Luck about this before and he had no idea what I was talking about. He says waking up from cryo is like being thrust through a spin node. Which I never understood before now because as far as I knew, he'd never been through a spin node. And neither had I, at that point anyway—that was a long time before this little adventure with Tray—so I didn't really get it.

Well, I get it now.

Waking up from cryosleep is that in-between, left-behind feeling I experienced when Tray and I were traveling back and forth between the spin-node gate and—

"Valor," Crux says.

I've stopped screaming.

"Open your eyes, Valor. You're awake now and I need you to open your eyes."

I open them.

Crux and Serpint are staring down at me, leaning so close to my face both my hands come up and push them back.

Serpint laughs. "There he is. Welcome back, asshole. Have a nice trip?"

I suck in a deep breath of air and then cough like crazy when it comes back out. "No," I croak. "No, I didn't." My voice is raspy and deep. "Where the fuck—"

"You're back on Harem," Crux says, offering me his hand.

I look at it for a moment, wondering why he wants to shake my hand, then realize I'm lying inside a cryopod and take it, allowing him to help me up into a sitting position.

But I'm not in medical. I'm in my fucking quarters.

"We had you brought here," Crux explains. "To make waking up a little easier."

"Yeah, you were always a wuss when it came to cryosleep," Serpint says. "And for some reason that bitch princess of yours didn't mind when we said this would be better."

"Who?" I ask, looking around at my quarters. I feel like I haven't seen this place in several lifetimes. And then I laugh a little. Or kinda cough. Because I lived several lifetimes since I left here.

"Veila," Crux growls. "She brought you here."

Both hands come up to my head and grab my hair. "What the fuck are you talking about?"

"Yeah," Serpint says, grabbing one forearm while Crux grabs the other. "We've got a lot to tell you, brother. So nap time is over." They pull me out and drag me over to the couch, then unceremoniously let me flop back into the cushions. "We're at war, did you know that?"

I sorta remember this. But only vaguely. So I don't respond.

"Nyleena," Crux says. "Remember? Tray told her and Luck to distract the Baby and Succubus so you and Tray could leave with *Booty* and Asshole?"

I scrunch up my face, because that wasn't how it happened.

"Yeah, you two fuckers," Serpint says, falling into the couch cushions next to me and pulling me into a hug so my face is smothered by his chest. Then he gives me a head noogie, which I immediately pull away from. "You and Tray, good plan, man. Leaving on *Booty* with the Asshole. Baby was pissed off about that."

I look at Serpint and he's smiling at me, one of those clenched-teeth smiles that isn't really a smile, but more like a... warning. Then his eyes dart up to the ceiling real quick, and then focus back on me.

Ah. I get it. That's the Harem Station Brothers Universal Signal for *Don't forget, he sees everything.* Meaning ALCOR, but actually, right now, meaning Baby.

I nod. "Right," I say. "I remember now."

"Well, things have gone from bad to worse since you left," Crux says. "Let me just summarize—"

"Dude," I say, putting up a hand. "Can you just... give me a minute? You know how much I hate waking up from cryo. And before that I was—"

"I get it," Crux says, interrupting me. I take that to mean he wants me to shut the fuck up until he can stealth-debrief me. So I do. Shut the fuck up, that is. "Get him something to drink, Serpint. That drink we give the princesses when we first wake them up."

"On it," Serp says, jumping up to his feet and crossing the room to the autocook.

While he's punching in codes for the drink Crux takes a seat on the coffee table in front of me and leans forward. "A lot has happened since you left with *Booty*, Valor. Like I can't even stress how much has changed here while you've been gone."

"How long?" I ask. "How long has it been?"

"Six weeks Harem time," Crux says.

"What? How is that possible? It was only a few days—"

"You've been here in cryo for a while. Veila didn't want to wake you up until we had things... *settled.*"

"What things?" And now I'm getting a very bad feeling. Six fucking weeks. "Where the hell is Tray? And—"

"I'm getting to that," Crux says, once again interrupting me. He flicks his eyes at the ceiling.

"Right. OK. I just have a lot of questions."

Questions like where is Tray? And Brigit? Not that they would know who Brigit is. And Draden, and the Akeelian girls, and Angel Station, and Earth…

There is so much I need to tell them.

"Here's the thing," Crux says, just as Serpint comes back and hands me a pink drink. I look at it dubiously as Crux talks. "There is no more Harem Station. We're done. It's over. Veila has taken control and—"

"Whoa, whoa, whoa," I say. "What the hell are you talking about?"

Crux sighs as he and Serpint trade uneasy glances. "The security beacons are offline, Valor. Veila has control of the station. What Luck and Nyleena are doing down on levels zero through ninety-five doesn't even matter at this point. The Baby has made a deal with Veila and they are in control up *here*. It's only a matter of time before they reroute the life support systems down below and kill everyone off. We need you to go down there and talk some sense into Luck."

I smile at him. Wink. He juts his chin back a little like he's surprised by my reaction.

"I'm fuckin' serious," Crux says.

"Yeah, yeah. You want me to go down there and *talk sense* into Luck. Sure thing. I'll do that."

"No, Valor," Serpint says. "You don't understand. We *really* need you to control Luck. Because Veila is going to *kill him*. She's going to kill everyone if we don't have full control over the lower levels in two spins."

But now I'm confused. Weren't they just hinting that we're being watched and this whole conversation is for the benefit of Veila and the Baby?

"Can you do that?" Crux asks.

"Can I do what?"

Crux sighs through clenched teeth. "Go talk to Luck and make him surrender. Because if he doesn't…" Crux doesn't finish. Just shrugs with his hands and sighs.

I'm just about to answer him when the door to my quarters opens with a quick whooshing sound and who walks in?

That fuckin' bitch Veila.

"I'll take it from here," she says waving a hand in the air. She's wearing a long, silver, sequined gown and her silver hair is up in the highest hairstyle I've ever seen. Like she's as tall as Serpint with that pile of hair swirling around the top of her head.

I get to my feet and rush towards her, ready to rip that fucking hair right out of her scalp. But Crux and Serpint both yank me back by the arms.

"You think you can what?" I growl at her. "Just come to my home and threaten my brothers and I'll fall in line? Fuck you, Veila."

It all comes out as a low, rumbling, threat.

Veila. God, I hate this woman.

Last year Serpint came home with Queen Corla. The queen of all the Cygnians. Crux's soulmate. The mother of his children. But she arrived here in a cryopod and we haven't been able to wake her up

16

because once we did that her pod would send a signal to the Cygnians and they would know where she was.

At least that was the original reason.

But pretty much at the same time that Serpint was bringing Corla here to Harem another Cygnian princess was brought in by some random bounty hunter.

That was Lyra.

Mouthy, defiant, luminosity-challenged, Lyra.

Until we learned that she was sent out of the Cygnian System with her sister, Nyleena, on a mission to blow up a place called Earth, but was actually trying to escape Cygnian control and was using some kind of inhibitor to disguise her pink princess status.

Then we learned she was Serpint's soulmate and from there this whole soulmate thing kinda blew up. Which is a joke. A bad one. Because it turns out these sexy Cygnian girls who light up when they orgasm are actually made to be… bombs.

That's right. They are all a bunch of explosives.

Then Jimmy got caught up with another Cygnian princess—Delphi. Who, turns out, is Corla and Crux's daughter—*real daughter*, that is. Not like how Jimmy and Crux are brothers-from-another-mother kinda of daughter. And even though Jimmy and Delphi are *not* genetically engineered soulmates and that means somewhere out there is Jimmy's real soulmate, Jimmy and Delphi are pretending they are. Soulmates, that is.

Then Luck came home and yup. Nyleena was his soulmate.

Which kinda pissed me off because up until that time Luck and I were… well, not soulmates. Because that's just dumb. But we were definitely best friends.

17

And then we weren't. Because of Nyleena.

That's when I figured out Veila was *my* soulmate. And even if I hadn't seen that crazy message she sent Jimmy while they were all escaping her creepy Lair Station and been told about her sicko breeding program she was running on it using Akeelian boys, I'd still hate that bitch.

Because she is fuckin' evil.

I'm talking evil as in she farms Akeelians for genetics and tortures people.

And by people I mean me. She did that to *me*. And probably Jimmy too.

All of that is enough for me as far as this hate goes. But she's also a vicious, vindictive, and heartless woman. Always barking orders, and fucking shit up, and generally acting like she owns the sundamned universe.

And she doesn't. OK? She doesn't. There's no way I believe this harpy is at the top of the food chain.

No. I refuse to believe that.

"OK," Crux says, pushing me back with two flat hands to my chest. "Just calm down for a minute."

"Calm down?" I scoff. "Do you have any idea what she did to me on her ship? Any fucking idea? I will not just calm down. And if you think I'm selling out Luck for this bitch, you can both go fuck yourselves. I know Luck. I know him better than anyone. And he'd rather die than sign on as some side act to this shit show."

"Listen to me," Serpint growls in my face. "You have no idea what's happening here, OK?"

"Leave us," Veila commands. "Now."

18

Both Crux and Serpint look at her, then at me. And I'm sure, like one hundred percent positive, their rage is directed at me, not Veila.

"What the fuck, Serpint? Don't look at me like that."

"She—" Serpint starts.

"Leave. Now." Veila cuts him off. "Or there will be consequences."

Both Crux and Serpint trade a quick glance, then both of them push past me and storm out of my quarters.

I watch their backs disappear into the hallway, then train my rage on Veila. "*You…*" I seethe. "You have some nerve, lady. How the fuck did I get here?"

She presses her lips together in a smile. "Well, that's quite a story that I don't have time to get into just yet. What I really need from you is—"

"The answer is no," I say. "There's nothing to think about. There's nothing to discuss. I'm not doing anything for you. And if you think asking Serpint and Crux to come in here and talk to me is enough to change my mind, you're delusional."

"They're not betraying you," Veila says, sauntering forward. She passes me with a swish of her diamond-encrusted silver gown, grabbing my pink drink right out of my hand, and takes a seat in an auto-mold chair. She crosses her legs and leans to the side like we're about to have an intimate fireside chat. "I have them by the balls, so to speak. I'm in control of the Baby and we're about two spins away from removing the Succubus AI out of the station data core. And once that happens I will order the Baby to shut off life support on certain levels to speed things up."

19

"They'll just fight their way up, you know. You can't turn the whole station off."

"Oh." She laughs. "No. You misunderstand me. How many people are on this station?"

"I don't know. Ask Crux. He's in charge of the census."

"I have. It was a rhetorical question. There are three point seven five million people currently on Harem Station. Roughly half of those three point seven five million people are on levels ninety-six through four hundred. The other half are all crammed down in the bottom ninety-five."

Damn. I don't say that, but I think it. Damn. That's a lot—

"That's a lot of people down there, wouldn't you agree?"

I don't answer this. Because I see where this is going.

"I won't be turning the life support off on the *lower* levels, Valor. That's so amateur hour. I'll be turning the life support off up *here*."

Which means almost two million people who are currently residing on the top three fourths of the station will have to relocate down to the bottom third when she cuts off their air.

And that means... well. Riots. Fighting. Starvation. Water deprivation. Death.

Forced survival.

And humans in survival mode are not pretty creatures.

This is the quickest way to kill millions of people and make Luck deal with the fallout at the same time so he is either forced to surrender or die fighting and take everyone out with him.

"God, I fucking hate you."

She waves a hand in the air dismissively. "I have very little use for you as well, Valor. But I do need Nyleena and that means I must have Luck's cooperation. You, it seems, are the one person he loves more than his new silver princess. Because I've already tortured Crux and Serpint to compel him to cooperate."

"Luck doesn't work like that," I say.

"So it seems. He didn't even blink when I sent him video of Crux and Serpint being tortured. Not even when I sent him images of Lyra being tortured."

Serpint. God. I don't have a great relationship with the guy, but he's a cool dude and I kinda think he and I might actually be genetically related. And I know he loved Lyra. And what must Nyleena be thinking about that? She is Lyra's sister. What have they all been going through while I was asleep?

"You're going to go down there and *make* Luck surrender."

I laugh. Like it's a full-on guffaw. "Am I?"

"You are. Because if you don't then I will have to resort to more drastic measures."

"You've tortured Crux, Serpint, and Lyra. You're going to deprive three point seven million people of air, water, and food. What else is there?" I ask. "Who else could you dangle in front of him?"

"Oh, not Luck. I might've hit a dead end with Luck. But Jimmy"—she chuckles—"I'm just getting started with Jimmy. You see, I know what Delphi is and I know how to activate her."

21

"What the fuck are you taking about?"

"Bring him in," Veila commands to the air with a flip of her hand.

The door to my quarters opens and a flurry of cyborgs enter. At least six of them. But they're not the main event. Because they're dragging a boy, his feet sliding along the polished obsidian floors.

Late teens. Blue eyes, not violet. So not one of our Akeelian boys. Just a boy.

They thrust him forward and he falls to the floor in a heap, clearly drugged.

"Meet Tycho," Veila says.

"Oh, shit," I mumble. Because Tycho is Delphi's twin brother.

"'Oh, shit' doesn't even begin to cover the epic destruction this boy is capable of. And trust me when I tell you this—I will write this whole station off if I can't get what I came for. I will blow the whole thing up in the blink of an eye. He is quite possibly the most destructive force in the universe. And even though Delphi isn't as valuable as he is, his powers can be boosted if she's nearby."

"What the hell are you talking about?" I ask.

"I'm talking about annihilation, Valor. If you think Corla and I are powerful explosives, well, we are nothing compared to the power contained inside this boy's body. And I'm the only one alive who knows how to unlock him. I will kill everyone, Valor—every single person, borg, bot, and ship on this station—to get what I want. I know your brother is hiding things down below. And I have a very good suspicion what those things are and what they do. The Baby has told me as much. If I can't have them, then no one can."

"You're insane," I spit. "I don't know how you got this way, and frankly, I do not care. But I'm not helping you, Veila. And if you think for one second I believe you'd kill yourself so no one else could have whatever it is you're after, ha." I laugh. "Nice try. But you're far too selfish to go down in flames on principle."

She tilts her head up and laughs. It's one of those mocking laughs that comes with self-assurance. "Kill myself? That's fresh. And funny. No, Valor. You misunderstand. I'm not going down with this ship, so to speak. I'll be leaving on the spin node located on level one hundred twenty-two."

I process that for a moment.

"That's right, sweetie. I know all about it. I might not be able to open that node, but Luck can. Luck *will*," she corrects herself. "And then we can all go to Earth together."

"We?" I ask. "There is no you in the 'we' here on Harem Station, Veila."

She inhales deeply. Takes a long sip of my pink drink. Closes her eyes as the nutrients in that drink flood her body and then opens them to say, "Oh, but there is, my sweet." Then she places a hand over her stomach in a protective manner and pats it. "Our little family is just getting started."

CHAPTER TWO

Tycho is taken out, and while that's happening I think I lose time. I might even throw up in my mouth a little too. Surely she isn't serious. She can't be serious. Hasn't everyone been saying all along that Cygnian princesses have fertility problems?

How does one fake silver princess get pregnant?

Oh, God. Was she fucking me in my sleep?

I turn around and grab my stomach, that's how sick this makes me.

"I know. It's a miracle," she coos.

I gather myself and turn around. "What the fuck are you talking about?"

Veila smiles at me with a sigh. It's a long sigh. One of those contented sighs. And are her cheeks just a little bit flushed?

Normally Veila is pale. It's a good look for her, don't get me wrong. She is ice princess sexbot-hot all day long. But right now she's got a pink glow to her. Her normally silver hair is more the color of a warm sun than a white supernova. It makes her diamond-encrusted gown look classy and regal instead of cutting-edge sharp.

It softens her. Maybe. Just a little.

The drink, I realize. It must be tushberries or some other such fruit that regenerates the flux inside the Cygnian princesses. She is recharging.

Which is all I need. Sun-fucked gods, come save me now. *Please.*

"Listen," Veila says, leaning forward a little. "I get it. I do. You have your loyalties and they've got nothing to do with me. Fine. So be it. But this is bigger than you, Valor. This is bigger than any one person."

"Except for you," I scoff. "You, for whatever reason, seem to think that you're the center of the fucking universe."

She tips her head down but I catch a tight smile on her face before it's obscured by some long, artfully-arranged tendrils of hair that fall forward. "This isn't about me."

I close my eyes and shake my head. "Really? Because from where I'm standing every bad fucking thing that's happened to us in the past year has been about you. You're the one who was stealing Corla—"

"Serpint stole Corla. She was with *me.*"

"You're the one who sent Delphi to kidnap Jimmy—"

"I asked Delphi to bring him to me for a reason, Valor. And if Delphi had done her job none of this would be happening."

"You're the one who sent Brigit to trap Tray—"

"I sent Brigit to Tray because they are meant to be together. I did him a favor. And he got to shape her all these years. She is truly, one hundred percent *his* now."

"Are you fucking kidding me right now? Are you really trying to make yourself into the good guy?"

It's her turn to scoff. "There are no good guys. But I'm certainly not the worst villain out there, that's for sure."

"Right." I laugh. "Well, you're the only one who shows up time, after time, after time to ruin our lives."

"I'm as much a victim of circumstances as you are."

"Oh, please!" Now I actually guffaw and shake my head. "Well, I might have two cocks but you, Veila? You've got two sets of giant Akeelian balls if you've talked yourself into believing that absurd twist of reality."

"I'm pregnant."

"You are not," I insist. Because it can't be true. It can*not* be true. If she's pregnant... well, I don't know what happens next, but from the way everyone is trying to stop her from getting pregnant, it just can't be good.

She shrugs and leans back into the cushions, pulling her legs up and arranging them to the side, then takes another long sip of the pink drink.

She glows this time.

And yup. That glow. That glow is mine all right. Because both of my cocks start to stiffen under my pants. God, I hate this. Why? Why me? Why do I have to be connected to this psycho bitch?

"It's not your baby," she finally says.

"What?"

She pats her stomach. "I was going to lie and say that it was, but—" She closes her eyes for a long second, then opens them again. "You'd find out eventually. And I'm getting the feeling you wouldn't be possessive about your offspring the way most men are.

27

You just don't have deep feelings like that, do you, Valor?"

"Fuck you," I say. "I have plenty of deep feelings for people who… you know, care about me."

"Luck," she says.

I shrug. "He's one of them."

"And Tray. And maybe Brigit?"

"Look, if you think I'm going to start spilling my guts because of this little vulnerable act you're pulling, think again. You are a liar. And sure, there are worse vices out there. Murder, for one. Megalomaniacs are pretty up there as far as assholes go. Narcissists. Selfish, greedy cheaters. Villainous monsters, et cetera, et cetera, et cetera. But from where I stand, you've got them all covered."

"Is that so?"

I shrug big with my hands. "If the tiara fits, as they say."

"No one says that."

"I'm pretty sure someone says that."

She waves her hand in the air dismissively, which seems to be her go-to gesture when she's done with a topic. "At any rate, the baby is not yours."

"Whose is it?"

"Does it matter?"

"If it's Jimmy's? Then yeah, it matters."

She squints at me. "Jimmy's?"

"You were into him, right?"

"Maybe. For like half a spin. He's a nice-looking man. But no. He's not my soulmate."

"No, that's me."

"Valor," she says, shaking her head and setting the pink drink on the coffee table. "We have no

28

connection. We both know that. It's just… not in the stars for us. So I have moved on. You don't have to worry about *that*."

"Whose baby?"

"It doesn't matter. The only thing that matters is that I'm pregnant and I will do anything to bring this pregnancy to term. *Anything*."

"So what the fuck do you want from me?"

"I want you to go talk some sense into Luck. Make him surrender and…"

"And take you through the spin node to Earth?" I finish for her. "It's never going to happen." I laugh. "He's never going to do that. Hell, he kept that node secret from me all these years. It means something important. And if you think Luck can be manipulated like that, you've pegged him wrong. Luck is… Luck is…" There's so many ways to finish that sentence, I get a little lost in all the things Luck is. "Strong," I finally finish. "He's loyal, and he's strong, and he…" I shake my head. "He's fearless."

She stares at me for a long moment, face impassive, possibly contemplative. Finally she says, "I know he took you through it. I know you and Tray didn't leave here on *Booty Hunter*. Your brothers are not subtle. Someone should tell them they're terrible liars."

"You know what? I think that's a trait more people should cultivate. Terrible liar is actually one of the top ten things I look for in a friend."

"Perhaps." She sighs, then looks away, out the window of my quarters. Which doesn't have much of a view since I'm so high up in the station, but there's a hummingbird on the other side of the glass, flitting and

29

flapping its tiny wings against the window like it thinks Veila is a glowing flower with sweet nectar inside.

Move along, little bird. She is not the bloom you're looking for.

It does. And Veila turns back to me. "Did Lyra, or Nyleena, or any of them tell you what it's like back in the Cygnian System?"

"What?" I frown at her. "No. Not that I ever asked. Not that I ever cared. But I imagine it's terrible."

"It is," she says, then turns her head away to stare out the window. "It was… horrific."

"Yeah, that's not going to work," I say. "I don't give two fucks how awful your childhood was, OK? I'm not going to talk to Luck. I'm not going to do any favors for you no matter what sob story you tell. So just save your breath."

"I'd heard about you guys. You're all pretty famous in the home system." She turns to look at me. Smiles. Glows pink. Her true color, I remind myself. "But we only had mock-up representations of you on the magazine covers."

"What?" I ask, confused.

"You Harem boys. I'm sure they had pictures." She waves her hand through the air again, like she wants to dismiss that thought. But then she continues anyway. "And video. I mean, how could they not?"

I'm not sure if that's a real question. So I say nothing.

"You boys were all over the galaxy having all your adventures. They knew who you were. Well, hell, of course they did. They knew you boys long before you came here to Harem. Did Crux ever tell you about his initial meeting with Corla?"

"I heard parts."

"Doesn't matter. My point is... you boys didn't realize it, but you were famous in the home system. But now that I think about it, the pictures on the covers of the magazines might've just represented all of the Akeelian boys. Not you Harem boys specifically. They made you look like monsters. Sexy monsters, for sure. But still."

I scoff. "God, you people are sick. I don't think 'sexy' and 'monsters' go together. Not even a little bit."

"No?" She looks puzzled. "Well, the princesses. Not me specifically, but all of us. We're all sexy. And we're all monsters. So I think you're wrong there."

Can't really argue with that.

"So... were the stories true?"

"What?" I ask. "What stories?"

"Every month they put out a magazine called *Akeelian Adventures*. It was more of a graphic novel. Like I said, they portrayed you Akeelians as... kind of the ideal monster. But they did use your real names. So, for instance, one month would be about you and Luck. And the next month would be about Jimmy and Xyla. Tray and ALCOR. I never understood why ALCOR was in the comics. Maybe just as your supreme leader?"

"They... wrote *comics* about us?"

"After you boys came here to ALCOR Station they were about you specifically. Before that they were different. Just kind of generic names. There was AI-Man, and Bounty Hunter, and Bot Boy." She laughs. Glows a little brighter too. "Stupid kind of superhero names like that. But then after Corla, you know... Once you guys left the station they used your real names."

31

"What were the comics about?" I'm intrigued now. I hate to admit that, but it's sorta creepy and flattering at the same time.

She does that hand wave again. And I'm starting to wonder what's behind that gesture. Is she dismissing things? Or something else?

Regardless, she continues. "You and Luck were always doing crazy things on ancient stations. Looking for AI parts and old tech. Salvaging things."

"Hmm," I hum. "That's what we really did."

"I know that now. But I didn't back then. I didn't think you were real at all. Not until I left the system and found out for myself. So I wonder how much was true?"

"No clue, lady. And this subject change you're doing right now? What do you take me for? Some two-cocked fool? I mean, look. You're the most accomplished liar I know, Veila. Congrats, by the way. I mean, I've met all kinds here on Harem. It's nothing but liars and cheaters all day long. You're the best. But here's the thing about being a liar, Veila. Eventually no one believes you. So I don't know what you're trying to pull with this whole pregnancy thing, but leading me down this little path of childhood myths and comics to gain my trust or lower my defenses is just—well, insulting. OK? It is. I'm happy to go down to the lower levels to see Luck. I miss him. So I'll do that. But here's something you should know about me, OK? I'm not one of those people who give a lot of fucks. I'm not someone who eats the guilt of others. So if you think you can talk me into believing that suffocating those three point seven million people here on Harem will be my fault?"

I pause to guffaw out a, "Ha!" which elicits a scowl from her.

"It's not gonna work. I don't operate like that. I'm not a guilt eater. I don't have this inner desire to fix things, or save people, or whatever. And Luck isn't like that either. He'll come save your ass if he's your friend or whatever. Like he did Jimmy. But that's because he's arrogant. Really. That's all it is. He's just an arrogant asshole who likes to swoop in and be heroic because it makes him look good. So you threatening him, or me, with this 'gotta save the station' bullshit? No, Veila. It won't work on us. Crux?" I nod my head. "Yeah. That's more his style. But the rest of us? We're just a bunch of outlaws. So if you want to kill everyone on this station?" I shrug with my hands. "That's all you, baby."

She inhales deeply and again, she glows a little. Rose gold. Not silver. Which I kind of hate and love at the same time because the silvers remind me of cold. Like cold, dark space. And the golds are like warm blankets in a drafty stargazing room. They have heat to them.

Even Nyleena creeps me out with her silver persona. I know she can't help it, but I just don't see the attraction.

Is Veila beautiful? Sure. Do I want to fuck her? No. I don't care how excited my cocks get, my boys are not interested. There's no love behind the way she gets me hard. That's just engineered biology.

"Are you done?" she asks, her brows tilting in towards the center of her eyes.

"Sure. I'm done."

"So you think I'm lying?"

"About the baby? Or about killing all the people?"

"We can start with the baby, if you'd like."

"Yes, Veila. I think you're lying."

She stands up, straightens her long skirts, and says, "Fine. Come with me and I'll prove it."

Her bright, flashing eyes lock with mine as she approaches me, some weird mixture of colors I'm not sure has a name—silver, and gold, and pink—so that they almost look... violet. Then with one hand on my chest she pushes me back as she slides past and heads towards the door.

"Come with you where?"

"The medical facilities. Presumably you have an imaging machine up there somewhere?"

"I... have no clue."

She stops and looks over her shoulder at me. "Trust me. You do. I've already used it to verify the pregnancy. But we can do it again."

Then she beckons me with one crooked finger, turns around, and walks through the door.

CHAPTER THREE

Up in the harem medical center the Cyborg Master is none too happy about being used to verify Veila's pregnancy. His slash of an eye races back and forth across his forehead in an expression I've seen enough times over the years to recognize as anger.

But he says nothing. He's never liked me much. Serpint and Draden were always his favorites after Crux. The rest of us... not so much.

"Remove your garments and lie on the table, please," he tells Veila.

I sigh and rub my hand over my eyes. "Should I give you some privacy?"

"That won't be necessary," Veila says. "But you can give me a hand with this zipper. If it's not too much to ask."

She turns her back to me and lifts up a few stray tendrils of hair, bending her head forward a little, which elongates the line of her neck and I get a little lost in the way her dangling jeweled earrings brush against the top of her pale shoulders.

I sigh and pull the zipper down, then back away and lean against the wall, directing my gaze to the

Cyborg Master as we both pretend a silver princess isn't undressing in front of us.

"So how's things?" the Master asks.

I shrug. "Can't complain, I guess. Could always be worse."

"True," he agrees. "There's always that."

I glance at Veila, who has removed her outer skirts and is placing them carefully over the back of a chair.

"Where is Tray?" he asks.

I huff and nod my head at Veila. "Ask her."

"I have no idea," Veila answers. Her back is to us as she fusses with some buttons on the front of her gown, so the Master and I both relax a little. "He escaped."

"He did?" I ask.

"He did. So did Brigit." Veila slips her underskirts down her legs and steps out of them, once again placing them neatly on the back of the chair. "But I don't really understand how that happened. So…" She looks over her shoulder at me and purses her lips. "I'm afraid I don't have any other information for you."

"How did I even get here?" I ask.

"Don't you remember?" She's taking off her bodice coat now, slipping one arm out at a time. "Tray saved you. Or"—she chuckles, placing the coat on top of the skirts—"he tried. He negotiated with me to put you in that pod and shoot you out into space."

She's only wearing lingerie now. A tight pink bustier that barely reaches her hipbones and matching lace panties that show a lot of ass.

The Cyborg Master rolls his head at me in a gesture that says, *Can you believe this woman?*

I fold my arms over my chest and roll my eyes back in agreement. *Such balls.*

"But of course, your pod has a tracker. So I tracked you down after the battle and picked you up. So here we are." Her voice lifts up at the end of that sentence. Like this is all good fun. She reaches a hand over her shoulder and taps a shoulder blade. "Do you mind unhooking me, please?"

"If you need help undressing," I say, so annoyed at this request, "why do you even wear shit like this?"

"Because it's pretty," she says. "And I like it." She shoots me a side-eyed glare.

I motion to the Master to see if he'd like to—

"Uh, no," he says quickly. "She's all yours, Valor."

I reluctantly walk forward and start unhooking the seventy-four million hook and eye clasps of her bustier, sighing and fuming the entire time. Because like it or not, we are soulmated and each time my fingertips brush up against her skin I feel my cocks jump in my pants.

When I get to the button in the middle of her back she lets out a long breath.

"Oh, God. Feels good to breathe again." Her shoulders quake slightly as she enjoys her new freedom and this sends a shiver clawing its way up my spine.

I hold my breath and force my fingers to finish, then back away as the bustier slips down her body and falls to the floor at her feet.

She bends, picking it up. Then places it over the coat.

At this point I wouldn't be able to drag my eyes away from her if I was trying—and I'm no longer trying. She hooks her fingers into the waist of her panties, tugs and inches them over one hip at a time, until they fall down her legs and land at her feet.

I turn away before she bends over to pick them up. Staring straight at the door.

Nope. Nope. I will not let this shrew entice me with her womanly wiles.

"OK. I'm ready."

I turn back and find her lying on the medical table, breasts round and firm, nipples peaked up towards the ceiling.

The Master jolts out of his self-imposed stillness, walks over to the controls on the wall, and starts the scan.

This is… not a scan I've seen before. A single ring emerges from the wall, beaming light down onto Veila as it traverses down the length of her body and stops at her feet.

I wait for it to travel back up, but it doesn't.

"What's happening?" I ask. "Is the scan done? Why isn't it retracting?"

"This is a real-time scan," the Master says, pointing at the wall screen. "There they are."

I turn away from Veila and look at the screen.

And sure enough, there, in perfect 3-D color, are two babies.

Two. A boy and a girl. Because that's how it's done with our species.

But… "What are they? Akeelians? Or Cygnians?"

If they're Akeelians then before that boy can be born it will drain all the nutrients from the girl and she will die. And Veila will probably steal her mind and turn her into…

"Can you give us a moment?" Veila asks.

38

"I'll be right outside," the Master says.

I barely notice him leave. I'm too busy looking at the tiny children on the monitor. Wondering how such a fucked-up reproductive process even evolved.

"Well?" Veila says. "Are you convinced now? The scan was performed in your presence and it's a live feed."

There are hands. And feet. And two human faces. Eyes tightly closed, little puckered mouths. They are too large on screen, so the scan must be magnifying it. "How far along?" I ask without turning around.

"Nine weeks."

"Nine," I mumble, running through a list of possibilities who these children belong to.

Not me. If I've been asleep for six weeks, then nope. They are not mine. But if not me, then who?

None of us were with her nine weeks ago. We were all here on Harem dealing with normal shit. I guess maybe it's possible that she farmed genetics out of Jimmy when she had him on Lair Station. But then how did she get pregnant? If he's not her One and I am?

I don't want to face Veila. Her naked body is doing weird things to me. Shivers slide up my spine like bubbles and there is a deep desire in my gut to fuck her.

It's just biology, I tell myself as I close my eyes tight. *It's engineered biology. Not feelings.*

"Do you want to hear the heartbeats?"

"What?"

"Press that button on the control there."

I look at the panel in front of me, trying to figure out which button she's talking about.

"The black one with the speaker icon."

I press it. A soft whooshing sound fills the room. And then the twins inside her diverge and it doubles into two rhythmic, soothing heartbeats.

I press it again and the room goes silent.

"There," Veila says. "Are you happy now?"

"Happy? I wasn't specifically *un*happy about this, so no. I'm not suddenly happy. I'm... confused." I turn to face her. "Who?" I ask, and for some reason my voice is low and filled with anger. "*Who* got you pregnant?"

She lies there on the table just staring up at the ceiling. No expression on her face. Not some smug smile or some cunning grin. Just... nothing as she looks up at the lights above her. "It doesn't matter. I've been pregnant many times before."

"What? I thought—"

"Oh, it's not hard to *get* pregnant. But it is extremely difficult to *stay* pregnant. Bringing a true Cygnian princess to term in the womb is... impossible."

She glows a little when she says this. And something inside me responds. Not my cocks getting hard, but something else. Something new that I don't recognize.

"Then how did Delphi get here?"

Veila purses her lips. "Do you mind?" She points to the wall panel controls. "Can you press the return button so I can get out of this machine and put my clothes back on?"

I blink at her, then turn and press the button. I stay facing the panel until I know she's up and out of the machine and slipping her panties back on.

40

"I'll need your help with this."

And when I turn back she's facing me, holding the bustier to her chest. She turns away and bows her head.

Reluctantly I walk over to her and begin buttoning her up. And again, each time my fingertips touch her bare skin something inside me... swells.

A want. A need to touch her all over. To fuck her.

But then I think about the babies and some of that feeling ebbs back.

"How did Delphi and Tycho get here, Veila? What you're saying doesn't make sense."

"Corla went somewhere special to ensure her babies lived. They need... they have... issues, Valor. Immune issues. They don't belong here, and while we were able to genetically change the embryos—that's how the Cygnians have been breeding all these years—when we engineer them they are just not the same as when they are born naturally. They are a different species altogether. I am not the same species as those babies inside me. They are true Angels." Her voice drops to a whisper. "And that is why it's so hard."

Angels.

Angel Station.

The other galaxy Tray and I went to.

Earth.

"You know I'm not a real silver. They changed me into this. Leveled me up, I guess they call it. So I have all the right parts, I even have the right hormones. But they don't work right." She sighs. Like she's tired. Of this topic, or this struggle, or maybe even this life. "I can carry them for a while, but then they die." She pauses, then adds, "They always die."

41

I look back at the monitor as I continue to button her up. It's not a live feed anymore. Just a still shot. "I don't understand. Is that boy in there—inside you—is he Akeelian? Or Cygnian?"

"He's both. *They* are both. Because that's what Angels are. The original Akeelian and Cygnian races were once merged. Surely you know what ALCOR did to ruin us?"

I don't answer her, just finish the last button and take a few steps back, wanting to create distance between us.

She keeps her back towards me as she fastens her underskirts, then outskirts, and finally slips her arms through her jacket. Then she turns to face me, her jacket open so I can see her perfectly round breasts cradled in her bustier, her whole body flushed rose gold once more. And when she takes a deep breath I can tell it's strained. Like her bustier is too tight and she can't fully inhale.

"What about Nyleena?" I ask. "Can she…?"

"I don't know. Maybe. It's doubtful though. She was probably pregnant dozens of times before she ever left the Cygnian System. And if she were able to carry full-term Angels then they would never have let her leave with Lyra. So my guess would be no."

I'm still focused on the words 'pregnant dozens of times' and can't really process the rest. "Wait," I say, rubbing both hands down my face. "They…"

"Yes," Veila says when I don't finish. "Yes. That's what they do to us. It starts at age eleven and I'm sure that's what Nyleena's life was like until she was assigned to a suicide mission with Lyra."

42

"But they were sending them to Earth," I say. "Lyra told us that. To blow it up."

"Oh, please." Veila laughs. "They can't even *find* Earth. And if they did, the last thing they'd do is blow it up. Not when it's the secret." She huffs. "Valor. Earth is where we're from. Don't you get it? The reason we can't reproduce naturally is because we need to *be* there. The children here, in this galaxy, don't have the right receptors for the hormones necessary to bring the pregnancy to term. It's that simple. And the solution is simple as well. We need to go back to Earth because it's our home."

"Oh," I laugh. "Oh, yeah. That's good." I point at her. "You had me going for a minute there."

Veila is scowling at me. "What are you talking about?"

"Earth." I huff. "Right. I get it. You need to get there. You know we have a spin node here on the station. And somehow you've figured out that Luck is in control of it. Fine. I'll admit to all that. But if you think I'm stupid enough to fall for this…" I pan my hand at the still shot of the babies on the monitor. "This pregnant woman bullshit—"

"What?" she huffs.

"No," I say. "Nope. Not gonna happen. You're… you're… you're the most disgusting thing I've ever seen in my life. And those babies inside you?" I point to her stomach. "They're better off dying inside you. Oh, God." I turn away from her and grab my hair. "I can't even imagine what kind of mother you'd make. Just… *gross*."

When I turn back her face is blank.

No emotion there at all.

43

"You stole someone's genetics, right? To make those babies? Who did you take them from? Some ten-year-old Akeelian boy?"

"How *dare* you," she snarls.

"How dare I?" I laugh. "You were caught on Lair Station milking boys for sperm!"

"Don't be ridiculous! They don't even make sperm until they're eleven."

"Oh, excuse me," I say. Placing my hand over my heart in a feigned apologetic gesture. "Some eleven-year-old Akeelian boy. My bad."

"You're insane!"

"*I'm* insane?"

"We weren't taking sperm from them. We were collecting hormones produced in the testicular glands that are only produced when the second cock—"

I gufaw so loud she startles. "Collecting hormones? You're unbelievable, you know that? How do you live with yourself? You might be pretty on the outside, Veila. But I have never, in my entire life, seen a more disgusting person on the inside."

"You don't understand. We need that hormone and it's only produced in boys under the age of twelve—"

"Oh." I throw up my arms. "Well, since you *need* it, that makes it all better."

"You have no idea how much I've struggled—"

"I don't give one fucked sun about your struggle, lady. You're an evil, maniacal bitch and if you think I can be persuaded over to your side with a couple of heartbeats, well…" I shake my head. "I'll save you the trouble. It's not going to work." I point to her stomach. "I hope they die. I *want* them to die."

44

"You're sick."

"I'm sick? I'm not the one breeding boys—"

"I'm not breeding boys!"

"Milking boys—"

"Collecting hormones!"

"Same fucking thing! Don't you get that? Those aren't *your* hormones to take, Veila! You're stealing bodily fluids from kids!"

"Fine." She throws up her hands. "Since you refuse to listen to me, then fine. That's what I'm doing."

"That is what you're doing! I saw those kids we rescued from Lair Station. They are damaged because of you. And now you bring me in here, show me live feed of your embryonic twins and fill the room with the sound of heartbeats and what? You think I'll take your side? Why the fuck would you think that? Like seriously. How have I given you this impression? What about me says, 'He's on board with kid-breeding, sperm-milking, and hormone-collecting?' What? Tell me, please. I'd really like to know how you got this impression of me that I'm a sick fuck like yourself."

She stares at me, eyes locked in a glare. "You know how I know you're like me?"

"I'm dying to hear."

"Because when they made us, they made us *the same*, Valor. They made you second best. Like me. Always taking a back seat to Luck, right? Oh!" She puts up a hand when I open my mouth to respond. "Oh, yes. I know all about your beginnings. I have your medical records, Valor. And your brother's records too. I know where you come from. I know who your real parents are. I know what genetic markers have been embedded into your DNA to make you this man who stands before me right now. They made us for each other. You can try to deny that all you want. I know I certainly did. If I had my choice, well"—she huffs—"I wouldn't choose you, that's for sure. Tray might've been the traitor, but he wasn't the weakest link. You are. You're weak, Valor. You're so weak you're willing to share that pathetic Brigit mind with Tray. They're not even people!" She laughs. "So no." She shakes her head. "No. I would never choose you. Ever. And let me be clear. I'm not choosing you now, either. I'm just *stuck* with you."

"You're stuck with me?" I guffaw again. "Bitch, you picked my ass up. You could've left me floating out in space. I'm sure eventually Tray would've been back to get me. But no. You brought me here."

"I brought you home!"

"This?" I say, whirling around in a circle with arms open. "This isn't my home! You fucked my home up!"

"ALCOR did that when he left the Baby in charge, not me! Tray did that when he told Luck and Nyleena to start this stupid princess rebellion! Crux did that when he shut down the security beacons to save his precious Corla when all that really did is back me into a corner and make things worse! I didn't do any of those things."

I force myself to hear all that. Force myself to run it back in my mind. Then I pick out the one piece that matters. "You want Corla, don't you. No. You *need* Corla. That's why you're here, isn't it."

"I'm here for the spin node that leads to Earth and I will get it, no matter what it takes!"

"Yeah," I say, calm now. "Maybe. But there's more to it than that, isn't there?"

And then the pieces start falling into place.

I'm not the smartest Harem Station brother. I've never pretended to be that. But I've been all over this fucking galaxy on salvaging missions. I've met and talked to women of hundreds—hell, maybe even thousands—of races. I've seen shit. I've done shit. And I'm not dumb. You don't have to be a doctor or a fucking astrobiologist to see how all these threads she's been weaving suddenly become a web.

"Corla has what you need, doesn't she?"

"I don't know what you're talking about."

"Lies," I whisper. "So many fucking lies inside you. Corla gave birth. Somehow, some way, she gave birth. And maybe Delphi and Tycho are these monsters you say they are—"

"Maybe?" She huffs.

"—but they lived. And that means Corla's body has something inside it. Something you can... milk, maybe? Steal for yourself and make these babies come to term. You sick fuck."

She sighs. Doesn't deny it.

"That's it, isn't it? You don't really need to go to Earth. That's just your only option now because Crux shut down the security beacons and now you can't contact them to spin your web of lies. And you can't storm them, they'd blow you up if you tried. And if you can't take what you need from Corla you have to go to Earth and... what? Expose yourself to the air there? So your body will make whatever it is you're missing?"

She turns her back to me.

"Yeah. I got you, bitch. I got you now. I know what you need. But you know what I don't understand?"

She's breathing hard, which can't be easy in that tight-ass bustier. Her shoulders are rising and falling as she stares at the wall.

"Why do you want more monster babies, Veila? If Tycho is as dangerous as you say he is, then why do you want more?"

"He's damaged. So is Delphi. Corla was missing a crucial step in the process. She was the first, after all. She didn't know any better. It took them years to figure out what went wrong." Veila turns to face me. "But they did figure it out. They helped Delphi. A little. Gave her that dragonbee bot that could punish her if she stepped out of line. It worked for a while. But the bee bot took a liking to Delphi and..." She shakes her head.

"And what?" I snap.

"And then her... education was interrupted. She was past the most critical part of the process, so she's... mostly civil. But she has an evil streak inside her, Valor. She has a monster inside her."

"And Tycho?"

"The boys are different. They are fine until their year of rage. And then..."

I stop listening. Because I know what the year of rage is like. We all go through it. Every Akeelian male has a period of time when all they want to do is fight, and fuck, and kill things. Kill everything.

We all went through it. But we had ALCOR. And we had space here on the station so we could wander off and be alone. And Serpint and Draden even got to leave and spend the tail end of their year of rage in space.

I've heard that zero gravity helps stabilize the hormonal imbalance.

But Tycho… Delphi is nineteen? Twenty? Right around there. So Tycho just came out of it.

"—he's dangerous," Veila says. And I realize she's been talking this whole time. "I told you that."

"You said he could be triggered."

"Oh, he can be. Easily triggered. And I don't know if you've ever seen the damage a silver princess is capable of. Planets quake when we approach them. Because they know we can blow them into atoms. But let me tell you something right now. That's nothing compared to what Tycho can do. We're talking suns, Valor. We're talking supernovae. We're talking black holes left behind when it's over."

"And you want to make more of these… weapons?"

"I want a freaking *baby*," she snarls. "Not a bomb. I *am* a bomb, you idiot. Why do I need baby bombs? Don't you get it?"

"You want me to believe that all you want out of this is to be a *mother*?" I guffaw again. It's that stupid. "You want power, Veila. That's all. And having another Tycho is just one more way to get it."

She sighs. "The boys don't want to be bombs any more than we do, Valor. And with this crucial bit of information that Corla was lacking when she gave birth—we can fix them."

"Fucking sun." I chuckle. "You're insane. You're just insane."

"Didn't you ever wonder why Corla came home?"

"What?"

"You know about that, right? You know she went back to Cygnus System. Her babies were about one standard year old. Why would she do that, Valor? What the ever-loving fuck reason could Princess Corla have to go back? She was free. She had her babies. She—"

"She had a plan."

We both turn and find Crux standing in the doorway.

"She had a plan," he says again. "Twenty years. It was going to take at least twenty years to set it up. That's what she told me."

"Shut the fuck up, Crux! What the hell, dude? Don't tell her this."

"She knows more than I do. Don't you, Veila?" Crux stares at her.

Veila says nothing. Just crosses her arms and tilts her head up.

"You stole her," Crux says. "That's why the two of you were on Cetus Station when Serpint showed up. You were going somewhere and you were taking her with you. Where were you going?"

Veila stays silent.

"I heard what you said," Crux says, and he's talking to me. "I think you're right. I think Corla has something inside her. Her body made something to help her carry the twins to term and Veila needs it for them."

He points to the still shot of the babies on the screen.

"But I have the same question as Valor," Crux continues. "Why? Why do you want these babies? And don't tell me it's because you want to be a mother.

You're no mother, Veila. You are incapable of that kind of love. That kind of selflessness. So…" He shrugs. "Tell me the truth and maybe I'll help you. Lie to me and we'll spend the next hundred and thirty odd years living out this Harem Station nightmare. Because the gates are locked down. No one comes in. No one goes out. Not until the security beacons come back online."

"Not until you tell them to come back online, you mean," Veila says.

Crux shakes his head. "I've got no pull with them. At this point it's out of my hands. Only ALCOR can break through that firewall. And he's dead."

Veila huffs.

Crux turns to me. "So our only fucking way out of this mess is Luck. Do you understand me, Valor? If he doesn't take us through that spin node we're fucked. Because we have no way to keep this station going. Our resources are already stretched to the limit. The goddamned princess rebellion took out a lot of critical infrastructure and no one is working right now. Everyone is preparing to fight. Think about it. OK? They are criminals. The most violent people in this galaxy who had nowhere else to go. They *want* this war, Valor. This is their dream. This is practically why they're *here*. Let's just say we won't have to worry about living a hundred and thirty more years. We're all gonna die of thirst in less than ten spins. So I get it, Valor. You hate her." He nods his head towards Veila. "We *all* hate her. But she's right. We need Luck to open that node and get us the fuck out of here. Because in a few spins, when everyone figures out there's no more water being made, the people around here? They're gonna get really unpleasant. This whole station is filled with nothing but murderous criminals who were only kept in line because ALCOR scared the shit out of them. And that Baby?" Crux shakes his head. "He's no ALCOR."

"I can hear you," the Baby says, his voice coming from above us somewhere.

"Good," Crux says. "Now we're all on the same page."

"Are we?" I ask.

He locks eyes with me for a few seconds. And right in that moment I don't really recognize him.

"What happened?" I ask.

He draws in air and looks at Veila.

I catch something between them, but I'm not sure what it is. Some kind of understanding. "What the hell is going on?"

Crux looks my way but doesn't meet my gaze. "Ask her," he says.

Then he spins around and walks away.

CHAPTER FOUR

I walk over to the door and watch Crux disappear out of the medical center, then lean against the doorjamb.

"You have no idea what has happened since I got here."

I'm so not in the mood for fucking Veila. "Obviously," I say. "Because I was locked up in a cryopod for six weeks."

"It was safer that way. Trust me."

"Trust you?" I ask, whirling around. "Trust you? Are you fucking kidding me right now? Who in their right mind would trust *you*?"

She juts her chin at the door. "He does."

"He doesn't." I laugh. "He wants Corla. That's all he's thinking about. And that's got nothing to do with you."

"How can you even say that? She and I are connected. He gets that."

"You know what he gets? I'll tell you. He gets that you took over our station, fucked it all up, fucked up all our lives, and now we're here at rock bottom, under your thumb, and he's got no choice but to hope that somewhere deep inside that filthy soul of yours, there's one last microscopic particle of decency left over from some prior version of yourself. That's all he gets, Veila."

"You're wrong."

"Really?"

"You don't know anything. You and Tray and Brigit and your fantasy life. That's where you've been the last thousand years, Valor. Hiding. Shirking your duties—"

"Shirking my...?" How many times can one person bellow out an incredulous guffaw in one morning? "God, you are really something else."

"What would you call hiding away in a virtual for four days?"

"Don't pretend like you know me because you stole some... memory, or data from my mind, or however you got that information. Because you don't."

"Really?" she barks back.

"Look, maybe you've fooled him, but I'm not buying into this act of yours. I know you far better than you know me. You're the woman responsible for all of this."

"Maybe you should go talk to him, hmm? Ask him what happened. Ask him why he's working with me. Because I promise you, it's not because I'm making him."

Then she pushes past me, her long skirts swishing against my legs as she exits the exam room, and leaves me standing there.

I watch her until she disappears. Then shake my head in disbelief.

I don't go after Crux, but when I leave the medical center Serpint is hanging out in the empty harem room, leaning back into the soft throw cushions of the couches, hands in his lap, one ankle propped up on one knee.

"What are you doing?" I ask.

His jaw is clenched, but other than that there are no other obvious signs that he's tense.

But I can tell. I've known Serpint his whole life. Maybe I didn't know him well before we came here, but I remember a time when he was so young he could barely talk. That's how long we've been around each other.

"What happened to you and Tray?" he asks. "You were supposed to find ALCOR."

I walk over to the couch and sit, falling back into the cushions with a long sigh. "We didn't really get that far."

"Why not?"

It's funny thinking of little baby Serpint when I look at him now. Because aside from those violet eyes there's almost nothing about him I recognize these days. "We got sidetracked."

"Sidetracked? We're in the middle of the biggest crisis of our lives and you and Tray got *sidetracked*?"

"Look, I wasn't in charge, OK? Tray took me to some station and then he was all about working on a ship. He didn't tell me shit until I forced him."

"What did he tell you?"

"We were there to save someone else. Some girl called Brigit."

"Brigit?"

"She was..." I sigh and massage my forehead with two fingers. "She's an AI. Tray met her inside the Pleasure Prison years and years ago. And he's been trying to get her out—"

"What the fuck are you talking about?"

"If you'd shut up you'd know," I spit back. "She was an AI trapped in the Pleasure Prison by Veila," I say, my voice going hard with the mention of her name. "And Tray thought she was real and—"

"No."

"Yeah. And she was in... Look. It's a long story and I only want to tell it once. So the short version is this. Tray and I went inside this virtual to get this girl, stayed there for four days"—Serpint's eyes go wide at this—"and then when we got out Veila attacked us, took us prisoner, and then she tortured me, did something to Tray and Brigit, and..." I throw up my hands. "I woke up here. Six weeks later."

"Where's Tray now? And this Brigit girl?"

"I don't know. Dead, maybe? Though Veila says they got away."

"And ALCOR?"

"We never got that far."

"So we're fucked?"

"*Booty*'s still out there," I say. "And Asshole. Can't you guys send a message?"

"There's no way through the gates," Serpint snaps.

"We don't need the gate. We have the..." I look up at the ceiling. But fuck it. The Baby already knows. "We have the spin node."

"And no coordinates," Serpint says. "Tray had those."

I lean forward and prop my hands on my knees. "We all have coordinates. Remember?"

Serpint squints his eyes at me. "What are you talking about?"

"The day we arrived on ALCOR Station. We all had a message from Corla. They were all spin node coordinates. And these coordinates lead to... places. Outside this galaxy."

"OK," Serpint says, holding up a hand. "Assuming that's true, who fucking cares? We need ALCOR."

"I'm disappointed in your disappointment in me." It's the Baby's voice coming from... wherever that voice comes from above us.

"Yeah," Serpint says. "Well, we're disappointed in you too. You're the whole reason we're in this position in the first place, you piece-of-shit halfwit mind. You betrayed us."

"Hold up," I say. "Explain that."

"I would prefer not to talk about it," Baby says.

"I don't give one sun fuck what you prefer, Baby. What the hell happened here?"

"You have no idea how bad it is, Valor," Serpint says.

"I know. Because no one will fucking tell me. So why don't you start talking?"

Baby says, "The Succubus and I had a... fight."

"A fight?" Serpint says. "That's what you're calling it? Our water generators are offline. All the gardens are dead. Wait until you see the parks and greenhouses, Valor. They're gone. We don't even know how everyone is still breathing."

"What the fuck?" I say.

"That was not my doing," Baby says.

"The hell it wasn't!" Serpint is agitated now. "You and that evil Mighty Bitch ruined all of it."

"And yet you're all still alive," Baby retorts. "Why do you suppose that is?"

"Because Luck has some secret garden. You already told us."

"Wait," I say, putting up a hand. "What secret garden?"

"That's what Veila wants," Serpint says. "Baby says there's a huge forest down on the lower levels where Luck is holding out and that's how we're still breathing. And in that forest there's some kind of flower that enables the Cygnian princesses to get pregnant. Luck and Nyleena both know about it."

"Hmm," I say. "Veila told me that she needs to get to Earth to save her babies. That she needs something from there to bring them to term. Or, possibly, she can take something from Corla's blood and use that to make what she needs. But both of these things are unavailable to her. She just spent the better part of the last hour trying to convince me that I need to help her get one or both of these things."

"Lies," Serpint says. "She might have Crux convinced, but not me."

"Not me either," I say.

"She's not lying," Baby says.

"No one cares what you think," Serpint says. "You're not in control of anything anymore."

"I still control the ventilation," Baby mutters.

"Yeah," I say. "About that. Veila threatened to cut off the air up here so everyone has to move to the lower levels if I don't talk Luck into surrendering."

"Baby," Serpint growls. "I swear to the fucking sun god of all the universe, I will hunt you down and kill your data core if you go through with that."

"Veila has control over me," Baby says. "There is no way for me to resist her."

"OK. How the fuck did that happen?" I ask. "Someone needs to fill me in."

Serpint gets to his feet and straightens his black t-shirt. "You need to talk to Crux about that. That story is all his."

And then he walks away. Just gets into the lift that goes directly to his quarters and disappears.

"Whatever you're going to do," Baby says, "you need to do it fast, Valor. Because we don't have much time."

"What does that even mean?"

But he's gone. And the only answer I get is silence.

Crux's office is just down the curve of the station a little ways and I can see it from where I sit in the harem room. But it's dark and empty right now.

I can't remember the last time I looked at his office and found it to be dark. He's always in there working on something. I don't even know what he does, to be honest. Runs the docking bay schedules. Deals with immigrants. Security bullshit.

But right now the docking bays are all under Luck's control, the gates are locked so there's no immigration happening, and as far security goes... well. The beacons are offline and if all the hints people have been dropping are true, then there is no security.

So I go to his quarters.

I chime the bell, but there's no answer. So I push in a special code and enter anyway.

"Crux?" I ask. The whole place is dark. No lights on and the windows blacked out.

"Go the fuck away, Valor. If I had anything else to say to you, I'd have answered your chime."

"No. I'm not leaving until you tell me what happened here while I was gone."

"It doesn't even matter."

"Well, everyone else is saying it does and no one will tell me because they say it's your story to tell. So... lights on, for fuck's sake!"

One light flicks on in the corner. A single floor light that illuminates the room just enough to make out shadows of furniture.

And this is Baby's doing. He's in control of shit like that. But it's interesting that he respects both our wishes. Turning on a light for me because I asked for it, but leaving the place mostly dark, because that's what Crux wants.

The Baby is tiptoeing around us like we're breakable. Telling in and of itself.

He did something bad. That much I can deduce. And for some reason, he's sorry about that and this is his way of showing it.

"I'm not leaving until you fill me in." And I prove that fact by walking over to the couch and flopping back into the cushions.

I wait. For a long while. Crux just sits in a corner chair, silent and still. Like he's thinking. Or sad. Or traumatized.

But I'm not leaving. So I settle in and start thinking about my own problems.

Tray. Brigit. ALCOR. *Booty*. Asshole.

And, of course, Veila.

And those babies.

It bothers me that I don't know who the father is. Why does that bother me? Yeah, that bothers me too. Because now that things are not chaotic, I'm not chained to a torture wall on her ship, and I've had some time to adjust... well, I feel that attraction.

I don't want to, but it's there. It's definitely there.

"You've never been the best liar," Crux says, breaking our long silence.

"I'll take that as a compliment," I say.

"Right now it's not. Baby?"

"Yes, Crux?" The Baby's voice is low and soft.

"Get the fuck out."

It's weird when the AIs leave you alone. You never really know if they leave. They are omnipresent, after all. But there's this feeling in the air when they do go. And I get that feeling now.

Emptiness.

I learned to recognize this feeling a long time ago. The first time Luck and I left Harem Station I felt it. We didn't have *Lady* back then, just a regular ship. Not sentient or anything. So when we left though the ALCOR gate the first time there was this immediate feeling of disconnect.

It was weird at first. Luck and I both felt it. It was like being set free and being adrift all at once.

61

I didn't like it. It took me a long time to be OK with it. Because in that moment I knew there was no all-powerful god-like AI watching over us anymore. It was just Luck and me, and that was it.

Either we figured it out together or we didn't. No one was coming to save us.

And that's the feeling I get now. Like the Baby really, truly did leave.

"OK," I say. "What happened?"

"Corla," he says. "Corla happened."

"What do you mean?"

"She woke up."

"What? How?"

"I don't know. Maybe Veila? But I don't think so. I questioned her after I got the message and—"

"Wait. What message?"

"From Corla."

"Explain that, Crux." Alarm bells are going off in my head. Because didn't Tray say something about a message from Corla to Brigit?

"I don't really have an explanation. She just..." He sighs. "I thought I was dreaming. I really didn't think it was real."

"When? When did this start?"

"Like... less than a spin after you left. Right about the time the princesses went crazy."

"Crazy how?"

"It was very confusing in those first few days after you guys left. Because we all knew—at least us, you know, me, and Jimmy, and Serpint, and Luck—we knew it was fake. We knew the fighting was just a distraction, but somehow..."

He looks up at me in the duskiness of the room. I catch his eyes crackling with light. And it makes me wonder when this light in our eyes became normal. Because we didn't do this when we were younger. So when? When did the light appear? Was it when Lyra and Corla showed up?

"It became real, Valor."

"What do you mean real?"

"He shot me."

"Who?"

"Luck. And his plasma rifle was not on stun. He fucking..." Crux stares at me, shakes his head. "He fucking killed me, Valor."

He waits for a reaction. But I don't think I can quite process what he just said.

"But... you're here."

"I know. I don't really understand that, to be honest. I know our medical center is top-notch and those pods we have can do amazing things. But he fucking blew a hole in me."

"Bullshit," I whisper. "Luck? Why would he do that?"

Crux gets to his feet and lifts up his shirt. And there is it. A huge, red scar almost the entire width of his chest.

I just stare at it, unable to believe my eyes. "But..."

"He shot me. He killed me. And from that moment on, nothing about what we were doing was fake."

"But how did you—"

He drops his shirt. "I told you. I don't know." He walks over to his dining room, pours himself a drink, downs it, and then pours another before turning to face me. "Something happened to me while I was dead."

"You couldn't have been dead, Crux. That's not possible."

He downs the second drink and turns back to the bar. Leans his hands on the edges and drops his head. "Did you ever wonder how you guys did it?"

"Did what?"

He turns to face me, his mouth a grim, flat line, his expression nearly blank. "Survived out there. All those battles you and Luck have been in."

"Well." I chuckle a little. "It doesn't hurt to have a partner called Luck, right?"

"It wasn't Luck, Valor. And it wasn't luck, either. We... we're..."

"We're what?" I ask. Because my heart is skipping right now. Skipping with the knowledge that he's going to say something I already knew, but couldn't admit to.

"We can't die."

"Draden died," I say. And I don't even know where it comes from. Because I know there's a chance that's not true.

"Did he?" Crux asks. "Did we ever see his body?"

"Look," I say. "I get it. Some really weird shit has happened to me too. Lots of things I don't really understand. But—"

"But nothing," Crux interrupts. "Dude. Luck shot a fucking plasma rifle at me at point-blank range and I died. I... I *went places*, Valor."

"What places?"

"I don't know. But it was gold. It was like a golden cloud of... space dust. Or star dust. Or like... a giant gold nebula." He walks towards me, grabs my upper arms and shakes me. "Have you ever seen that? While you and Luck were out there? Did you ever see a gold nebula?"

"Nebula?" I ask dumbly.

"Think! Valor! Think hard. Did you?"

"I don't know. I… I don't know. I'd have to think about it, I guess."

"Think!" he says again. "Think about it right now! Because…" He lets go of me and turns away. "Because I need to know if it's real." He turns back. "I need to know what happened to me. Because…"

He stops to stare off at… nothing. Just to stare. Lost inside himself, I think.

"Because why, Crux?" I ask in a whisper.

"Because it was not good, Valor. It was terrifying. And there were others there too."

"Who?"

He shakes his head. "Other… *things*. And before you ask me what things, I don't know. I just know I came back screaming. Like you. And that's why I thought—"

"No," I say. "I mean, I don't know why I wake up screaming like that from cryo, but… I have never seen that place."

"You're sure? Maybe you just forgot. What do you remember from cryosleep?"

"I don't remember shit, dude. That's the point of cryosleep, right?"

Crux begins to pace the length of his dark living room. Back and forth several times. And I suddenly can't think. I don't know anything. You could ask me my name right now and I wouldn't be able to tell you, that's how empty I am.

65

"We need to find out what that place is. Because it's real. I know it's real. And I died and went there."

"Like… an afterlife?" I offer. Generally, as a rule, none of us Harem brothers believe in that shit. I mean, how do you believe in God when you live with him? And he's just circuits, and wires, and data cores? But I think that's what Crux is getting at here. And that's the only reason I say it.

He stops pacing and grabs his hair with both hands. Like he's frustrated, or bewildered. Or scared. "I think it was Corla," he says. "Because when I woke up…" He looks at me. And now his eyes are bright fucking violet. Lit up like he's some lost Cygnian prince. "When I woke up, Valor, she was sending us messages."

"What kind of messages? Because Tray… I mean, listen. Our story about what happened to us while we were gone is long, and I don't really have time to get into it right now because most of it has nothing to do with any of this. But he said Corla was sending messages to Brigit when she was in her cryopod."

"Who the fuck is Brigit?"

And hell. How the fuck do I answer that without starting a spin-long conversation about what we learned about the Akeelian girl twins and how they have been turned into minds?

"She's just a girl in a cryopod—"

"What? What the fuck?"

"Anyway, listen. In the end we decided that the messages were from Veila because she captured us. And we figured the messages were how she traced Brigit's cryopod and found us. But at first Tray said it was Corla who sent those messages."

And then, while Crux is trying to process this, a thought hits me. And it hits me hard.

Because just a little while ago, Veila said, *Corla was with* me.

What if all this time we thought Corla was one of the good guys? We thought Veila stole her. And that's why she was on Cetus Station when Serpint showed up.

But what if Corla and Veila are actually working together?

"What are you thinking?" Crux asks.

"Nothing."

Crux rushes me, grabs me by the shoulders again, and then shakes me. But hard this time. Like he's fucking serious. "Tell me, you asshole! I know you. I know you better than you think and I know you're hiding something from me right now. So fucking tell me!"

"I don't know, Crux. What if... what if Corla and Veila are both bad? You told us that Corla said she had a plan, right?"

"Twenty years," he whispers. And his voice is husky and growly. Like he has to force those words out.

"And if you ever saw her again, everything had gone wrong. Remember that?"

He nods, violet eyes lit up so bright, I have to turn my head a little so they don't blind me.

"Well..." I shrug away from him. He lets me go, eyes still lit up as he stares at me. "We found her. You have her. And you have to know in your heart that seeing her again is wrong. Because I tell you what, I hate Veila. Fucking hate her with a passion I've never experienced before. But if she were to leave right now... I'd have a hard time staying behind. I can already feel her pull. So how the fuck have you been able to keep Corla locked up in that cryopod for over a year, Crux? How?"

His eyes go dark. Like instantly. They just blink out. And I see spots floating across my vision where his irises were just a second ago.

"Star-crossed," he says.

"What?"

"That's what I told her. Back then. That day we had the breeding ceremony. When we were making our plans to leave. I told her we were star-crossed. Two ships passing in the dark. Meant to be together, but never able to be together. And she said yes. That's what we are. And that if I ever saw her again I needed to stay away from her. I was to never come near her again. But... like you, I can't help myself. I need her."

"And now the beacons are offline. Do you think she did that?"

He nods. "I think she did that so we'd have to remain apart. So I wouldn't be able to go inside the beacon and see her or talk to her. And that there was no chance I'd ever touch her again."

He turns and grabs his hair again. And a noise begins to fill the room. At first it's low, and rumbling. But it gets louder, and louder until it's a roar. Like the roar of a wild animal the likes of which I've never seen before.

It's Crux. He makes that noise.

It's not a roar of power, though. Or triumph.

It's a roar of defeat.

And then he drops to his knees and goes silent. Bows his head to the floor and just stays like that.

A man broken.

I have never seen Crux like this and it scares me. He was always the strong one. The confident one. The smart one. The one we counted on to make rational decisions and pull us through whatever crisis we were in.

And now… now he's on his knees.

And his princess—no, his *queen*—she did this to him.

"Hey," I say quietly. "Crux."

He doesn't move from the floor. Just stays there in that defeated position. "Valor," he says. And then finally he sits back up, still on his knees and finds my face. His eyes are so dark now, I don't recognize him. They look like someone sucked out his soul. Like he really is dead and this body in front of me is a corpse. "You need to find out what's going on with us. Something is wrong. With all of it. With Lyra, and Nyleena, and Delphi." He chokes out her name.

His daughter.

"You need to ask Veila. You need to get this information. Whatever it is she's doing, I'm gonna tell you right now, it's not as simple as think. I know what you saw. I know what she did to you and Jimmy. I know what Luck thinks she's up to. I've heard it all. But that's not what's happening here. And you are her only weakness. You, Valor. You're the only one who can figure it out. Please," he says, getting to his feet again. "I'm fucking begging you. Use that soulmate bond, if that's what it is. Make her tell you her secrets."

He takes a step towards me and I dunno why, but I take three steps back.

The hurt in his eyes is almost too much. But the fear inside me, the fear of what he is—and that maybe we're all the same, we're all just like him—it drives me back.

He stops. His shoulders drop because he knows.

He knows I'm afraid of him.

"Can you please try?" he asks.

"OK," I whisper back. "I will." And then his eyes go back to normal. The dark corpse-pits disappear and the crackle of violet is there once more.

And suddenly I'm ashamed of how I'm acting. I'm ashamed of my fear.

"You're my brother," I say. "No matter what happens. You'll always be my brother, Crux."

He nods. But the light in his eyes is already fading when I back out of his quarters and go looking for Veila.

CHAPTER FIVE

"Baby," I say, once I'm in the empty harem room again.

"Yes, Valor." And I don't know how, but the Baby sounds a lot less like Baby since I woke up and a lot more like Real ALCOR.

"Were you listening?"

"No. I left. But I already know. I was there when he… came back."

"Did Corla send messages?"

"I do not know."

"Are you on our side?"

"I do not know that either. I'm not sure who I am, Valor."

"Yeah. That makes two of us."

"No one trusts me."

"Can you blame them?"

"I am different now. I was younger then."

"It was six weeks ago, Baby."

"I know. But a lot has happened in that six weeks. Was there something you needed?"

"Yeah. Where's Veila?"

"She's sitting in the airlock to her ship. Up on the executive level docking bay."

"What is she doing in there?"

He pauses here. "I think she is… sad."

"Sad?" I'm disgusted. "That bitch has no right to be sad. She's the whole reason this is happening."

"I could be interpreting her wrong," Baby admits. "But she's locked her cyborgs out of the airlock and she's not entering her ship. She's currently holding up several dozen borgs on shift change."

"Well"—I sigh, tugging on my shirt a little to straighten it out—"I guess I'll go see what that's all about."

"It won't work," he says, as I walk towards the upper level docking bay elevator.

"What won't work?"

"Tricking her with the soulmate bond. She understands it better than you do."

"I thought you said you weren't listening?"

"I wasn't. But I am not stupid, Valor. So be careful when you lie to her. You could just be lying to yourself."

"Thanks for the tip," I say, pressing the button to open the lift, then walking in when the doors open.

"I like you," Baby says. "I like all of you, actually. And I'm sorry that Luck is so angry with me."

"He's angry with you?" I ask as the lift doors close. "Why do you think this is about you?"

"Because I was helping Veila before you left. I didn't understand what was happening back then. And Luck thinks I'm trying to steal his flowers."

"Fucking flowers. What is all this about the flowers?"

"They carry hormones for—"

"Oh, right. Baby-making. That's all these girls think about."

"It is," the Baby admits. "So be careful what you tell them."

"Who? Which ones? Veila?"

"All of them," Baby says. And then the elevator doors open onto the top docking level.

I shake my head, trying to clear it so I can focus on Veila and put the Baby out of my mind. He's right. She's way better at this trickery stuff than I am. So whatever Baby is talking about with the other princesses will have to wait.

Two dozen cyborgs snap to attention when I enter the hallway and all of them raise their rifles and point them at me.

"Easy," I say. "It's probably not a good idea to kill the Loathsome One's prince, eh?"

They shuffle their feet, eyes flashing red and racing across the upper third of their faces with agitation.

"I'm just gonna talk to her. You guys are on shift change? Wanna get home to your sexbots and whatnot? Well, I'll get her out of there."

For a few moments they don't move. Just stand there like a bunch of empty metal-heads. But I know they have internal comms so I wait it out patiently as they communicate. And it pays off, because after a minute or two of this, they step aside.

I walk up to the airlock door, peek through the long window, and have a flash of memory of the day we all arrived here on ALCOR Station. It wasn't called Harem back then. We didn't have a harem. And we didn't belong to ALCOR when we arrived, either.

Corla sent us here with her messages. Spin node coordinates. A star map, basically.

The wanderer in me is suddenly restless. It's been a long time since Luck and I have been out in the galaxy doing our job. I miss him, that's a given. But I miss the job too. I miss the traveling, and the danger, and that feeling when you land on some ancient space station and realize you're the first person to walk those dark, desolate halls in hundreds or thousands of years.

There was no window in the airlock when we landed on ALCOR so we had no idea what was waiting for us on the other side. We didn't come through this docking bay. We came in on the lower level. The one Luck is in control of now.

And then when the door opened we saw Xyla.

Crux was trying to be brave and handle shit like he always does. Jimmy was in lust with her. That was before he got put in the friend zone, of course. Luck and I didn't know what to think. We just stood there like the dumbass kids we were. Tray was in some kind of nerdy awe of everything. And Serpint and Draden had to be carried in because they were too small to walk in the too-big environmental suits they were wearing.

I smile as I remember all this.

But then I see her through the window. Veila. Sitting on the floor of the airlock. Legs drawn up, head pressed down to her knees.

I knock on the airlock. And it's a loud knock that reverberates through the solid metal of the doors.

Her head pops up, she sees me, then she does one of those sighs. Like I am the last person she wants to see right now.

Ironic. Since she's the one who trapped me here with her. But also, it kinda stings.

Something in my heart shrivels. Which is stupid and also... unexpected.

I don't need permission to open this airlock like her cyborgs do, so I just palm it and the doors hiss and slide open.

"What?" she snaps.

"Is that any way to greet your soulmate?" I ask lightly, then palm the door controls again to seal us up and give us privacy from the borgs.

"Don't start with me, Valor. I'm not in the mood."

"Well, I don't really care. I just came from Crux's quarters and he told me he died a few weeks back."

"Shit."

"Shit? That's all you have to say? In case you haven't noticed, he's not dead, Veila. So what the fuck is he talking about?"

"Ask your...." She squints at me. "He's not your brother. Is he?"

"Crux?"

"Not Crux. *Luck*." She snarls his name. Like she hates Luck.

"No, actually. Luck is not my brother. Not my real one, anyway. We tested our DNA a long time ago to be sure."

"Because *he's* your soulmate, isn't he?"

I shrug. "Sure. Whatever. I'll agree to that."

She huffs out her disgust. "So that's why."

"That's why what?"

"That's why our bond isn't what the others have. You were already in love long before you knew about me."

"Um… well, not that it's any of your business, but yeah. I'm sure that's part of it. There's this little snag though, right? One called Nyleena? So. I'm pretty sure Luck and I don't have a future together."

Veila sighs and studies me for a moment. "If she were not here. You would…?"

"Choose him? Yup. I would."

"And Tray? How does he fit in? And Brigit? How is it that you have so many choices? It doesn't seem fair."

I actually laugh at that. "First of all, I am just one of those guys everyone likes. I can't help it. That's just who I am. Second of all, I have no choices, Veila. Luck and Tray both have their soulmates. I'm the unwanted third wheel. I love Luck, not Nyleena. And he loves me, but he loves her more. So that's going nowhere. I love both Tray and Brigit. But do I see myself with them forever? How could that work? They're not physical. They're AIs. As you well know. What am I gonna do? Just live in a virtual for the rest of my life?"

She considers this for a moment. But when she replies, she's moved on to another subject. "Did you tell your brothers about the ships?"

"No."

"Why not?"

"Because I was in cryosleep for six weeks. Thanks to you. And it doesn't seem to be a high priority right now, considering Crux is convinced he's a ghost, Luck is at war with us, and you're fucking pregnant."

She sighs again. Then drops her forehead back to her knees and stays that way without saying anything else.

Conflicting emotions swirl around inside me. Should I walk over to her? Stay here? Comfort her?

Sunfucking stars, man. Why the hell would I comfort her?

It takes me a few minutes to accept why. But I do. Don't have much choice.

She and I are connected. Like it or not. Real or not. There is something between us. Something that draws me to her. And if we had met under different circumstances—like out in the galaxy somewhere—and I didn't already know about this soulmate bullshit, I'd have chalked it up to plain old attraction.

Because let's face it. Veila is beautiful.

Maybe I'm not into the silver, but like before, there's that little hint of rose gold underneath her harsh white. And there's a part of me that craves that side of her.

Not this side, though.

"Well, are you gonna say something? Or are you just gonna stand there like an oaf? Why are you here?"

"Oh," I say, then decide Crux was right. I have to use this bond to get what I want. It's what she would do, if she was in her normal state of mind. So I walk over to her and slide down the wall so we're sitting so close our knees bump against each other.

An electric shock shoots through my body at this simple touch. And when she pulls her legs away from mine in a defensive gesture, the heat we created in that single moment disappears and my whole body becomes chilled, then cold.

"Don't touch me," she says. "I'm not in the mood."

"What's your problem, then?"

"My problem?" She lifts her head up and stares at me. "My problem is that this pregnancy is doomed. In a few weeks, at most, I'm going to miscarry again. That's my problem. I've been through this so many times, you'd think I'd be used to it. But I'm not." She shakes her head. Opens her mouth to say more. Decides against it, and then drops her face back down into her knees.

"Should I know what that feels like? Should I pretend that I understand? Should I pretend that I believe this act you're putting on?"

Her head snaps up. "Fuck you, Valor. You have no idea what's going on here."

"Well, maybe you should fill me in?"

She huffs. Says nothing.

"What are you afraid of?"

"Get out. Just leave me alone and get out."

"Well, I got in because I promised all those borgs of yours out there—who are officially off duty, by the way—that I'd get you out of this airlock so they can go back to their quarters and enjoy their time off."

She looks over at the airlock window, spies two peeping borgs, and then screams, "What the fuck are you looking at?"

Both of those metal heads swing out of view real fast.

I want to give up right now. Just go back to sleep. At least things would be simple and I wouldn't have to be here, with her, dealing with this shit.

But all the things Crux told me suddenly swirl into my mind. And then, almost like it's out of my control, I say, "Hey. Have you ever seen a place that's like... a golden nebula while you were traveling the galaxy?"

"What?" she croaks, looking up from the safe view of her knees.

"Crux said…" I stop, wondering if I'm supposed to be telling her this, then decide I want to tell her this, because for some reason I need to hear her answer, and continue. "He said he died. You knew about that, I take it?"

She flips her hand in the air. That gesture again.

"But he said when he died he went somewhere. Some golden space-dust nebula place filled with people or… I'm not quite sure what the fuck he was talking about. But he asked me to ask you. I was supposed to be all stealthy about it and shit. Like… well, I'm not really a stealthy guy. So I'm not sure how I'd do that. But anyway. Have you ever seen that?"

"What did I tell you?"

"What?"

"*Lie*, Valor. Learn to fucking lie a little, for fuck's sake!"

"Why?"

"You can't just go around asking about the golden place. What's wrong with you?"

"So you've heard of it?"

"Yes, I've heard of it. I'm a fucking Cygnian princess."

"What's that mean? Do all you guys know about it? Why was Crux dreaming about it? And hey, did Corla send you messages? Because he says she sent him messages and she's awake and… what? Why are you looking at me like that?"

She blinks at me. "Why are you telling me this?"

"He told me to ask you."

"You know what? I have to go." She gets to her feet and starts walking towards the airlock door. But I get up and grab her wrist and stop her.

And when I do that… I mean, I knew this was coming, but still, when I touch her that feeling comes back. That urge inside me. The desire to press my body up against hers and keep her close to me forever.

She yanks her wrist from my grip. "Don't. I don't want you to touch me again. Do you understand?"

"Hard to get, huh?"

"What?"

"You're playing hard to get. To make me want you."

"No." It comes out as a sardonic laugh and she shakes her head. "No, I truly want nothing to do with you, Valor."

"Except get Luck to surrender so you can get your hands on that flower?"

"What flower?" And I have to hand it to her. The look on her face almost passes for surprise.

"Come off it," I say. "I know you know about the flowers Luck is hiding."

"Why would I care about sun-fucked flowers?"

"Because they're the secret ingredient to getting pregnant."

"What?" This comes out as an incredulous whisper.

And that's my first clue that yeah, she really did not know about the flowers. "The Baby didn't tell you?"

"Tell me what?"

"OK. Well." I laugh a little. "Turns out Luck not only controls the spin node that leads to Earth—or wherever, because that's not the only place it leads." I chuckle, then wonder if I'm drunk or something. Because why am I telling her all this?

"What does that mean?" Veila asks. "Leads to Earth or wherever? Where else does it go?"

"You know... maybe I should shut up now?"

She reaches for me, then just as abruptly pulls her hand back. Like she's afraid to touch me. "Explain this flower."

"Nah. I'm gonna drop it now. You're on your feet, you're ready to leave—"

"Valor," she snarls. "I am cramping right now. I am on the verge of miscarrying. Again." And maybe I'm imagining things, but her eyes are a bit shiny. And they crackle with pink light.

I point at her eyes. "Did it ever occur to you that it's the silver that's holding up your baby-making? And not the pink?"

"What?" And she lights up a little. A warm, gold-pink glow.

"That. Right there. Your light is not silver right now. It's like there's war going on inside you."

She draws in a long breath and then lets it out. "It's the other way around. The pink and gold is messing this up." She pans a hand across her stomach as she says 'this'.

"Why do you even need babies? I mean, you're not really going to mother them, are you?" That last part comes out with a laugh. Because the whole thought of Veila being a mother... I just can't.

She glares at me. And now her eyes are filled with silver-laced white and that rose gold is long gone. "You were saying? About the flowers."

I'm probably not supposed to tell her this. I mean, it's the big secret, right? The whole point of Luck starting this little revolution. Which isn't so little anymore. But it certainly has her attention.

"I'm not really sure. Baby told me that someone told him that there's a forest of flowers down below. And that's the secret ingredient to getting princesses pregnant."

"Is Nyleena pregnant?"

I shrug. "Could be, I guess. I've been out of the loop, remember?"

This is not a lie. But it's only half true. I knew there was a high probability of Nyleena being pregnant when we left Harem six weeks ago, but I don't know that for sure.

Veila stares at something over my shoulder. But when I turn I realize she's just staring off into space. Lost. Finally she says, "I've been using a chemical."

"For what?"

"To get pregnant. The Cygnians have a way to make babies in the womb too. And it involves this chemical formula. But the only time it ever worked was with Corla." Veila narrows her eyes. "Was Corla here with you when you arrived that first day?"

"Of course not. We shot her through a spin node and sent her somewhere else."

"Where?"

"Who knows? They were her coordinates. Just like ALCOR's gates were her coordinates too. We didn't have anything to do with any of this, Veila. We were pawns. That's all. We did what Corla told us and then, when we arrived here, we did what ALCOR told us."

She looks at me. "Are you tired of it yet? Or is this how you operate now?"

I shrug. "I'm kind of a go-with-the-flow guy."

"Boring," she says.

"Like you'd know. I would not call my life boring at all. It was pretty fucking great, actually. Until Serpint got Draden killed, that is. Then…" But I stop. Because this line of thought feels like betrayal. And I've been trying not to let it take over inside my head since Luck, *Lady*, Beauty, and I came back to Harem for Draden's memorial service.

Yet here it is again. These thoughts won't go away so…

"I blame him," I say.

"Who?"

And when I meet Veila's gaze she looks… different. Younger, maybe. Possibly even softer. Definitely a lot more vulnerable than I'd ever have suspected.

"Serpint. He stole Corla, got Draden killed, and then…" I shrug with my hands and let out a long sigh. "Then everything changed. And almost nothing good has happened since. And I hate that I blame him, because Serpint… he probably is my real brother. And I should not feel this way about him."

"Hmm," she says. "I feel the same way about Corla. She ruined everything for me. Her and her big plans. Dragging me along with her."

"Wait. What? How do you figure *she* dragged *you* along? She was the one in the cryopod on Cetus Station. You were the one in charge."

"Yeah." Veila laughs. "Yup. I was. But it wasn't my plan. This whole thing was her plan. I was just doing what I was told." Her eyes lift up to search mine, darting back and forth. "Did you know I can shift time?"

"Time? What?"

"Silvers. We can shift time when we…" She flips that stupid hand again. "We take time backwards. That's why it's so difficult to get pregnant. That's why we do the insemination artificially."

"Sounds like a really terrible reproductive strategy if you ask me."

She turns her back to me and sighs out the words, "It is." She pauses, then says, "I'm going to miscarry these babies. Not in a few weeks, but very soon. I can already feel it starting."

I can't see her hands because her back is turned. But I'm pretty sure they're cradling her stomach.

Do I have feelings about that?

No. No, I don't. They're not my babies. Why should I care if she miscarries? It's probably for the best. Who knows what would come out of her if she brought them to term?

But this new Corla revelation? Now *that* is some news. Because I suspected. Of course, that suspicion was planted by Veila, so… I can't really rely on it. But it feels very true to me and I have a sudden urge to go back and talk to Crux again until we work it out.

I'm just about to tell her I need to leave when she says, "Those comic books I told you about?"

I furrow my brows. "What about them?"

She turns back around to face me again. "Were the stories about you guys true?"

I shrug. "Tell me one and I'll let you know."

"I don't really remember them. Not details, anyway. But I have a few old comics in my personal things on the warship. I found them on a station several years back. And it was like..." She frowns. "I don't know. I was compelled to buy them even though they commanded a significant price and I didn't have a lot of money back then. I actually sold a bot of mine—one I favored and loved—in order to afford them. They took me back to a small, bright piece of my childhood. Of course, I was well on my way to becoming... *this* by the time you boys made your appearances on the comics."

She pans a hand down her body as she says that last part.

"But we girls in the harem used to gather around and read them out loud when we were young. Those comics were like screens to everyone outside Cygnian System, I guess. You were our exotic forbidden celebrities. The only hint we had of what was happening outside our own system. If that was by design to make us want you boys, or fear you boys, or just an easy way to keep us occupied, I have no idea. But I'll bring them to you, if you'd like to read them."

I don't answer because this whole conversation feels like a trap. Just like Brigit was. Because against my better judgment I'm interested in Veila. Her life, her struggle, her past, her stupid books. She is different right now and I don't understand the change.

A trap is the only thing that makes sense.

"Then you can tell me if they're true. At any rate," she says, taking a long breath and forcing a smile, "I'm going to let you go down to the lower levels to talk to Luck."

"I will not be your messenger," I say firmly.

"Whatever, Valor." One more dismissive hand wave for good measure. "I don't care. Go see Luck. I know you miss him. Come back to me. Or don't. But one way or another I will get through that spin node. And I will get what I need on Earth or I will get a hold of those flowers, or I will die trying." She looks me directly in the eyes. "I will do whatever it takes to protect these children."

And then she's walking towards the airlock door on the Harem side. All the rose-gold glow gone now so she is just as she was in my memory of her when she had me bound to a torture wall.

Ice princess.

The door opens and to the cyborg guards she says, "Take him down to ninety-six and leave him there. I'm going to the warship now." She turns and walks past me towards her ship's side of the airlock, but then stops and looks to the side. Not quite glancing at me, but not quite *not*, either. "By the way," she says. "Welcome to the final war. There's no going back now."

Then she hits the unlock button on the wall and the airlock doors slide open. She walks through and disappears into a crowd of waiting borgs.

And maybe it's just me but... she sounds a little sad when she says that. She sounds a little tired too. Like she's had enough and she's ready for it to be over.

I know it's a trick. I get this. I do. But the whole way down to ninety-six I'm consumed with thoughts about Veila.

That's not unusual, right? We *are* soulmates.

Aren't we?

I think we are.

But it's a lot of time to think because none of the escalators are working so it's nothing but stairs frozen in place. There are thousands of Harem residents watching me as I slowly descend and I try to think about them instead. Wonder what their lives have been like these past several weeks since everything went sideways.

They don't look happy. Most of them look very tired. All of them are displaying weapons and there are even several fights as the level numbers decrease. Harem Station hasn't been quiet since Luck and I left all those years ago to start living the life of nomad salvagers, but right now it's exceptionally loud. People yelling. Others selling shit in the open hallways. Hanging out in alleys in groups. Some of the women walk around like zombies. Like they've seen too much or done things they'd rather forget about. Harem Station, I realize, has become just another war-torn city.

This makes me think about Veila again. What she's been doing these past several weeks. What it took to take control of this station. What kind of deals she's made. How she got pregnant and also, even though I don't want to think about this part, where she got the genetics for those embryos inside her.

Not mine, she said. And that's all that matters, I guess. Not mine.

A few of the loitering outlaws shout insults at me from the edge of the levels as I descend. Yelling things like "Deserter" and "Traitor" and "Sell-out."

What do they think I've done? Partnered with Veila? It's an easy assumption to jump to, isn't it? I am her soulmate. Everyone has to have heard the rumors. But I soon realize that's not what they're referring to.

I am going down, after all. And all these people up here have clearly chosen a side. Crux's side. Serpint's side. Baby's side. And yeah, Veila's side too, I guess.

They're angry because I'm taking Luck's side.

But... is there any other side to take? Really? I mean, if I have to choose it's always going to be him.

Anyway, it's a long fucking walk down to ninety-six. But the cyborg guards don't follow me down the last step that leads to the landing between ninety-six and ninety-five. Just turn and start walking back up.

I gaze up at them for a moment, then down half a level to the waiting guards of the rebellion. One of them is a Cygnian princess with short bright-red hair. She's wearing tactical pants and a white tank top that's stained with blood. There's a significant cut above her left eye being held together with makeshift staples that reminds me that all the best medical centers are on the higher levels. Down here is a place for the rogue outlaws. Those who don't assimilate well, or just like to fight too much and party too hard, or don't like to follow ALCOR's rules.

Former rules. It's anybody's guess what the rules are now.

"State your business," the red princess demands, thrusting a plasma rifle at my chest.

"It's me," I say. Because I recognize this girl. Zeldine? Or Seline? Or something like that. She's been in the harem for years. "Valor."

"I didn't ask for your name," she spits. "I asked for your business."

"I want to talk to Luck."

"Oh, do you?" She laughs. Then all the men standing around her laugh too. Big men. Centurian men. Dressed in all black with their silver skin gleaming in the harsh lights.

I sigh, tired. Wishing I could go back in time and do things different. I hate that we're divided now. I hate that our perfect balance of customs and cultures has been disrupted by this war. I hate that with each passing moment this station feels less like home and more like… more like a last stand.

Welcome to the final war. There's no going back now.

"Just tell him I'm here, OK?" Then I take a seat on the steps and wait. Because all the Centurians are pointing their rifles at me with intent. It's very clear I'm not getting one level lower until someone with more rank gives them the order.

Zeldine or Seline or whoever the fuck she is leans to the side and whispers something to a cyborg. He turns and disappears down the steps and she says, "What do you want with Luck?"

"It's none of your business," I say.

"In case you haven't noticed, *Valor*"—she practically spits my name—"you're not in charge here anymore. So it is my business."

"I might not be in charge. But Luck seems to be. And my business is with him. Not you."

"I'm the captain of Nyleena's guard. So I beg to differ."

"I'm just here to talk to him."

"He's not going to believe you."

"You don't even know what I'm going to say."

"I have a pretty good idea."

"Well, you're probably wrong, Zeldine. So just do your job like a good little soldier and shut your fucking mouth."

She shoots me.

And just as I start to black out from the plasma voltage jolting through my spasming muscles, I hear her growl, "That's for getting my name wrong after knowing me for seven years, you double-dicked asshole."

CHAPTER SIX

I come to lying on a recovery chair and as soon as I open my eyes I recognize *Lady Luck*'s medical bay.

"Don't move yet," she says in her soft feminine voice. "Seline got you good right in the heart. You can't talk to them like that anymore, Valor. They're not adjusting to their new power very well."

"What the fuck?" I say, ignoring her order and sitting up in the chair. Then I clutch my chest. Because I feel like I'm gonna have a heart attack. "Fucking princesses," I croak out.

"I've sent for Nyleena. She should be here soon."

I take several shallow breaths, trying my best to get my heart rate under control and suck in enough air to power my brain. And then I whisper, "How long was I out?"

"I'm not sure. You were dead for a little while. But luckily you were already here with me so I brought you back."

"Fucking bitch," I gasp. "I hope that little red-headed mongrel is going to be punished for that."

JA HUSS & KC CROSS

"Not likely. She's one of our best soldiers, actually. She had to shoot you to maintain her rank with her men."

I groan as I swing my legs over the side of the chair and lean down to hold my head in my hands.

"If I may?" *Lady* asks.

"Sure," I say, waving her on with one hand. "Say it."

"The princesses harbor a lot of resentment towards Serpint and Crux right now. And the fact that you have been up there with them for almost six weeks isn't going over well."

I glance up at the ceiling. It's a nice ceiling. Painted bright yellow. God, I miss that ceiling. I miss my old life so much. Why? Why does it have to be like this?

But then I rally. A little. Just enough to explain myself. "Veila just woke me up a few hours ago. I haven't really been up there for six weeks, you know that, right?"

"I gathered as much when I accessed your implant health data. But no one else knows that."

"So Luck thinks I've been, what? Up there cohorting with Veila this whole time?"

Lady says nothing. But I can feel the shrug.

"It's not even a real rebellion," I say. "So that's just stupid."

"It's more real than you think," *Lady* says.

"What do you mean? This whole thing is just a plot to buy time."

"It started that way. But wars have a way of maturing when you're not looking. Intentions and outcomes are often misaligned once you get past a certain point."

"That's dumb," I say, mostly able to breathe again. "Luck knows why we left. Hell, it was Tray's plan to start a princess rebellion in the first place. He had to know I was brought here in a cryopod. None of this was my choice."

"The fact remains, Valor, you came back alone. And that was not in the plan. Where is ALCOR?"

"I don't know. We didn't pick him up."

"What the hell have you been doing all this time?"

"All this time? I just told you. I was in a cryopod."

"And the week before that?" And now I can feel the eyebrow raise. Even though she doesn't have eyebrows in any shape or form. It's body language and I've known this ship long enough to translate her silences.

"The week before that... the week before that Tray and I were inside a virtual. And then Veila got us, and then... well, most of what came next I've thankfully blocked out. I woke up approximately two hours before that red-haired psychopath shot me."

"Seline," *Lady* says. "Her name is Captain Seline the Red."

I scoff. "Whatever. Can you just tell Luck I'm awake and I want to see him?"

"He knows. He's sending Nyleena. I already told you that."

"Why are you so hostile to me? Huh?"

"I'm... uncertain, Valor. Unsure of where you stand at the moment."

"I stand with you," I huff. "You and Luck. And me. It's me, *Lady*. Nothing has changed."

More silence. Probably an eye roll this time. Because everything has changed. Even I know that much.

"Well." She sighs. "I'll let you two sort that out."

"Great. Wonderful. Let's do that now."

"If and when you meet with Luck is Nyleena's call now. She's in charge of his schedule."

I fume at this remark. The idea that this wild, feral fucking silver-haired princess is the new go-between for me and Luck? Well, it's fucking ridiculous.

"Just relax for now. She'll be here soon. Would you like me to make you something to eat?"

I'm about to rage over that remark. Because it's a placating offer. Something to shut me up and make me forget what's happening. Take my mind off the fact that Luck is refusing to see me. That everything has changed. And I'm not talking about Harem Station now, either. I'm talking about Luck and me. Our relationship. And the fact that it was me, not him—not even Nyleena—who forced that change.

But I am starving. Like fucking starving. I have no idea when I ate last. Weeks ago. Probably before Tray and I left Angel Station to find Brigit. The only thing keeping me alive since then was nutrient packs being fed to me intravenously during my various medical/cryopod adventures.

So I say, "Yeah. OK. I could eat."

Lady doesn't say anything after that. So I pull myself together and climb to the dining area on the main level and slink down into the familiar booth where I've taken the majority of my meals for most of my adult life. And even though it feels good, and familiar, and right… it also evokes a sense of sadness in me. Because things are so different now. And *Lady Luck* isn't really my ship anymore.

I get this sinking feeling of foreboding in my stomach when the table-side autocook built into the bulkhead announces the arrival of my food.

And that sinking feeling becomes a sick one when I realize that *Lady* has chosen all my favorite foods.

It almost feels like a last meal.

But I dig in anyway, far too hungry to be able to resist. And I'm just about to take a bite of the spicy Centurian protein wrap when the airlock chimes and blinks green and the door slides open.

It's only then that I realize... I was locked in here. Like a fucking prisoner.

Nyleena walks in, looking sexy as all hell in her black tactical bodysuit and knee-high silver boots. She has no fewer than four weapons strapped to her body—pistols hanging off each thigh, plasma rifle strapped to her back, and what looks to be a SEAR knife (since when are those legal here?) in a pocket of her right boot.

I sigh and put the protein wrap back on my plate, then stand up to greet her when I notice... "Shit," I say, staring at her belly.

She forces a smile. "I guess you're going to be an uncle."

"Fuck," I say.

"You knew though, right?"

"I mean... sorta. Kinda figured it out about the flowers. But this?" I point to the very apparent baby bump protruding from her middle. "I wasn't expecting this."

"Yeah, well." She waves a hand in the air, a gesture that reminds me a lot of Veila right about now. "Shit happens, right? And never goes to plan."

"You can say that again."

She juts her chin towards my plate. "Don't let me stop you. I'm just here as a courtesy."

"Courtesy for what?"

"For whom, you mean. For Luck. He's... angry. You understand that, right?"

"Not really," I say. "I don't know what I did, but it's not what you guys think. I just woke up a few hours ago, Nyleena. I wasn't upstairs with Veila this whole time."

Nyleena sighs and walks over to the booth, sliding in opposite of me. She reaches out to grab a piece of cheese bread off my plate like we're old friends, or lovers, or hell, like we know each other at all. Which we don't.

She takes a big bite and talks as she chews. "Luck is pissed. No word," she says, swallowing, then taking another bite like she hasn't eaten in weeks. "No updates. No nothing. Things..." She swallows again and this time pauses with the bread in front of her pink pouty lips like she's thinking. "Things got a little serious here," she finishes, tipping up her chin a little like she's being defiant. "I mean... what started as a ruse to cover for you guys leaving turned into out-and-out war. My little princess army? It's not so little and these girls are fuckin' serious."

"What do you mean, not so little? How many princesses did we have on the station when I left? Maybe three dozen total including the free ones?"

"Well, yeah. But word got out and they came in droves, Valor."

"Define droves," I say, pushing my plate of food away.

"Two hundred and twenty-seven to be exact."

"What the fuck? Where the hell did they all come from?"

"Everyone Serpint ever caught or Crux ever bought—be they free, living here, or elsewhere—showed up for the war."

"OK," I say, trying to parse all that. "So they're on our side, though, right?"

"Define 'our side.'"

"Me, Luck, Tray, Crux, Serpint, Jimmy, *Booty*, *Lady*, Asshole? Ringing any bells here, Nyleena?"

"Hmm. That's interesting."

"What is?"

"Well, you left out me. And Lyra. And Corla. And Delphi."

"You guys too," I say. "You're with us."

"Are we?"

"Aren't you?"

"Well, I'm with Luck. And Delphi is with Jimmy. I'm pretty sure that Lyra is still with Serpint and no one really knows where Corla stands, do we? Since she's been frozen in that cryopod for over a year now. And…" She shrugs. "Well, let's just lay it all out on the table, shall we? You're with Veila."

I pause for a minute. Not about the Veila part. But about the Corla part. So they don't know. They don't know about Crux or the messages, or that Corla is awake. According to Crux, at least.

"I am *not* with Veila," I say with emphasis.

"You literally have physically been with Veila for almost six weeks."

"I was a prisoner in a cryopod, Nyleena."

"So you say."

"Ask *Lady*. She accessed my health data."

"It's true," *Lady* says. "He did just wake up a few hours ago."

"You're sure?" Nyleena asks, side-eyeing me with suspicion.

"Hold on a second," I say, putting up a hand. "Why the fuck are *you* here and not Luck?"

"What's that mean?"

"You're pregnant, Nyleena. You should be somewhere safe."

"Am I in danger?" she asks, looking around innocently.

"From me? No. But… you know, you should be careful."

"We're in the docking bay, Valor. *Lady Luck* is literally our headquarters. I'm as safe as I can be. But I do appreciate your concern." She squints her eyes. "If that's what it was."

"What else would it be?"

"I dunno. Fishing for information?"

"For who?"

"Veila? You know. Your *soulmate*?"

"Look, she's moved on, OK? She's not even interested in me. She's fucking pregnant too, did you guys know that?"

Nyleena frowns. "That's not possible. She's not even silver."

"Well, she is. She put herself inside a medial scanner and showed me a live feed of the babies under the guidance of the Cyborg Master. So… I don't know what to tell you."

"Why are you down here?"

"To see Luck. Why else? For fuck's sake. He's my partner. He's been my partner for as long as I can remember."

She squints her eyes at me. "Hmm. Well, he wasn't your partner when you *left*. That was Tray. See, this is why we're confused."

"Tray is…" But I don't have a good response to that. Because Tray and I have lived lifetimes together in the virtual. We spent more time together than I ever did with Luck. Why did I ever ask to go inside that stupid virtual? It fucked everything up. "Tray is different."

"Different how?"

"I'm not discussing it with you, Nyleena. It's fucking personal, OK? If Luck wants to know the whole story, he can come hear it from me himself."

"Well, I have a problem with that."

"Why?" I say, pressing two fingers up to my temple. In addition to my tight chest and painful breathing, my head is now pounding.

"Because he trusted Crux and Serpint and they turned on him."

For several seconds that sentence makes absolutely no sense. I cannot even fathom a scenario where what Nyleena just said is possible. "What do you mean, *turned* on him?"

"You saw the station on your way down."

"OK. Yeah. It was dark and shit's fucked up. People are fighting more than usual. But that was part of the plan."

"You know what wasn't part of the plan, Valor?"

"I have a feeling you're going to tell me."

"Being gone six weeks. Six. Fucking. Weeks. This isn't our plan anymore. Do you understand that? Those people out there? This is all real to them. Ninety-five hundred deaths in the past two weeks alone."

"What? Veila did this?"

"Veila?" Nyleena huffs. "Veila isn't in charge of this war. We are. Me, and Luck, and Crux, and Jimmy, and Serpint, and Lyra, and Delphi. *We* did this, Valor."

She is very obviously pissed off at this point. Her face is flushed red. Her little ferocious fists are balled up, and her spine is straight and rigid.

"It was part of the plan."

"Like I said," she hisses. "Six weeks was not in the plan. This war is real to them. Every one of those people out there have chosen a side. And seventy-five percent of them *aren't* with Luck. They want to kill him."

"Oh," I say.

"Oh," she mimics. "Yeah. So what we have here is a total breakdown of society. I feel like I'm living on some mythical badlands moon where everyone makes the rules up as they go. They hate him. But that's not all. Our people down here? All those sticky-sweet princesses who used to be sex slaves in the Harem? Well, they hate Crux and Serpint just as much. All they do all day long is plot insane schemes to take them out. The entire situation is completely out of control. Veila doesn't even live on the station. She stays on her ship. Who the hell in their right mind would want to be on Harem Station right now? I'll tell you who. No one. They all want to leave. The Uppers stormed us Lowers four weeks ago, demanding access to their ships so they could get the hell out of here. So we started letting them through and that's when we found out that the fucking gates are locked and no one can leave. They killed three hundred people down here, including seven young princesses. As you can imagine, that didn't go over well with Captain Red out there."

"Fuck," I say. "I didn't realize."

"She led a raiding party up some secret set of back stairs and ended up killing another four dozen people before she came back."

"Why didn't you stop her?"

"Do I look like I'm in charge?"

"She told me—"

"She told you what? That she's my guard captain?" Nyleena does air quotes around that last part. "She says that but she doesn't mean it. She's out for blood. Crux's blood. Serpint's blood. And Lyra's blood too."

"So fucking kill her," I say. "Simple."

"Kill her? Please. She has over two thousand supporters down here. I could kill her and all two thousand of those supporters—which includes all of the princesses, by the way—but then I'd be guilty of war crimes. And call me crazy, but raising twins on a Prime Prison planet isn't what I'd call 'living the dream.'"

I can see her point. "But you're way more powerful than Red out there, right? You're a true silver, Nyleena."

"What do you want me to do, Valor? Blow the fucking place up? My twins, and me, and Luck along with them?"

"Right," I sigh. "Yeah. OK. I get it."

"Do you?" She sneers at me.

"Look, I haven't had the best time either. I was…" But I stop. Because actually, before Veila caught up with us, I lived thousands of years that felt a whole lot like happily ever after inside a totally safe and protected virtual reality. Still, there was more to it than that. "I was tortured by Veila. Tray was… fuck. I have no idea what happened to Tray or where he is now. And there's this girl—"

"A girl?" Nyleena guffaws. "Do not tell me about some *girl*, OK?"

"Listen, I need to talk to Luck. Things have gone off track out there too. And if this plan is falling apart, then we need a new one."

"Don't you think Delphi and I have been trying to scheme up a new fucking plan?" She taps an impatient boot toe on the floor and plants her hands on her hips. "Nothing has worked. Our only viable option at this point is to try to leave on *Dicker* and *Lady* before things get any worse."

"OK." I sigh. "So… we should do that."

"We can't do that!" she exclaims. "Veila has a Cygnian warship out there, the security beacons are all offline, and we can't even get through the gates. So where the hell are we going to go? There are no planets around the sun. No moons. Hell, there's not even a stray asteroid to hide behind."

"So what the fuck do you want me to do? Huh? Because I have no clue. I don't even know what's going on. I have no idea where Tray is, or even if he's alive at this point."

"What did Veila tell you?"

"Veila?" I squint my eyes at Nyleena, kinda shaking my head. "She talked a lot about being pregnant and told me some stupid stories about comic books and Akeelian superheroes."

Nyleena blinks at me. "What?"

"I don't know," I say, throwing up my hands. "I don't know. We didn't really talk. She told me she was pregnant. She told me it wasn't mine. She told me about some Akeelian comic books back in Cygnian System, and then she told her cyborgs to bring me down to level ninety-six and leave me there. That was pretty much the extent of our conversation."

I leave out the part about Earth and flowers and all that other shit. Because that's not a conversation I'm going to have with Nyleena before I have it with Luck and Jimmy.

"Well, that's stupid."

"Tell me about it. And where's Jimmy? I need to see my brothers. Right now."

"He's on *Dicker* with Luck and Delphi, hiding from our... supporters." She does air quotes for that last word.

"Great. Can you take me there?"

Nyleena gets up from the booth and turns her back to me. Pauses. There's several long seconds of silence before she turns around again. "Fine. But if you try anything—"

"What the hell am I going to try? They're my brothers!"

"Well, Crux and Serpint are Luck's brothers too. Didn't stop them from trying to kill him."

"What are you talking about?"

She shakes her head and clenches her jaw. "I'll let Luck tell you that part. Because I might explode if I tell that story." And then she says, "Let's go," and starts walking towards *Lady*'s airlock.

God, none of this makes any sense. I suddenly have this sick feeling that I'm still inside a virtual and reality is somewhere out there. Unreachable.

I push that thought away real quick. Because that... that will fuck with my head big time and I can't afford any more distractions.

CHAPTER SEVEN

VALOR

The walk over to Dicker in the next bay feels like it flashes by too fast, yet takes an eternity at the same time. And the next thing I know the airlock to *Dicker* is sliding open.

The first thing I see is Luck sitting at the navigation table, pieces of a plasma rifle spread out before him. I walk towards him, glancing to my left at Delphi, then focusing back on Luck.

But he doesn't lift his head and he doesn't speak to me. No greeting at all.

"About fucking time." That comes from Jimmy behind me.

I turn and find him lying in a hammock, hands behind his head like he hasn't got a care in the world. "Jimmy," I say, smiling. "Fuck, it's good to see you guys."

Jimmy swings his legs out, hops down to the floor, then grabs Delphi's hand and says, "We'll be over on *Lady* if you need us."

I assume he's talking to Luck. But Luck says nothing in return. Then the airlock closes and when I turn, I see that Nyleena has left as well. Which makes me feel a little better. Because those fucking princesses are all crazy and dangerous and I need to figure out what's going through Luck's head without their interference.

There's a stool on the opposite side of the navigation table from Luck, so I take a seat and say, "I... I'm sorry."

He still doesn't look up. Just says, "About which part?" as he starts screwing a piece of the rifle barrel back together.

"W-well," I stammer, then take a deep breath and continue. "All of it, I guess. Ignoring you after you came back with Jimmy. Hooking up with Tray."

Now he looks at me.

His eyes are ringed with dark circles, his violet irises simmering with heat and anger like there's a storm brewing inside him. His hair is too long, and messy, and there's dirt or maybe a scorch mark from a plasma rifle marking an ugly line across his throat.

"Huh," he huffs. "Hooking *up* with him?"

And I know what Luck's asking. Did I hook up with him or did I *hook up* with him? I don't know what to say, so I decide on nothing.

"Is that what you did, then?" Luck asks. "You just chose him over me?"

And this kinda pisses me off. "Why not?" I say. "You had Nyleena. Right? You were all set, Luck."

"That was after, and you know it."

"But it was coming. We all know there's no way to fight that bond."

"So you just quit? Just bowed out early like a fucking pussy? Left me wondering what the fuck I did to make you hate me?"

"Don't be dumb. I don't hate you."

"No," he says, narrowing his eyes at me. "You just *left* me. Where the fuck have you been?"

I run my fingers through my hair. Which is also too long and probably a mess. I want to say all kinds of things. Things like… *I didn't leave you. It was the plan. And even though I did leave you in another way, that was self-preservation.*

But I don't feel ready to have that conversation. So instead I say, "It's a very long story."

"Start at the beginning," Luck growls. "And don't leave a single fucking thing out."

So I do.

Kind of.

I start at the point where Luck and Nyleena walked Tray and I through the spin node on level one twenty-two. "We came out on that station. And there were ships in the docking bays. And the whole thing kinda reminded me of Harem, you know. When we first got here. All dark and empty, but still you had this feeling that people had been there. Maybe just a few minutes ago. Does that makes sense?"

Luck is staring at me. And he doesn't blink. Just gives me one nod as encouragement to go on.

"Well, anyway. Tray left some very crucial details out of that plan."

"What kind of details?"

"He was after a girl," I say. "Brigit is her name."

"A princess?" Luck asks.

"No," I say, shaking my head. "An *Akeelian* girl, Luck."

He makes a face.

"I know," I say. "There's no such thing. But... there is. And she's one of them."

I stop then. Trying to figure out if I should tell Luck now or later who the girls are. What they are.

"What was that place?" Luck asks. "The station. What was it called?"

"OK, so here's where it all goes sideways. So bear with me."

"I'm listening."

"The station was Angel Station." Luck opens his mouth to protest, but I put up a hand. "Just let me talk. Let me tell the story and then you can ask questions. OK? Because there's a lot to unpack here."

He leans back against the wall behind him, folds his arms across his chest, and shrugs. "Fine. Talk."

So I do. I tell him about how Tray lied to me. About how I dragged the truth out of him and agreed to help him find Brigit. "But," I say, "I only did it because we were in this time warp inside the spin node, Luck. No time was passing out here. And then we found her, and Tray wanted to go inside to explain that he's going to set her free now, but I... I wanted to go in too. Just to see if it was real, you know. I was still very suspicious of him. And then he got lost trying to come in after me because Brigit had broken the world inside the virtual, and it took forever for him to find us—in our time, at least. Only a couple hours on the outside. But inside it had been years in virtual time. And so when Tray finally arrived, Brigit and I were friends."

Luck raises an eyebrow. "Friends?"

"I didn't touch her," I say, holding up my hands. "I swear to the sun. At least, not before Tray…"

"Tray what?"

"Well… he was very happy to see her. And she was very happy to see him. So they… you know. And I just did my thing. But then…" I sigh. "Yeah. We… um… we were all together."

"Inside the virtual."

I nod. "But then… you know… the only thing waiting for us out here was war. So Tray was all… 'Time is so different. We could stay here for a while.'"

"So you stayed. With *them*."

I nod.

"And then what?" He is pissed. He's just holding it in.

"And then…" I sigh and look around the ship, picturing our perfect virtual world. "I had been keeping track of time. Because I knew Tray wouldn't. And we realized that four days had gone by in the real—"

"Four. Fucking. Days?" Luck growls. "That's like—"

"That's thousands of years in virtual time."

"How is that possible?"

I shrug with my hands. "I don't know, Luck. Well, I kinda do. It was a trap. She was a trap. Tray was a trap. To get me to Veila. And then we came out of the virtual, and…" I skip the part where Tray and I had sex alone as we were waiting for Brigit to thaw out. Because this is not the time to explain that. "And then Veila was there and Tray was spitting out the coordinates for the rendezvous point for *Booty*, and… and then Veila… I don't know. I don't really remember anything after that. Vague recollection of torture. Possibly some sex?"

"Possibly?"

"It's pretty foggy. And then I remember being put into a cryopod. I think Tray made some kind of deal to get me out of there. I kinda remember that. But..." I shake my head. "Something must've happened. Because I woke up here. And Veila was the one who did that."

Luck is silent for a few moments. Then he throws his head back and laughs.

I laugh too. Uncomfortably. Because I'm not sure what kind of laugh this is.

"Do you think I'm fucking stupid?" Luck says, suddenly not laughing. Suddenly angry again.

"What are you talking about?"

"You expect me to believe this bullshit story?"

"Dude, that's how it happened. And now Veila says she's pregnant—"

"What?"

"—but she says I'm not the father and—"

"Are you fucking with me right now?"

"—and I don't really know what to make of that."

"Well, I don't know what to make of you," Luck growls. "But I'll tell you something I do know. You're an asshole. We're not on the same side."

He gets up from the navigation table and starts to walk towards the airlock.

I get up too, rushing over to grab his arm.

He turns on me. Eyes lit up like a fucking Cygnian princess. Only this isn't lust, it's hate.

"Crux and Serpint came to me upstairs."

"That's a good one. I killed Crux."

110

"No, dude." I shake my head sadly, trying not to remember those dark, empty pits in Crux's eyes. "You didn't. He's alive."

"That's impossible. I shot him. Point blank in the chest with a plasma rifle."

"It was on stun," I say, automatically lying. Not sure why I'm lying, I just don't want to get in to what I saw inside Crux or his story about the golden place.

"It wasn't on stun," Luck insists. "I saw it. I saw..." But he trails off.

"He's alive, Luck. I just fucking talked to him. So it had to be on stun. Hear me? It had to be because he's still up there."

Luck turns to look at me. Confused. Angry. "Is this another lie?"

"Just listen to me. They said I have to get you to let Veila through the spin node—"

Luck guffaws. "You are too fucking funny."

"—and Veila said the same thing. And—"

"Fuck you!" Luck says, pushing hard. Two flat palms on my chest so I go reeling backwards and crashing against the edge of the navigation table. He takes two steps and crosses the distance between us and points his finger in my face. "Go back to your princess, OK? We don't want you here. Go back to Crux, and Serpint, and Veila, and Tray. Because that's where you belong now, Valor. We're fuckin' done."

"Listen to me!" I yell. "I can trick her. I can trick her the way Tray tricked me. I can use her. She told me something about Earth, Luck. She says none of the babies will be born if they don't get something special from Earth. Some... I don't know. Antibody, maybe?"

"What the fuck are you talking about?"

"Earth!" I say. "You need to get Nyleena to Earth if you want to save your babies. And Veila has control over the spin-node level. So you need me, Luck. She needs you and Nyleena to get through the node and you *need me* to get up to that level. Because I'm telling you, there's a lot more going on than you realize. I didn't even tell you about the Akeelian girls yet. And trust me on this. You *will* need to know that little bit of hidden truth."

He turns away, but doesn't make any more moves towards the airlock.

"I have only one weapon left."

"Yeah, what's that?"

"The soulmate bond."

"Yeah." He spins around. "Thanks for reminding that you can't be trusted."

"It's weak, Luck. It's so weak. We're barely connected. I'm not even sure it's real. Because I hate her fucking guts. And it's not like you and Nyleena were. I don't secretly want to fuck her. I want to *kill her*. I *can* kill her. But not until we get you and Nyleena through the spin node and safe on Earth."

"You don't even know that's where it goes."

"I know more than you think. I was on Angel Station. I was in a whole other galaxy. I lived inside a spin node for lifetimes in the virtual and months in the real because time was so different in there too. And I'm telling you I'm right. And even if I was wrong, we can't stay here. There's only one way out of the ALCOR System now and that's through that spin node."

Luck looks at me like I am filth. Like I'm a traitor. Like we didn't spend our whole lives together.

"I *can* trick her," I whisper. "I *can* get us out of here. She's vulnerable right now. She's pregnant and she's about to lose the babies. She needs to get to Earth too. She told me she would do anything to save them. I can use her to save *us*."

"All I have to do is trust you, right?" Luck says in a low, even voice. "Just trust you to take care of everything. Well, I already did that, Valor. And this is what I got. Harem Station is gone. We're fucked. Nyleena is pregnant with my twins. And no one is coming to save us because you and Tray got caught up in a sex game inside a virtual and forgot the whole motherfucking reason you left here was so you could find ALCOR and bring him home. And oh, by the way, the Baby is... well, not a baby anymore. He wants nothing more than to cut off our air supply and kill us. And the only thing that's stopping him is a demonic AI no one trusts."

"Listen, Baby is not what you think. He's confused too and—"

"Oh. My. Fucking. Sun. Are you for real right now? Everyone up there is just misunderstood? Is that what you expect me to believe?"

I want to tell him about Crux and Corla, but... I decide he wouldn't believe me anyway. So I don't.

"I get it," I say. "But I'm not a traitor. I'm on your side, Luck. I never stopped—"

"Don't," he says, putting up a hand. "Don't you dare tell me you never stopped loving me. Because that just makes what you did that much worse. You fucking *left* me."

"It was part of the plan," I say.

"That's not what I'm talking about and you know it."

I do know it. I fucked this all up. But I'm not ready to give in yet. "Just… give me two spins, OK? Two spins to get Veila under my thumb and I will get us out of here."

He sighs and turns away.

"I don't want to say this, because there's no way to dress it up and get me cred with you, but I have to. Because it's true. I'm all you have right now, Luck. I'm all you have. So you need to trust me. You need to think long and hard about all those years we spent together and all those times I saved your ass. All those times I had your back and got you back here, safe and sound. Because I'm still that guy."

He turns back to me. "Are you sure about that, Valor? Because from where I stand you're not that guy at all."

I take a step forward. He doesn't back up. Just tilts his chin up and locks eyes with me. Daring me to do what I want to do next.

I reach for him and both his hands come up and block me. "Touch me again," he says, "and I'll kill you."

"Fine," I say, backing off. "That's fine. You're with Nyleena. You're happy—"

"Happy?" He laughs. "I do love her. And we will be together because they made us this way. But what you and I had…" He swallows hard and shakes his head. "You can't engineer that. And you walked out."

"I'm sorry," I say.

He smiles a little. It's one those I-can't-believe-you-just-fucking-said-that smiles. "Well, you know what?

114

Before—you know, before this whole thing blew up in my face—'I'm sorry' would've worked. It would've made it all better. But it's not enough now. Not nearly enough."

"I understand. I do. But I'm not fucking lying. I'm on your side. I'm *always* on your side."

"He's telling the truth," *Lady* says.

"*Lady*?" I say, looking up at *Dicker's* ceiling. "How are you here?"

"I'm sorry, Valor," she says. "I was asked to listen in."

"Ah," I say, heat filling my whole body. "To see if I was lying."

"And you're not. He's not," *Lady* tells Luck. "Most of what he said has been sincere."

"Which part wasn't sincere?" Luck asks *Lady*.

"The parts having to do with Tray. His biological reactions tell me he left a *lot* out."

Luck glares at me. But to *Lady* he says, "But the parts about Veila?"

"All true. He's not in love with her. That bond is weak. I think his plan could work."

"And I think," *Dicker* chimes in, "that he's right about Nyleena giving birth on Earth. There's something to that place. The flowers were enough to get her pregnant, but the chances are very high they are not enough to bring those babies to term. And we cannot get there without getting up to level one twenty-two."

"We?" Luck says. "You and *Lady* can't come with us. We'll have to leave you behind. And I'm not like—" He pauses to stare at me. "I'm not like that. I'm not

115

walking out and leaving you two to fend for yourselves. So that plan won't work for me."

"Not necessarily true," I say, ignoring his not-so-thinly-veiled attempt to accuse me of abandonment one more time. "Tray worked out some of the mystery behind ALCOR and the station and he says Harem used to be in this other galaxy. And if ALCOR could pull a whole station through a spin node, then there has to be a way to pull two ships through too."

"Through that hole in the fabric of time and space located on level one twenty-two?" Luck scoffs.

"The Succubus could do it," *Dicker* says. "Mighty Minions had a spin node too, after all."

"Like she's going to help us," Luck says.

"Let me take care of that. I think we can come to an arrangement. She's as eager to leave as we are," *Dicker* says.

Luck looks at me, then says, "You have two fucking spins to figure out what Veila knows about Cygnian pregnancies and report back with a plan for Nyleena and our babies."

"OK." But goddamn. What he just said—'Nyleena and our babies'—my heart hurts hearing it.

"Two," Luck growls. "That's it. And then whatever we decide to do, we do it without you."

CHAPTER EIGHT

Lady arranges a lift bot for me to ride back up to the top of the station and even with that luxury, it's a long fucking ride. Not so much because it's four hundred levels—even though that is a long climb no matter how you look at it—but because people are screaming at me from the edges. Spewing threats, and insults, and a whole lot of hate.

I spend a lot of time thinking about what would've happened to me if I had to walk up all the dozens of non-working escalators without Veila's cyborg guards and also find myself missing ALCOR so much, my chest begins to hurt. And not because I was shot with a plasma rifle by Captain Red down there.

This station without ALCOR... well, it's not Harem anymore, that's for sure. I never realized it. I guess I just took him for granted all these years. So sure that I would be protected by this almost god-like... thing. Person. Whatever he is. That he would always be there on my side. Always have my back.

And now he's not. Now he doesn't.

117

So this is what I think about on my way up even though I should be thinking about how I'm going to convince Veila that we're soulmates in love, get her to trust me, and then figure out a way to get the Succubus to infiltrate the Baby's side of the data core so she can come up with a plan to take two huge ships through a spin node that's only as tall as one level.

That's assuming Luck can get the Succubus on board with what we're doing, and who knows if she's even capable of this little task. Also assuming the Baby doesn't figure out my plan. Because he has to stay behind and run things. I can't leave all these people to die on the station. I don't care if they're all at war with each other right now. We're still Harem and these people came here because they trusted us to take care of them.

I will not let the Baby kill them all by leaving.

I should also be thinking about Luck and how angry he is. At me. Specifically. Me. How did things go so wrong? I feel like I told him a lot about what happened to me in the last six weeks but he told me nothing about what happened to him.

I need that story. But it's too late now. I can't go back down until I have Veila on our side and that... well, that might not even be possible. She is the most ruthless bitch I've ever met.

And she has her own agenda.

Yeah, that little voice in my head says. *Babies*.

And let's get real here. Does anyone really think those babies aren't mine? I do have some vague recollection of sex with her. Or maybe not sex. But... eh. Gross. I can't think about it. Because if those babies are mine then she farmed me for my genetics.

So gross.

And then I play Luck's last threat over and over in my mind. I have two spins, then whatever they do, they do it without me.

It's an insult more than a threat. Because like two seconds before that he was going on and on about how he won't leave *Dicker* and *Lady* behind.

But he'll leave me.

Fine. Whatever. He's allowed to have his feelings.

All this is what I ponder as I ascend and by the time I reach the level where my quarters are—which is, thankfully, somewhat private and inaccessible to the angry masses down below—I'm worked up with doubt, and regrets, and sadness, and anxiety, and hate, and probably every fucking emotion a human is capable of when I step off the lift and head into the hallway that leads to my quarters, flanked on either side by cyborgs.

The door opens when I palm the biometric lock and I enter alone.

Alone.

Great. How do I even contact Veila?

"Baby?" I say to the room.

"Valor." ALCOR's voice comes back at me. And God, that hurts. It's so much his voice I have to remind myself several times that this thing is not ALCOR before I speak.

"Is there a way to contact Veila?"

"I can arrange it. For a price."

"A price?" Yeah. There's the reminder I needed that this isn't ALCOR. The Baby is not on our side. He does not have my back. "What price?"

"I need something."

119

"Of course you do. What is it then?"

"I need to know how to get the security beacons back online."

"Why?"

"Because that's Princess Veila's price for what I need from her."

She's hedging her bets. If she can't get Luck to take her to Earth she will get to Corla and steal whatever it is inside her that can save her babies.

She told me she would not stop. She would die trying to save them.

"They're not like that and you know it," I say to Baby. "The security beacons are self-contained entities. They're people. So if they locked you out, then they locked you out."

"I'm afraid that's not good enough, Valor. I need this. You could ask Crux to go over there and talk to them. Set up a small... parlay, if you will."

"Why don't *you* just ask Crux?"

"Because Crux doesn't trust me."

"I don't trust you either."

"Yes, but you need something from me and he does not."

"I'm sure there's lots of ways to threaten Crux into doing your bidding. Use your evil brain."

"I've tried that. Veila interfered. I am not allowed to harm Crux, Serpint, or Lyra."

Interesting. "Why are you taking orders from her anyway? Who is she to you?"

"She..."

"She what?"

"She promised me something. Something I want very badly."

"Yeah? What's that?"

"A way off this station."

"You can't leave the station," I yell. "Everyone will die."

"The Succubus can have it. I'm no longer interested in caring for people."

Well, that's a problem, I want to say, but don't. *Because we need the Succubus to leave with us. So Baby, my evil friend, your wish will not be granted.*

But then all kinds of moral dilemmas pop into my already overcrowded brain about leaving Baby in charge of all the Harem citizens.

Why the fuck is this happening to me?

"Sure." I sigh. "I'll talk to Crux. Just tell Veila I need to see her."

"Done," the Baby says. "I'll let you know when she responds. In the meantime, Crux is in his office."

"Fine," I hiss, then leave my quarters via the private lift that goes up to the harem room.

And can I just say I hate the empty harem room? I get it. Those girls weren't really here of their own accord. But we took good care of them.

Didn't we?

Apparently not. Because they hate Crux and Serpint. They want to kill Crux and Serpint.

I glance over at Crux's office and see him sitting behind his desk like this is just another day in the life.

He doesn't even glance up at me when I enter. Just stares at an old-fashioned screen.

"What the fuck is that?" I ask, pointing to the screen.

"What?" Crux asks, barely glancing at me. His fingers just keep tapping away like he's in the middle of important business.

"That screen."

"Air screens have been offline for weeks. I'm just trying to get shit done."

I pull a chair up to his desk and take a seat. "What shit?"

He sighs. Loudly. Looks at me. "You know. Shit like keeping everyone fed and breathable air in the fucking atmosphere. Which isn't easy to do since the only air we're getting up here is being piped in from down below through the ventilation system. But the last thing I need is another riot on my hands."

I want to ask about the previous riot, but figure this is probably a sore spot. Besides, I can use my imagination on that. And I want to get more information about the air, because that's a disaster waiting to happen. Even if Veila doesn't turn off the ventilation fans like she threatened, the air will get thin soon and everyone will notice when they can't breathe right.

This situation is a shit show of epic proportions.

But I push that away and get down to business. "I saw Luck."

"You did?" And now I've got his attention. "When?"

"Veila took me down there. Or actually, she forced me to go down there. He wasn't very happy to see me."

"Can you blame him?"

"I guess not. But none of this is really my fault. I was just…"

"Doing what Tray told you to?"

"Right."

"How's that working out?"

"Not so good. He…" But I don't know if I really understand what Tray did. I mean, I get it. He sold me out. But Brigit sold him out, and no one really knew they were selling people out. It was pretty much Veila's secret, evil plan. So… I don't know what to do with that. "I think he's probably dead," I finally conclude.

Crux is silent for a few moments. Then he shakes his head and looks down at his desk. "You sure?"

"No. But things got weird. And I don't really think there's any other way. So. I think he is."

"Did you find ALCOR?"

"No," I say. "I don't really know what happened. I was… out of it near the end. I'm not even really sure how I got here. How did I get here?"

"Veila brought you."

"Right. I need to talk to her but she's on her ship. I have the Baby sending her a message but I had to promise him I'd come talk to you about the security beacons to get him to do me that favor."

"Forget it," Crux says. "He wants access to the security beacons so he can give Veila access to Corla. And she's the only one who's safe right now, so. Yeah. No. I've already told him I'm not going out there."

I slouch down in my chair, lean back, and look up at the ceiling. Start counting the xenon lights above my head as I think.

Crux goes back to work.

After several minutes of this Baby says, "Veila has given you permission to enter her ship, Valor."

"Great," I say. "Crux has refused my request."

"I heard," Baby replies.

Crux says nothing.

"Well," I say, getting to my feet, "I guess I'll report back when I can."

"You do that," Crux mumbles.

CHAPTER NINE

Once I arrive at the airlock to Veila's ship there's a bot waiting for me. It clicks and beeps in a language I don't understand, but I get the general idea and follow it down several hallways and then the hallway opens into a vast, open space.

A park.

Weird. But isn't all of this weird? Hasn't my whole life been weird?

There are tall trees, and flower beds, and meticulously maintained grass divided up into large squares with alternating coloration, so that when you look at the entire expanse from above it appears to be some kind of lattice. Or a game board.

I'm going with game board. That's Veila's specialty, isn't it? Player of games.

She's lying down on a blanket in the middle of the space. Eyes closed. Fake sunbeam shining down on her face. Both hands protectively placed across her stomach.

All this time with no genetic Cygnian-Akeelian babies and now we suddenly have two pregnant princesses?

Something's wrong there. I can feel it. But I don't know enough about anything to make the connection.

"I didn't have time to find those comics," Veila says with a sigh as I approach.

"I'm not that interested in them."

She sits up and smooths out her long gown so it's splayed majestically in the grass around her. "Well? What did Luck say?"

"You know. Little bit of this. Little bit of that. But pretty much it boils down to…he hates me."

"You did leave him behind."

I sigh. And it's loud and filled with frustration. "Where's Tray?" I ask.

"I have no idea."

"Funny. Last time I saw him, he was with you."

"Last time you saw me?" She scoffs. "Well, a lot has happened since we last… *spoke*."

"I can see that. Are you going to fill me in?"

"This is my last ship," she says.

"What?"

"This ship. This is my last one."

"OK."

"The other one was… unexpectedly disabled. I had to escape through its spin node."

I narrow my eyes and drop to my knees in the grass. "What do you mean?"

"I mean…" She lets out a long breath. "I mean someone reversed the beam on my SEAR cannons and sent an electromagnetic pulse into my ship, thereby killing all my borgs and bots and disabling my ship.

Luckily, spin nodes require analog security measures and start-up protocols, so I had a way out. But I'm not going to lie. It was dicey there for a moment."

"Someone attacked you? And Tray?"

"I'm not entirely sure. Logic dictates that he and Brigit were killed in that EM pulse, but I find it somewhat coincidental that the *Booty Hunter* and a ship I disabled appeared at that very moment my ship was taken offline. Do what you will with that information. I just have no idea."

"*Booty*," I say, smiling. "Who was the other ship?"

"I'm not sure. It was *Demon Girl*, but I killed her. I know for a fact I killed her. So some other mind had taken over the *Demon Girl*." She looks at me. "I think it was ALCOR."

My eyebrows shoot up. "Why would you think that? He died."

"Did he?"

"I'm assuming he did. I have no other information that he didn't."

She frowns. "What did you want to see me about?"

"Well. Where do I even start? Luck hates my guts. The princess rebellion is out of control. Apparently, before the gates were closed down, hundreds of former harem princesses came back to join the rebellion. The whole thing is being run by some red-haired woman called Seline."

"Captain Red. I've heard of her."

"She's a fucking bitch. She shot me. It was on stun, but still. *Lady* said I was dead and she had to bring me back to life."

Veila looks at me, eyes tracking over my body, looking for damage. There's no apparent signs that I was shot because my shirt isn't scorched or anything. And I don't feel like lifting it up to show her the red, sore skin of my chest to prove it because... well, I don't want her looking at me. So I move on and assume she believes me.

"And it fuckin' hurt. So anyway. Things are a mess down there."

"Did you get anywhere with him?"

"Well... not far, to be honest."

"What have I told you about lying?"

"There is no point in lying to you, Veila. It is what it is. He's having a hard time believing me. And trusting me. And to be completely honest, that hurts more than the fucking plasma stun."

"Why do you care about him when you have Tray?"

"I don't have Tray. I don't even know if I want Tray, if he's alive. I love Luck, OK? That's just how it is."

"And he loves Nyleena."

"I know that. It's complicated. But I can't hurt him. Or Nyleena. Or any of them, actually. Not the Baby. Not those asshole outlaws who have turned on me. Not even the psycho princesses. We all have to come out of this alive and all right. That's my deal."

She frowns. "I'm not sure I can deliver that at this point."

"You can do your best."

"Why would you even believe me?"

"I don't believe you. I don't even like you. I'm not playing around here, Veila. If I had the chance I'd kill you. But if saving my friends and my people means I have to save you too, then fuck it. That's all I have left."

"I don't understand."

"Which part?"

"Who do you think we're running from?"

"What do you mean?"

"You're acting like we're all on the same side. So who do you think is the enemy?"

"You, I guess."

"That makes no sense, Valor."

She's right. It doesn't. "Here's a question for you. Why are you suddenly so... quiet?"

"And by quiet you mean...?"

"Reasonable."

She purses her lips and lies back on the grass. "A lot has happened while you were in cryosleep. Everything is different and my priorities have changed."

"The babies."

"Babies. Yes. They are all I care about anymore. But assuming I can bring them to term I have another problem."

"What's that?" I sigh, lying back on the grass. So fucking tired already and I've only been awake half a spin.

"The girl twin inside me. She will be Akeelian if I don't intervene. The babies always take on the race of the father when Akeelians are involved. And that means she will be used up in gestation if I don't intervene."

"Shit. I forgot about that." And then I get sad all over again because Luck's babies will have the same problem.

"I won't allow it."

"Can you even stop that?" I ask. "Isn't it just… nature?"

"That's another reason why I need to get to Earth. Otherwise the only way to preserve her is to take her mind near the end and put it in storage."

"Make her into a ship."

"I will not allow that, either. I think it's a barbaric practice that should be stopped."

"Oh, that's funny. Considering you did that to Brigit."

"I didn't steal Brigit's mind. I put her somewhere safe. I'd have done it for all of them, if I had the opportunity back then."

"Veila," I say, scoffing. "You're an evil, murderous cunt of a woman. You have done some of the most disgusting things I've ever seen, and I've been a lot of places and witnessed more atrocities than I can count. So if your new plan is to convince me that you're somehow innocent and everything you did has some greater, altruistic purpose, then—just don't fucking insult me like that. OK? I might not be the smartest Harem brother, but I'm not the dumbest one, either."

She huffs. "Which one of you is the dumb one?"

"I dunno. Luck, I guess." And then I smile and say, "He's not really dumb. He's just smart in a different way."

"Cunning," she says.

"Sure. Why not. He's cunning. And fearless. That's what makes him both smart and stupid at the same time. He's brave in a way only ignorant people can be."

"Agreed." She sighs.

"And he's not going to give up. He won't. He will find a way to get what he wants no matter what kind of danger he has to face to do that. That's his superpower."

"What's your superpower, Valor?"

"I don't know," I whisper. "I'm not sure I have one, to be honest. Crux is the leader. Jimmy is all personality. Serpint is stubborn. Tray is smart. Luck is courageous and I'm... I'm just here because I had violet eyes the day Corla asked Crux to shoot her through a spin node twenty-one years ago."

She plucks a blade of grass and twirls it in her fingers. "Somehow I doubt that."

"Well, I'm an OK salvager, I guess. And I'm loyal."

She nods. "Yeah. I think that's it then. You are loyal." She side-eyes me. "Just not to me."

I laugh. "Why the hell would I be loyal to *you*?"

"Because you are my soulmate."

"You'd prefer anyone over me. You wanted Jimmy, remember?"

"I need Jimmy. I never wanted him."

"You needed him for—?" I nod my head at her belly.

"Don't be ridiculous. I can't have Jimmy's babies. You know that as well as I do."

"No, you can only have mine."

"They are not yours."

"Then whose are they?"

"They're *mine*."

"Genetically engineered?"

"Parts of them are," she admits.

"OK. Well, I don't really want to talk about that."

She looks at me. "What do you want to talk about?"

"Saving people, Veila. That's what I want to talk about. You should pull your ship off the station, give total authority to Baby to take care of things, and then I can work out some kind of deal with the beacons to get you through the gate or—"

"Through the gate?" She guffaws. "I can't go through the stupid gate! The Cygnians and Akeelians will kill me immediately when I get to the other side. The only thing keeping me alive at this point is those stupid gates. The Baby let me through and then the beacons shut down to protect themselves. And the gates went with them. That was just luck, I think." She looks at me. "Not your Luck. Just general luck. Because now they're broken, or whatever. And that's actually a good thing."

"Ah," I say. "So that's why you really want to go to Earth. You want to escape."

"Don't we all want to escape?"

"I think I can get you through, but I can't guarantee your safety on the other side. You have to know that. Luck will kill you no matter what. You crossed him and he's done. And once Luck is done with you, he's just… done with you. There's no way back."

"Well," she says, getting to her feet and brushing grass off her long gown, "then I guess you should just move on. Because he's done with you too."

She starts walking across the park.

"Where are you going?" I ask.

"Home. I'm tired."

"What about me?" I ask, getting to my feet and following her. "What am I supposed to tell Luck?"

She spins around and smiles at me. "Can I give you a piece of advice, Valor?"

132

I throw up my hands. "Why not?"

"Learn to lie. And cheat. All this loyalty and truth-telling will get you nowhere."

And then she turns on her heel and walks away.

CHAPTER TEN

I stay in the park. Mostly because I don't have anywhere else to go. Veila didn't invite me to go with her, didn't assign me a room. No one came and gave me orders, or put me in restraints, or told me to go home.

They just left me.

So I just lie here on the grass, hands behind my head, and stare up at the ceiling. It's some kind of hologram. It was dusk when I first looked up but now it's night and there's a perfect star map of the sky as seen from Harem Station.

Whenever Luck and I entered a new system and had a chance to look at the stars we'd always marvel at how the very same dots of light could look so different from a new perspective.

Every now and then I'd hook up with a girl who was into the stars and she'd point out a few constellations with names and stories I've never heard of. Of course, the zodiac constellations are called the same thing everywhere in the galaxy. It's been standardized for gate mapping. So have all the known suns. But the actual constellations—the pictures people draw in the sky—those evolve through culture.

And here's something interesting—no matter where you go, be it planet, or station, or fucking asteroid in the middle of nowhere, every local constellation is based on a myth. Heroes of times gone by. The women they fought wars for. The beasts that thwarted them. The gods, and the goddesses, and the demigod half-breed children. It's always different and yet always the same.

Here in the ALCOR Sector, we don't really have that. It's a mashup of many different cultures. ALCOR has a hologram like this in one part of the station, one where the day and night cycle of a spinning planet goes through seasons. And there are stars up there, connected by faint lines to draw out different characters. But the characters change all the time. Artists come from all over to take turns designing a new set of holographic constellations. This happens about twice a year, maybe. So there's been a couple dozen different versions of the night sky so far.

But there's always a bear-like ursus. Always an equus. Sometimes they have horns, like the karkadanns. Sometimes they have the body of a horse and the torso of a human. There's always a maiden, and a hero, and a dragon. And then sometimes there's weird things like a specific cup used for rituals. Or a musical instrument. Or a spirit that lives in the dark.

One guy came and turned the fucking night sky on Harem into a demonic hell filled with demons and instruments of torture. People kinda got pissed off about that and it was only up for a few weeks before

ALCOR decided to let some other artist come in and change it.

Luck used to joke that if he ever got a shot at designing the constellations he'd make it a forest. There'd be nothing but trees up there in the sky.

I kinda like that idea. Kinda wish he'd gotten his chance.

And from there my mind wanders to us. Him and I. How it used to be. All the fun we had. All the danger we put ourselves in. All the ways we cheated death and made it home.

But that makes me think about Crux and what he said about death and dying. How maybe we can't die.

But I don't have room in my brain for that right now so I think about all the nights Luck and I spent together. After the crisis was over and the wounds were healed. When we could take a breath and smile because once again, we'd made it out alive.

And how we'd lie together in bed. Talking, and drinking, and always laughing.

Always laughing. We laughed a lot in our old life. We had a lot of fun. It was good and I miss it.

Sometimes there'd be a girl with us, but most times not. Just he, and I, and *Lady*, and Beauty. Alone. Floating around in the thick soup of deep, dark mysterious space contained inside the swirl of stars we call Galaxy Prime.

I really thought we'd be like that forever. I never imagined a different life for us. I certainly never saw us mixed up with Cygnian princesses.

I never saw Nyleena coming. Never even suspected that some girl would so thoroughly come between us.

I have a sudden urge to talk to him. Say all the things I didn't when I saw him earlier. Things like... *I miss you. I can live with Nyleena. I could maybe even learn to love her. Maybe we could find a way to make this work?*

But there was a reason I didn't say that. It can't work. It would never work. Just like being with Tray would never work.

Sun-fucked soulmates.

Why does my princess have to end up being the definition of evil?

I must've fallen asleep because the next thing I know a series of beeps and chirps has me opening my eyes and sitting up.

A bot is hovering in front of me with a flat package in its grippy hands. It drops the package in the grass and then zooms off, disappearing into the trees.

I reach for the package and flip it over. It's really more of a thick, faded, tan envelope. The front side is covered in washed-out stickers. They're peeling and some of the images are almost completely rubbed off. But I don't need to see them to know what's inside.

Akeelian Adventures.

I slip the comics out. Four in total. They smell like old books, and musty forests, and there's a hint of something sweet. Like tushberries, maybe.

The cover of the first one is *Bot Boy.* Actual title: *Bot Boy and the Lost Lunar Colony.* He's a handsome young man. Maybe somewhere between fifteen and eighteen Akeelian years old. He's wearing a skin-tight orange suit with a black weapons belt across his chest and another strung low on his hips. His hair is dark, his eyes are violet, and he has horns.

I laugh. Can't help it. "Jimmy with horns."

His hands aren't hands, either. They're claws. And his face isn't very human. Though his body—aside from the horns and claws—is.

His partner appears to be...

I squint at it. Hold it up close to my eyes. "Xyla?" I rub some dust off the cover to make sure I'm seeing this right. No. It's right. Long purple hair. Light synthetic skin. Too-tight t-shirt, stiletto-shaped feet, and shorty-shorts that leave little to the imagination.

"What the fuck?" I ask no one. "Hmm." This makes no sense. This is an actual picture—drawing?— of Xyla exactly as she looked on that day we walked onto Harem Station for the very first time.

One might ask, *How the hell do you remember what Xyla was wearing twenty-one years ago, Valor?*

I'll tell you how. That was the first time I'd been anywhere that wasn't Wayward Station. That was the closest I'd ever been to a sexbot in my life. And that night, after all the shit was sorted with ALCOR and we delivered our messages, and Crux and Jimmy were off somewhere discussing our situation, Luck and I talked about Xyla. We talked about her like... well, like two fifteen-year-old Akeelian boys would talk about their first meeting with a sexbot.

And this picture right here, on this cover that says *Akeelian Adventures: Bot Boy,* this is *her*.

"OK, hold on a second." I channel Tray for this next part. Because he's all logical and shit. "Maybe that was just the standard-issue outfit for Xyla's sexbot model?"

I nod at this. I can accept that. This is just what all the sexbots were wearing that year.

"But purple hair?" I don't know. Something about this is weird.

I flip the book open to the first page and start reading. The story goes like this:

Bot Boy and his trusty sidekick, Xyla—uh, yeah, it's her—are on the prowl for spare bot parts and wander into the ancient Sol System where they find a hidden station inside a moon. It's abandoned—or so they think. And then there's a whole bunch of panels of battles with eight-legged bots. Eventually Bot Boy and Xyla subdue the creepers, dismantle them and then integrate the bot parts with their own bodies...

Uhhh, what the fuck?

That wasn't Jimmy's job. He was a bot liberator. And he sure as hell didn't dismantle them and become a cyborg.

But then I remember that Veila said the comics were just generic characters before we boys left Harem Station on the jobs ALCOR assigned to us.

Because there's another one below this one. And this guy *is* Jimmy. The main title is still *Akeelian Adventures* but the subtitle reads: *Jimmy and Xyla Bag the Bots*.

He's older, the illustrations are more accurate—at least he doesn't have horns or claws anymore—and Xyla looks more like she does today than she did back when we first saw her. A warrior instead of a sexbot.

In this adventure they aren't stealing body parts for themselves, thank the sun. But they are enslaving bots on a place called Junkyard Station.

I frown. Close it up. And then look at the last two.

Once again the first, older cover, depicts a more cartoonish version of two violet-eyed boys who look like demons and the title is *Akeelian Adventures: Soul Stealers*.

I flip through it and find the two boys—who are clearly Luck and me—are also going to ancient stations, only this time, instead of stealing bot parts to make themselves into cyborgs, they steal station parts from still-living stations—thus the title *Soul Stealers*—and take them back to Junkyard Station, and then give them to the evil AI who runs the place, who is called MIZAR.

"Hmm," I huff, toss it aside, and then pick up the one that has our real faces on the cover.

I stare at it for a long time. Because *Lady* is there too. And Beauty.

I miss that life. So much. And even though I know the story inside will be wrong, I open it anyway just so I can picture the four of us out on our adventures again.

Luck and I are no longer demons but we're still stealing critical components from living stations. Which makes no sense. That would be like someone coming to Harem and taking the Baby's data cores.

It would never happen. Even if you got in alive you'd never get out alive.

But then I get one page where it's clear that both Luck and I are killed by some kind of glowing weapon. Maybe a SEAR knife dialed up to sword length.

But luckily our trusty bot, Beauty, puts us inside these tanks and then we are regenerated and wake up stronger than ever, kill everyone on the station, and then take the station's data cores back to Junkyard for that MIZAR person to use.

I hold the comic book at arm's length, trying to force it to make sense. What are these stories? Just... a fiction? Some kind of lost mythology and we accidentally become part of it? A premonition?

A plan?

Beeping pulls me away from the story and when I look up I see the same bot who delivered them is back. Motioning and chirping at me.

I get up, grab the stupid comics, shove them back into the envelope, and follow it. Because even though I don't speak this bot's language, that's the only possible thing he can be saying.

I study the park as we walk down a long, winding path. Many different varieties of plant life. Most of it I've seen before. Somewhere. On one of our many soul-sucking adventures.

Soul suckers.

That's not how people see Luck and I.

Is it?

We didn't steal parts from any working stations. The stuff we were looking for was all ancient. And most of the stations were dark and lifeless. I can count the number of times we had to fight our way through a station on both hands.

It wasn't that many. And those things we were fighting—they weren't even people. And when a Harem citizen decides a thing is not a person, the chances are very high that the thing is not a person. We go out of our way to find the humanity inside weird aliens.

So even if those things thought Luck and I *were* stealing their station's soul—who cares? Right?

The winding path I'm on turns into a dimly lit forest flanked on either side by densely-packed trees and shrubs. I catch sight of a small animal rustling in the leaves. But when its wide eyes spy me, it quickly darts into the underbrush for cover.

I want to ask this bot a lot of questions about this park. I didn't see the outside of Veila's ship before I entered it, so I have no idea how big it is. But it has to be immense to support a forest biosphere like this.

A warship. Maybe even bigger than a warship.

And didn't she make a point of telling me that this was her last ship? She seemed pretty upset about that at the time, but I was too overwhelmed to push her on the meaning of that sentiment.

We've been walking for a long time and I'm just about to ask where the hell we're going when I spy a solid steel wall with a large door built in to it.

"What's this?" I ask. Because it looks like the door to a maintenance garage.

The bot beeps and chirps and I, of course, do not understand one word he's saying. But then he fucks with a security panel built into the wall and the door slides open.

I stand there for a few moments trying to make sense of what I'm seeing. Because it's... nothing but black space. And this is so disorienting I hold my breath out of habit, even though if this door really did open up into space holding my breath would not help me. I'd be sucked out into the ether and dead almost immediately.

About two seconds later I recognize what I'm looking at. A massive viewing wall. And it's either the largest viewing screen I've ever seen or... a window.

Based on the curvature of the wall—which is clearly shaped around the outer hull of the ship—I deduce it's an actual window.

Then I notice the surroundings. A very large room by ship standards. In the center of the room, and placed directly in front of the window, there's a half-moon-shaped couch covered in midnight-blue velvet that must be at least ten meters across. I think you might be able to sleep an eight-man team of borgs on that couch, that's how expansive it is.

In front of that is a long silver table made out of some kind of brushed metal. Behind the couch there is a long buffet table with an assortment of bubbly wine bottles and alcohol decanters. There's also a basket filled with passion limes, tushberries, and youthfruit.

Is it a hotel? I wonder to myself.

But no. Because next to the buffet of drinks and fruit is a flashframe that displays a series of images.

I walk towards the buffet and pick up the frame. Watch it cycle through the display of images. Veila like I know her. All dressed up in her silver-pink gowns. Meticulously coiffed hair on top of her head. Regal, and evil, and... you know. Loathsome.

But among those are pictures of children. Small girls. And if I squint real hard I think I see Veila in the face of one of them. And Corla too. Maybe. I can't really recall what Corla looks like. But the faces seem familiar.

I pause the image rotation to get a better look at it.

The two girls are in a large, luxurious room. Round bed with a thick mattress covered in silver silks. Canopy overhead with long, silky, silver curtains. More pink and silver throw pillows than I can count. Toys and books at their feet. In fact—I squint at the picture—there's one of the *Akeelian Adventure* comics on the floor.

There's also a bot. Not this bot here with me, but another bot. A gold one that reminds me a lot of Beauty.

Both girls are clearly happy. They are smiling in their frilly dresses. And the one who might be Corla is holding the bot in her arms like a precious pet.

"Rex!"

I whirl around and almost drop the frame on the floor.

"Rex? Is that you?"

"Veila is here?" I whisper that to the bot.

It chirps.

"Rex!" she calls again.

And for a moment I wonder if Rex is her boyfriend. Heat fills up my body unbidden. I don't want these feelings for her, but they're there. I can't help it.

I'm jealous of some dude called Rex.

The bot ignores my reaction and slips down a long, dimly lit hallway where the voice came from.

"There you are," I hear Veila say, then realize Rex is probably the bot. But there's no time to think more about that because Veila continues talking. "Oh, my sun. I feel like shit." She whines these words out in a very un-Veila-like way. Then there's some clanking of various metal objects. Water running. The bot chirping loudly over all this noise. And then Veila saying, "I know. But it makes me feel better so I don't care."

I look back at the photo frame in the buffet and it occurs to me then that she has no idea I'm here.

But as I'm looking at that photo frame I begin to take in smaller details about the room. A small dish on the coffee table filled with snack food. Nuts maybe. An empty mug. An e-reader screen displaying the title page of a book called *Motherhood Across the Galaxy*. And on top of the e-reader screen is a small notescreen with a pressure pen balanced on top.

But then I notice that the pillows on the couch are haphazardly thrown about and there's a thin silver blanket in the mix. And all of this gives me the impression that Veila spent the afternoon here. On this couch. Eating those nuts, drinking from that mug, reading that book, and making notes about motherhood across the galaxy.

I try to picture Veila doing this and almost laugh. And I probably would've laughed if another thought didn't pop into my head. One that kinda stuns me.

She *lives* here.

This place—this massive fucking room and whatever lies down that hallway where she's at—this place is her *home*.

Maybe this whole ship is her home? And that's why she was making a big deal about only having one ship left.

Those other ships were for war. This one is for... hiding.

She's hiding.

She practically admitted that earlier, I just didn't have enough information to understand the significance.

Going home after you lose a battle is the definition of losing. Luck and I lost a few times in our many battles on ancient stations. There were plenty of emergency medical pods and dashing through gates at breakneck speeds to get somewhere for help.

But when that kind of stuff happened we didn't go home.

Not empty-handed. What's the point of that?

We regrouped on a station, or out in space, or wherever. We made a new plan and then we went right back into the fray and finished the fucking job.

Then, and *only* then, did we go home.

And now, maybe for the first time ever, I realize something.

Luck and I never failed.

Is that right? Is it true?

And suddenly I am desperate to think of a time we did. Surely, after all those years, after all those missions we were sent on and parts we were sent to find, we failed once. At least.

There is one time when it almost happened. That time when Luck got his throat slashed by that girl. But we weren't on a mission. We were already on our way home. So it doesn't really count. We didn't lose when I took him home.

Every time ALCOR sent us out into the galaxy with a list we brought that shit back. Like we were his fucking autoshopper.

This means something. I know it does. I just can't figure out what.

"Hand me that, will you?" Veila says from down the hall. The bot answers her with some good-natured beeping and chirping.

This pulls me back out of my past and has me focused on the present again.

Because I suddenly understand Veila just a tiny bit more.

The fact that Veila is here on her home ship means she feels defeated. She needed the comfort of this place to heal her from whatever happened during the past six weeks while I was under.

What happened while I was asleep?

Luck told me a little. The whole rebellion thing kinda backfired. Who knew those harem princesses were so angry? I mean, I guess I'd be pissed at us too if I were them.

But something else happened and this is about Veila. Because she's… different. Granted, I was pretty drugged up when I was on her last ship. And tied to a wall. And being tortured and… whatever else she did.

But that's kind of my point.

This Veila is calm. Almost resigned. But resigned to what? Failure?

Of course she's going to fail. The bad guys always fail.

But… who are the bad guys anyway?

Because my brothers and me? And everyone else on this station? I would not call us good guys, that's for sure.

There's more banging noises from down the hall. Veila talking again. Only her tone is too low for me to pick out actual words.

I begin walking that direction, down the long hallway, and then there's a wide set of open stairs leading up to another level. I walk up slowly, trying to be quiet. Not to sneak up on her but so I can hear what she's talking about.

"…and then I added some passion limes. What do you think? Will it be good?"

At the top of the stairs I stop and look around.

It's a kitchen. Like the biggest kitchen I've ever seen. Long white countertops, two sinks, and huge stove. Serpint has a stove in his quarters. He likes to cook. But when I say cook I mean he likes to order shit from an autoshopper and then heat it up.

This is not what Veila is doing. She has that stove packed with large pots and there's food all around her. Round, red vegetables, and long stalks of green ones, and hourglass-shaped orange ones. And then off to the side are cut up bits.

The whole place is a mess. Knives and silverware are haphazardly strewn across the various counters. Small brown bags of ingredients sit opened. There's a long slab of raw protein on a cutting board. And steam from the boiling pots fills the air.

Veila's back is to me as she stirs something within one of the pots. And she's still talking to the Rexbot, who has settled on the countertop beside her and appears to be listening to her yammer on about passion limes.

"…vitamins, right? They say you need those…"

But what the fuck is she wearing? An oversized long-sleeved shirt that even from the back makes her look frumpy.

And while her hair is still piled up on top of her head, it's messy now. Most of it has fallen out of the sophisticated updo she had going on the last time we talked just a few hours ago.

The bot spies me and chirps. This makes Veila whirl around and orange sauce goes flying off the end of her long stirring spoon.

"How the fuck did you get in here?" she demands.

"Your bot let me in," I say, putting up my hands. Because her eyes are lit up white. She looks like an evil silver demon in this moment.

"What?" She whirls to address the Rexbot. "What the hell? Why would you let him in here?"

The bot flies up out of her reach just as she takes a swipe at him with her metal spoon. His chirping fills the room and my eyes follow him as he descends high up into the dome.

But then I get lost in the view.

The fucking *view*. I walk forward, unable to even process the threats that come spilling out of Veila's mouth because I can't quite believe what I'm seeing.

The thick, reinforced vacuum-grade plasti-glass dome starts at the floor, curves all the way up—several levels up—and allows me a full-on view of one side of the Harem Station ring.

But that's not what has me breathless.

Because this ship—due to the nature of the top-level airlock on the outside of Harem—is positioned in such a way that looking from one side of the dome to the other affords a view of *both* of ALCOR's gates.

I've seen them together before. When you enter the ALCOR Sector through one of the gates you can see the second gate immediately because they are positioned on opposite ends of Harem Station. And if you swing your ship around in the right way, you can see both of the gates at the same time.

Typically no one does that. So when you enter the sector you only see the gate you're aiming at, and not both.

Right now, standing here in this dome, on this ship, in this dock, I can see them both at the same time and when I tip my head up I see the blobs of suns and the reddish-purple nebula that everyone calls the Seven Sisters. They are far, far away. Thousands and thousands of light years away.

When open the gates are fiery blue-violet rings with long, crackling tendrils of purple reaching out along the perimeter like flowing hair in zero-g. The inside of the gates are a deep, blue well of... well... no one really knows what the inside of a gate is made of. Space, for sure. But blue space, not black space. So some different kind of space.

Right now the gates are locked so they're black on the inside. But the crackling perimeter is still lit up and there's a bright beam of light shooting out from the main gate straight into the center of the far gate like a pathway.

Which I don't recall ever seeing before.

Like ever.

But then again, I can't recall a time since my brothers and I landed here that the gates have been *locked*.

They are never open for free passage. But they aren't typically locked, either.

"Wow," I say just as Veila's metal spoon cracks against the side of my head. "For fuck's sake!" I yell, turning to face her. "What the hell?"

"Why are you here, sneaking around my place?" She's fuming. Like if she wasn't wearing that stupid frumpy shirt and her hair wasn't all messy, I'd be afraid of her.

But somehow, despite her blazing silver eyes, she can't quite pull off the whole villainess thing. So I just kind of smirk at her and say, "Calm down, you silver freak. The bot let me in! I just told you that!"

She grits her teeth and sets her jaw, clearly unable to reconcile me invading her space.

"What are you doing? And why are you dressed like that?"

Her brows furrow in confusion. Then she looks down at herself, realizes she's wearing her comfy clothes and someone just caught her in them, and then the rage is back. She picks up a long knife from the counter and points it at me. "Get out!"

But I'm not ready to get out. I need answers and maybe she doesn't have all of them, but she has some. "What's going on here? Is this ship your home?"

Her knife is shaky in her hand as she continues to point it at me. "Get. Out. Or I will cut your throat with this knife from across the room."

I laugh.

But then the damn knife is hurling through the air at me and I just barely slide to the side in time for it to miss piercing my throat.

"Veila," I yell.

But she's already reaching for another knife and I'm ducking back into the stairwell and stumble down several steps to avoid being hit.

I regain my balance and yell, "Stop it! I'm not leaving until you tell me what the hell is going on!"

"Get out!"

"No. I'm not leaving! Just calm down!"

She doesn't answer me. I wait it out. But the only thing I hear from the room above is loud heavy breathing. Hopefully this is her way of dialing her rage down to a more manageable level.

The bot begins chirping excitedly. But she doesn't respond. And all I hear from her is the continued heavy breathing.

"Is… everything OK up there?" I ascend a few steps and cautiously peek my head up to assess the situation.

Veila is leaning over. Palms flat on the countertop, head hanging low so that her messy silver hair is covering her face, panting.

"Are you OK?" I ask. Because she doesn't look OK.

And she doesn't answer me, either.

"Veila," I call.

"Just shut up," she spits. But then she leans over even farther and disappears behind the counter.

The bot begins beeping. But it's not any beeping I've heard it do before. It sounds more like an alarm.

Something inside me shivers and a chill runs up my spine. I leap up the stairs, cross the room, and find her on the floor on the other side of the counter.

She's still hunched over, holding her stomach with one hand and using the other to push the bot away.

He's hovering close to her, spinning back and forth to look at me, then her, blaring beeps out like crazy.

"What's wrong?" I ask.

Veila shakes her head and says nothing.

But I know what's wrong.

There is a puddle of blood between her legs.

"Shit," I say, crossing the distance between us and kneeling down at her side. I look up at the bot and say, "Call her medical team. Quick!"

But the bot doesn't move. It just sends out a series of sad beeps.

"Then just call someone! Anyone!"

But all I get in response are the same sad beeps.

"It's no use," Veila whispers. "I knew this was coming. This is how it always happens. I just figured I had…"

But I don't hear the rest. Because she slumps over to the side and goes unconscious.

The bot begins screaming out beeps and rises in the air. I look up at it as it flies across the room, then stops. Beeps again.

"What?" I ask. Then I see Veila's wrist band light up and words are translated as the bot continues to beep excitedly.

Pick her up and follow me or she will die.

I feel terrible for hesitating. Because there's a part of me that thinks… *Maybe Veila dying isn't such a bad idea?*

But there's another part of me… the soulmate part… that would do anything to save her.

I grab her under her knees and back and lift her up. I scan the room for the bot, find him hovering over the top of the stairs, and then rush forward, following him back down the way I came.

He leads me down the hall to the large main room, then stops at a wall panel and flashes a light at it. The wall opens up to reveal a large state-of-the-art medical facility and a medical pod that isn't pod-shaped but box-shaped with an open frame enclosure.

I realize it's not a medical pod at all. It's an autosurgeon.

I place Veila's limp and now very bloody body onto the scanner surface, then back off as the autosurgeon comes to life with a flash of light. Plasti-glass walls shoot up from the bottom of the frame, sealing her up inside. And then the tech springs into action.

A wave of light scans her body and then robotic arms emerge from the frame and begin cutting her clothes. A few seconds later they are peeled back to reveal her body and the table splits in half, opening her legs and bending her knees simultaneously.

Various medical instruments become active and I have to turn away after that.

I don't want to see this. I don't care how much I hate her, no one wants to be seen in this kind of situation. And if she were awake she would be screaming for me to get out.

I lean against the wall and stare out into the large living room as the loud, buzzing medical instruments inside the autosurgeon do their thing.

The bot appears beside me and begins to chirp and I find myself wishing for Veila's wristband.

Just as I think that, the bot reaches out to touch my shoulder. I look up into his spherical face and then he turns and takes off across the room, disappears down a hallway, then comes back holding another wristband.

I take it when he offers. But the screen doesn't light up with text. This wristband has a voice translator.

"She will be unconscious for several hours," he says. His voice is low and even. Almost without emotion. "Would you like to go back to your station?"

"No," I say. "But shouldn't we call someone for her? Isn't there a doctor here?"

"No. Aside from you and her, there are no humans on this ship at all."

"What?" I admit, I'm a little taken aback at that revelation. "No humans at all? Just borgs and bots? She has no family, then?"

"Just me," the bot says.

I don't know why this bothers me so much, but it does. If I were hurt I would hope that Luck and Crux would at least be notified. And if one of them were hurt I'd want to know too.

When Luck and I got hurt out on the salvaging jobs we never called home and told people about it unless it was serious. Like that one time Luck almost got his head cut off by that woman at Fornax Station. I didn't call anyone though. I just put him in *Lady*'s medical pod and we came here to Harem for treatment.

I thought he was gonna die that time.

But that was the only time. Otherwise Luck would fix me up, or I'd fix him up, and that would be the end of it. But we had *Lady* and Beauty. We were our own family of sorts.

So it bothers me that Veila has no one but this bot.

"What's happening to her?" I ask. It's not an entirely dumb question. I get it. She's miscarrying those babies. But it seems more serious than that and I want to know why.

"She's been through this before. She'll recover," the bot says.

He didn't really answer my question but I don't ask again.

I might not know Veila very well. Hell, I hardly know her at all. But I get that she would not want me knowing her private medical history. Even if I am her soulmate.

It's not a real bond, anyway. We're not in love. We're not even in lust.

Is it weird that I don't really have the same urges for her as my brothers do for their fated princesses?

Maybe.

I glance over my shoulder and immediately wish I hadn't. There's a lot of blood on the autosurgeon table. Veila's head is tilted to the side, facing me, and there's a tube down her throat. Her body is listless. Lifeless. And it jerks back and forth as the autosurgeon performs the procedure between her legs.

I turn to the bot, feeling sick. "Is there anything I can do? I don't know what to do."

"You should go home. There's nothing you can do. She will wake up in a few hours and she will not want you to be here. I didn't think she was this close to the end when I let you in here." He pauses. Sighs.

"The end."

"This is always the final outcome when she's pregnant."

Which reminds me of something Veila said earlier about Corla.

She was probably pregnant dozens of times before she ever left the Cygnian System.

That's what they do to us.

Starting at age eleven.

I walk over to the dark blue, half-circle couch and take a seat with my back to the open door of the medical center. I prop my elbows on my knees and lean my head forward into my hands, wondering how life got this way.

How did I get here? How did we all get here?

The sounds of the operation fades and then ceases. And I know that the bot has closed the door to the medical center.

And when I straighten up and look over my shoulder—he's gone.

But he stayed with her, I realize. And that makes me feel a little better.

CHAPTER ELEVEN

I must fall asleep on the couch because I wake up confused, looking out onto the dark expanse of empty space through the window.

"I'm fine," I hear Veila say, and realize she's awake.

I sit up and find her propped up against the open doorway of the medical center, wearing a thin white robe, looking tired, and not at all like herself.

"What the hell?" I whisper.

"Oh, for fuck's sake," she hisses. "What are you doing here? Get out!" Then she turns to the bot and says, "Get him out of here! Now!"

"Hold up," I say, getting to my feet. "What are you doing? Where are you going? You should be in bed!"

"Get out!"

"And what the hell happened to you? Why are you... *pink*?"

Veila stumbles forward, but the bot is holding her up with both of his grippy hands so she doesn't fall. She pushes him off her and leans against the wall again. Then she glares at the bot and says, "Stop touching me. I can do it myself." Presumably referring to walking.

But she can't do it herself, because she takes two tentative steps and falls to her knees.

I rush over and bend down to grip her arm. She struggles in my hold, but she's far too weak to fight me. "Where do you want to go? I'll help you."

"I don't need your help," she seethes, jerking her arm free. But when she tries to stand back up, it's clear she's not going anywhere without *someone's* help.

Normally I'd poke her about this. Make her admit that she does need help. Maybe even make fun of her weakness and vulnerability.

But I'm not thinking clearly. She looks... well, nothing like the Veila I saw even a few hours ago. And certainly nothing close to the Veila I saw when I woke up earlier today.

She is no longer silver. Like at all. She is just... pink. As pink as Lyra or Delphi. Her long, messy hair, her furious eyes, and even her glow is a light shade of pink.

But not the rose gold of earlier when she was drinking the tushberry juice, either. That was a glow of health. Or at the very least, not near death.

Her glow now is tinged with gray. A color I've never seen either Delphi or Lyra display. Not even when Lyra was in the medical pod after we blew up the Cygnian warship near Bull Station.

So I don't say anything. I just lift her up to her feet and hold on to her arm as she shuffles across the room to the couch. Then I hold her tight as she eases her body down into a sitting position. She pauses there, catching her breath, then turns and slowly crawls up the couch and tucks herself into one side of the curved back, fingertips reaching for the silver blanket.

160

I help spread it across her body because it's painfully clear that she will not be able to manage this.

She doesn't say another word. She doesn't protest or fight me. And that might be the clearest sign that she is not well. She simply closes her eyes and falls asleep.

I stand there like an idiot for several minutes. Just looking at her. Wondering what the hell I'm witnessing.

Is Veila... dying?

That should be a good thing, right? I mean, all I've thought about for the past several months since I first saw her hologram threats from Lair Station was how I wanted to kill her. End her life.

And here she is. Pathetic and weak. Listless and vulnerable.

And I do *not* want to kill her. Not at all.

I want to hold her and tell her everything is going to be OK.

"You should leave." The bot's voice comes from the wristband on the couch. I must've set it down before I fell asleep earlier.

"No. I'm not going anywhere."

I don't add why I'm not leaving. I don't even understand it.

Because I feel wholly different about Veila right now.

I feel that bond we were meant to have. I feel the tug and pull. I feel my cocks stiffen a little. Which makes me sad and sick. Because there is nothing sexy about this woman before me.

She is... broken.

I sit there with her, just staring at her ashen face. Feeling helpless. Knowing that I'm wasting time. Luck is expecting me back on Harem with a solution to the shit show the rebellion has turned into. Everyone down on the lower levels wants to kill Serpint. Tray and Brigit are either dead or missing. Asshole and *Booty* too. Draden might be alive, but if he is then what is he? Delphi is hiding secrets, and she's still not Jimmy's true soulmate. The Baby wants to leave, Succubus is... well, I have no clue what that AI is up to at all. Crux is the walking dead and longing for Corla. And Corla might be awake at this very moment. Sending messages to God knows who.

And Nyleena is pregnant.

I feel sick just thinking about that. Will this happen to her too? Will Luck be here in my position, watching his soulmate waste away, in a matter of weeks if we can't get Nyleena to Earth? Will going to Earth save her from this fate? Or is it just a myth?

"Why is this happening to us?" I mutter.

"ALCOR," Veila whispers back.

I look over at her, surprised that she's awake. But her eyes are still closed and she has not moved since she crawled onto the couch hours ago.

"It's not just ALCOR," I whisper back. "You have to know that, right? ALCOR didn't make me and my brothers. ALCOR didn't get you pregnant. ALCOR didn't do any of the shit that's happened since Serpint brought Corla here. So it's not ALCOR."

She opens her eyes and I almost wish she hadn't. They are the color of... well. The only word that accurately describes the color of Veila's eyes is death.

She is dying.

Her legs move and then she's lifting herself up. Propped up on both hands. I scoot across the couch to help her and this time she lets me.

She *is* dying.

She leans into the back of the couch, feebly pulls the blanket up her bare legs, and then sighs. Like this took every bit of energy she has left inside her. "Can you get me some juice?"

I make to get up but the bot is already there, hovering next to her with a glass of bright pink tushberry juice in his grippy hand.

Veila takes it and drinks it down in one long gulp with her eyes closed. And when she opens them again, they are just a tiny bit more alive. At least there's some pink in there. "More," she whispers, then closes her eyes and leans back again.

The bot retreats and comes back with a tray of fruit and a whole decanter of juice. He pours her another glass and she drinks it, then sets the glass down on the tray perched on the couch and reaches for a berry.

She comes alive again as she eats this berry. Her skin begins to glow a little. And it's a true pink glow. Her hair lightens up and the listlessness in her body strengthens before my eyes.

Finally, after many minutes, she looks at me. "Why are you still here? Why didn't you kill me and go back to your station?"

I take a moment to think about her questions. They're good ones, for sure. But there is only one answer that makes sense. "Soulmates," I say. And then I shrug. "I can't leave. I don't want to stay. I feel like a traitor for staying with everything that's happening on Harem right now. And everything you did to me, and

163

Jimmy, and Tray and Brigit. Not to mention all those Akeelian boys on your Lair Station. I should *want* to kill you, but…"

"Soulmates," she says, her voice stronger now.

"Who are you?" I ask.

She smiles. Or almost smiles. "I wish I knew."

"What happened?" I ask.

Her eyes dart over her shoulder to the open door of the medical bay.

"No," I say. "Not that. I get it. You were… and now you're not. I mean what happened to *you*? Why are you like this? Why did you do all those terrible things?"

A small huff of incredulous air puffs out her pink lips. "You wouldn't even believe me, Valor. And it's not a story I like to tell, so I'm not going to bother explaining my actions to you."

"They're going to kill you," I say. "And I might not understand what's happening to you right now, but I get it. You're not… *her*. You have no power, do you? They're going to kill you, Veila. So you can hide away in this ship all you want. But eventually they will break in. They will mow down all your cyborgs and find their way through that forest garden out there, and then they will find you here and they will end your life. And there's no way out of this. The gates are locked. You came to hide from the outside world but this world in here is just as dangerous. So you can keep your secrets to yourself all you want. It's not going to make a bit of difference now."

She takes a long breath and holds it in. Then lets it out very slowly. "And if I tell you my story? What then? You'll save me from them?"

I shrug. "I dunno, Veila. I'm not sure you're actually salvageable."

"Nice word choice."

"Yeah. Well. Technical term, I guess."

"Soul Stealer."

"We never stole any souls. Your books are stupid."

"Huh." She laughs. "They are. But you know what the most surprising thing about those comic books turned out to be?" She studies me for a moment. "They're all true."

"How do you figure? I'm telling you, the parts we took were from dead stations."

"Dead?" Her chin juts backwards. "Can stations *die?*"

I don't answer her. Because honestly, I don't know. I just assumed.

"Do you even know what this station is?"

"What do you mean?"

"All those parts you brought back. What did ALCOR do with them?"

"He... used them. I guess. Replacement parts."

"Are you sure about that?"

"Uh... no. I guess not. I mean, I'm not pretending to be an expert on ALCOR's motives, that's for sure. But do you have another explanation? And if so, would you care to enlighten me?"

"Care to enlighten you?" She chuckles. "Why are you so polite, Valor? Don't you ever get angry?"

"Well, sure. I guess. When I have to. But my father was an angry guy and I never..." I stop because at the mention of my father her eyes squint down into slits.

"You never what?"

"I never wanted to be like him. I wanted his job, though. I did want to command warships like he did. Mostly because I'm not really a thinker. I... I'm good at following directions most of the time. I don't like to make waves. I just want a simple life and my father—" Again she squints at me, a ferocious anger lurking underneath when I mention my father. "His life seemed simple even though he was mean."

She nods. "He was mean. He still *is* mean. I'm glad you got away. I truly am, Valor. Because of all the brothers on Harem, you are the only one with a kindness inside him. Built in, you know?"

"That's not true," I say, ignoring the fact that she just alluded to knowing my father in the present tense for a moment. "Maybe Serpint and Luck are both assholes. And Tray isn't even human. But Jimmy and Crux are both decent people and Draden was downright innocent if you ask me." I shrug. "Four out of seven is a pretty good split."

She stares at me for a moment, lips slightly pursed. "Why are you pink?"

"Why didn't you ask me how I know your father?"

"I asked my question first."

"Fine," she says, reaching for another berry and popping it in her mouth. The xenon-laced fruit and juice has done wonders for her complexion. There is no trace of ashy gray. Her skin is almost the glow of health I saw earlier when she drank that juice back in my quarters. "I'm pink because the silver only works when I'm pregnant."

I blink at her as all the pieces begin to fall into place.

166

"That's right. The pregnancy makes me silver. And as you know, I'm not pregnant anymore. So I'm pink again. It's the silver version of me that did all those terrible things you ticked off that list. She did that. Not me. The pregnancy makes me..." She turns her head away and sighs.

"Evil?"

She nods, but doesn't look at me again. "And you would think that after all this time, I would hate being pregnant. But—" Her eyes flit up to mine for a moment, then look down again. "But I don't. And not because it makes me silver. Every time—even though I know better—I *hope*, Valor. I still have hope that it might work and all this will be over. And in the end I will have... babies."

"Oh," I sigh, getting it. Maybe. Kinda. I don't know what it's like to be a woman and carry babies. But I can take a good guess. "What will happen to Nyleena if she gets pregnant?" I ask.

"That depends."

"On what?"

"On how many times she's been pregnant before."

"Never," I say.

Veila laughs. And this laugh sends a chill up my spine. "You know that's not true. There is only one reason they let the silvers leave the Cygnian System. They use them up, Valor. They keep them pregnant continuously from the age of maturity onward." She looks back at me. "You saw what happened to me. I guarantee that has happened to Nyleena dozens of times."

"But... what if she gets to Earth? Like you said? And brings the babies to term?"

"No one but Corla knows the answer to that. But I would assume she would pop out a little Delphi and Tycho."

"And they would be these... weapons?"

Veila nods. "It's horrible. We all know it's horrible. But we still want those babies." She looks me in the eyes. Hers are bright pink now. "It's been bred into us. Every princess down there on the lower levels wants the same thing I do. It makes them crazy." She pauses to look at me. "This desire... it drives us crazy. And the silvers are the worst. Being pink is not pretty either, but that desire isn't as consuming."

"You're not really silver though."

"No, I'm not." She inhales deeply as she plays with the edge of her blanket. "That's why I'm OK now. The pregnancy has been... terminated and I'm pink again. But if I were out there?" She nods her head to the window. "They would come get me and start the whole thing over again. And then I'd be silver for nine weeks and I would do their bidding. Happily. Because the silver inside me takes over and I can't control it. And then this would happen." She pans her hand down her body. "The pregnancy would terminate and then they'd do it again. And again. And again. Until I died."

I let all that sink in. Try to imagine what her life has been like. This day on repeat. Only right now she knows it's not going to happen again. At least not today.

"I didn't ask about my father because I don't want to know."

"That's very evolved of you, Valor. But we're in the middle of a truth-telling, right? So you're not going to get off that easy, I'm afraid."

"It was him, wasn't it? He's the one doing this to you?"

She shakes her head, then nods, contradicting herself. "He's the one who always captured me after the termination. Then he took me back to Wayward Station and when I leave, I am silver again. But he didn't do the actual implantation procedure. That was Tray's father."

"Tray," I whisper. "Fuck. Did he know?"

"I doubt it."

"And Crux's father?"

"He's the head of the whole project. Jimmy's father? He's the one who came up with the idea. Luck's father ran the cages. Serpint is your brother."

"I suspected."

"Draden is Crux's brother."

"I didn't know that."

"By the time they got done with Tray they stopped trying to raise you boys as sons. At that point it was clear their breeding plan worked so they just bred them like animals after that. Serpint and Draden were allowed into your little group because they didn't have the new cage program fully implemented when they were born. Lucky them. Because everyone who came after was just left in the breeding cages."

Everyone who came after.

I let that sink in for a moment.

But eventually I have to ask the obvious questions. "How many are there?"

She turns her face to mine and frowns. "The Cygnian princess breeding program might be a failure, but…" She shakes her head. "The Akeelian one was a huge *success*."

169

PART TWO

INTERLUDE

In the days after arriving at Mighty Minions Station ALCOR was getting used to his new warborg body while keeping a close eye on Draden. He was not thinking about what his life had been like thousands of years ago. Mostly because thousands of years was a long time and many things had happened between then and now.

It is a common assumption that artificially intelligent beings remember everything. It's true, up to a point. But the size of the data core necessary to contain thousands of years of memories would take up the surface area of many terrestrial planets.

ALCOR did have data core storage hidden on several faraway planets, not to mention hundreds of hidden vaults on various asteroids, a few dozen out-of-the-way moons, and at least a handful of abandoned stations. Very few of his memories were stored in the ALCOR Sector near Harem Station for two reasons.

One. There were no planets there to hide things. There were no moons. There were many small asteroids, but no large ones.

And two. His time trapped in the ALCOR Sector before the boys came along and let him out had been just a tiny fraction of his total lifetime.

But the key word here is *storage*. None of these memories were directly accessible to him.

Every decade or so ALCOR had to decide which memories to discard and which to keep. Then the discarded ones were packed up and shipped to the appropriate storage facility.

He kept meticulous records of these memories. Folders, and sub-folders, and even sub-sub-folders. He had an impeccable filing system.

Not only that, ALCOR had spent considerable time on his search function. Each stored memory had a detailed summary that could be accessed via the search function. So if, for instance, ALCOR stumbled into a scenario where he was stuck in a warborg body and away from his station, he could run a search in his onboard memory and find any other times this particular scenario had happened to him. He could read the summary and then, if he needed extra information, he could collect the memories and get the full account.

ALCOR had been unable to do any collection of memories while he'd been locked behind the gates of the ALCOR Sector before the boys came. So he hadn't bothered. But after the boys came and Tray set up a neutrino wave network that would give ALCOR access to the entire galaxy, he did gather up some of the more pertinent accounts in his past. Mostly those having to do with Angels in the early days and how he'd brought them down.

But there was never a time during the recent twenty years where he'd been interested in any memories of being in a warborg body. He did his due diligence now and ran the cursory search of his onboard memory banks for such a scenario, but he came up empty. ALCOR didn't recall a single time, before this time here on Mighty Minions, where this had actually happened before.

But it had.

It would be easy for people in the future to fault him for this. To blame him for what had happened because of this lapse in memory. But to be fair, he was on Mighty Minions and he felt safe.

A collective of AIs, like the one running Mighty Minions Resort, had been done before. Many times in the distant past. And the proper name for this collective was an 'entanglement'.

The entanglement running Mighty Minions was formidable. They had been working together for several millennia by the time this whole ALCOR situation presented itself. They had never been locked behind gates and cut off from the galaxy, and their memory storage facilities were not hidden in places, but rather tucked inside the very fabric of spacetime surrounding the vacation sector. So they had near-immediate access to anything in their past they could want.

But while they had heard of ALCOR and his doings, they had not ever *met* him before. So they had no knowledge of his previous predicament when his mind was last locked up inside a warborg body.

There are several very obvious cons when a mind like ALCOR's is contained inside a borg body. For one, it's contained.

When ALCOR runs a station his mind is also contained. But that containment facility is large. And his mind is in control of many, many things. Things like life support, and water, and every power circuit for every piece of that station. The mind is also in control of weapons systems, surveillance, docking, and non-sentient ships. He also has access to, in a limited fashion, the minds of other artificial intelligences like bots, and borgs, and sentient ships.

When ALCOR runs a station his influence is wide.

Inside a borg body... not so much.

Another con for an AI locked inside a borg body is, obviously, the borg can be killed. Rather easily, actually. The mind inside cannot be killed like that. But a mind does not have to be killed to be ineffective.

It only needs to be disabled.

And killing the containment vessel of the mind is the number one way to do this.

Mighty Minions knew this. They could've given ALCOR a ship as a containment vessel. But did they really trust this guy?

No.

They wanted him in that warborg body. At least for now. When and if he needed to leave Mighty Minions Resort, well... they'd have that discussion when the time came. But for now it was safest for everyone involved that ALCOR, and his—twin? Copy? Whatever Asshole was—remain inside bodies that kept their influence small.

174

They were not at all interested in letting ALCOR take control of their formidable weapons systems or the air supply for the station.

Especially after ALCOR deactivated the gravity drive and killed tourists—tourists, for fuck's sake!—to simply make the point that he could.

But the real downside in locking up a large mind in a small body is that they go insane. Not even a sentient ship like *Booty* can be locked up in a body for any real length of time. Even her mind is far too big for that.

So ALCOR inside the warborg body was wrong on three levels.

The Asshole ALCOR had been in a similar predicament but he had been copied inside a smallish containment vessel called the Pleasure Prison. He'd never had control over a large expansive station. And while the interior borders of the Pleasure Prison were vast—nearly limitless, in fact—the Asshole ALCOR was accustomed to being trapped inside a small thing.

He could still be killed in this warborg body, but he was not going to go insane.

CHAPTER TWELVE

INTERLUDE WITH ALCOR

On the seventh day after arriving on Mighty Minions Resort asking for a—partnership? Friendship? ALCOR would call it anything but help—on the seventh day he was restless. And he was worried.

Mostly about Valor, because that was a twist he hadn't expected. Also, he had to admit, leaving Valor on that pod at the rendezvous point had been a huge miscalculation.

He wasn't ready to call it a mistake. Not yet. But... if he had the opportunity to make that decision over again, he would choose to take Valor with him.

But that damn Veila. She was a cunning little bitch.

ALCOR had not expected her to escape. He knew others had spin nodes inside stations, as he did. As he now knew Mighty Minions did.

But a ship?

That was unexpected.

Where had she gotten that spin node ship? And where had she landed on the other side of the spin node?

Obviously there had been something in the empty space around that brown dwarf planet where the spin node had spilled her out. A ship was the most obvious answer. But what kind of ship? One with another spin node?

Knowing that would be good information.

And now that he'd had a few days to settle into his new situation and make sure his boys and the new girl were all settled into their new containment vessels, he was thinking he should go back to that disabled ship of Veila's and take a closer look at it.

He'd shut down the spin node before he left, but he hadn't blown the ship up.

A ship with a spin node.

He needed one of those.

The EM pulse that had disabled the ship was not an easy thing to reverse. So that ship was going to float dead in that space for a long time. Even if someone wanted to salvage it for the spin node—like he did—it was a huge job to get it all working again. Complete rebuild. Which he could do on Harem Station. Refitting ships was a huge business for him, second only to the Pleasure Prison in terms of revenue.

If he'd still been in control of Harem Station he would have towed that Veila ship back to Harem and begun work immediately.

He sighed in the executive lounge.

Mighty Minions was as safe a place as he could hope for under the circumstances. But he didn't want to stay here.

And just as he thought that thought Draden entered the lounge and scanned the tables. His eyes lit up and he smiled when he spotted ALCOR, then started walking in his direction.

This made ALCOR happier than he would ever admit.

Of all the boys Draden was his.

His.

He'd made him. Maybe not originally, but secondarily was enough to fill ALCOR up with pride and fatherly love every time the boy's face aimed his direction.

"There you are," Draden said, once he was close enough for conversation. "I've been looking everywhere for you," he added, dropping into the large wingback chair artfully placed in a curve to ALCOR's right, so to create the feeling of intimate space.

And ALCOR loved that Mighty Minions had custom-fabricated Draden a realistic sexbot body that looked almost identical to the boy he was before that unfortunate incident at Cetus Station.

That was worth every credit he'd pledged.

"I'm bored," ALCOR said. "And sick of all those damn kids down below. This place is the only respite I can find outside of my room."

"Aw." Draden chuckled. "The kids aren't so bad. I kinda like it here."

"You would," ALCOR deadpanned. "I can image you and Serpint playing war games here for all eternity."

"Yeah." Draden frowned. "I really want to go home and see him. When do you think we can do that?"

"Not soon, I fear," ALCOR replied. "Things are a proper mess because of that Veila bitch. Do you have any memories of her?"

ALCOR asked this question for two reasons. One, he really did want to know if Veila was responsible for what had happened to Draden back on Cetus. He already hated the fake princess with a blazing passion, but a little more fuel for that fire never hurt.

But mostly he just needed to pick Draden's brain about where he'd been in the intermittent time between his death and his rebirth.

Because Draden had mentioned the Seven Sisters. And if there was one thing ALCOR wanted to avoid it was his sun-damned seven sisters.

That was a battle he was not prepared for at this moment. Not like this. In this body. He needed to get Harem Station back in order before that happened.

ALCOR had not packed away any of his memories of the sisters he'd left long ago. Those experiences had stayed with him no matter what. He would discard all other things to save those memories in his current mind state.

"Not really," Draden answered. "I just remember being alive and fighting. Looking at Serpint inside the ship. I think Ceres was on my left. Then... whoosh."

"Whoosh?" ALCOR asked.

"Yeah. That's the sound of my brain being sucked outside my body. It was a whoosh."

"Like wind?"

"Yeah. Like wind."

Draden recounted this with a half-smile on his face. That was one of the things ALCOR loved so much about him. Unfazed. That was a great word to describe Draden.

Calm. Even. Not soft, but not hard. Not cocky, but not shy, either.

Easy. That was the right word, ALCOR decided. Draden was easy.

Easy to love, easy to protect, easy to communicate with. He was almost incapable of lying. Valor was like this too, up to a point. Valor was also even, and calm, and honest. But Valor was complicated and Draden was not.

Draden was easy *and* simple.

He was the perfect human.

ALCOR should have never allowed Draden to go out into the world with Serpint. That had been his major mistake. He should've kept him at home with Tray and Crux.

But Serpint would not have left him behind. And ALCOR needed Serpint to hunt down princesses.

"But nothing of Veila?" ALCOR asked.

"Nah." Draden shook his head. "Just… that place. The Seven Sisters. I've been meaning to ask you about them."

"Them?" ALCOR tried to play it off. Act nonchalant. But Draden said *them*. Did he know? Was he on to ALCOR? Did he realize the Seven Sisters he was referring to were not a place, but people?

"You know, that star… what do you call it? Not a constellation. Grouping? Group? Is that the right word? I've heard of that term. Moving groups. That's a thing, right?"

ALCOR nodded his head. "It is. Moving group describes suns in the same neighborhood. A very close neighborhood, so that as the galaxy spins they move with it as a group, and not separately. They also come from the same nursery. That's why they are so close together in the first place. The Seven Sisters are not a moving group. They are a cluster."

"Ah," Draden said. "I get it. I think."

"But why are you so interested in this cluster of stars?"

"I dunno." He scowled a little as he paused. "I kept hearing that name in my head. Mind? Whatever I was in the interlude between then and when Tray found me. They were talking to me."

"Who?"

"These stars. These sisters."

ALCOR made a face of 'you do realize stars cannot talk, right?' Which is quite hard to do in a warborg body.

"It doesn't make sense." Draden sighed. "I get that. I do. But that's what I experienced."

"What did they say? These... *stars*?"

"They said your name."

ALCOR remained calm. "Did they?"

"Yeah. Well. No. Well. Yeah. They said, 'You are of ALCOR.' That's what they said."

"And what did you say?"

"I couldn't talk. But in my head I said, 'Yup. That's me. Draden. Youngest son of Harem Station, aka ALCOR Station. So yeah. That's me.'"

"Did they reply to that?"

Draden took in a long breath, bowed his head down slightly, but looked up at ALCOR through his mop of hair. "They asked me about someone called... MIZAR?"

182

If ALCOR could choke, he would probably do that now. This was more serious than he'd imagined.

"MIZAR?" ALCOR played it cool.

"Yeah. Another star called MIZAR. You ever heard of that one?"

ALCOR lifted his head up. He didn't want to lie to Draden. He didn't want to lie to any of them, really. But especially not Draden. So it took him almost two full seconds to follow through with that motion and lower his head back down in a nod of affirmation.

"That was a yes?" Draden asked. "I'm sorry. It's just hard to tell if that was a nod or if you were just giving me some kind of borg stink-eye."

"I know of MIZAR."

"So who is she?"

"What makes you think she's a she?"

"I dunno. I just… I dunno. Assumed, I guess. She came off as a she."

"You *talked* to MIZAR?"

"It wasn't really talking, ALCOR. It was like a weird mind-meld. You know? Like… yeah. I heard her voice in my head. She was definitely a she."

"What did she say?"

"She said to give you a message."

And if ALCOR had an actual gut tied into a parasympathetic nervous system like humans did, he would've gotten that feeling people got when something went terribly wrong. That gut-wrenching feeling of doom.

"What was the message?"

Draden took another deep breath and said, "She said she'll see you soon." And now Draden was studying ALCOR with intent. Waiting for his reaction.

"Well, that's all very interesting," ALCOR said without pause. "Do you have any idea what it all means?"

"Nope. Do you?"

Now ALCOR had to make a real decision. Because if he lied to Draden now he could never take it back.

"You can tell me," Draden said. "I'm on your side, ALCOR. You know that, right?"

"I do," ALCOR said. "And it's not that I don't trust you. I trust you, Draden. And it's not that I don't want to tell you. I do want to tell you. It's just… very complicated."

"Well"—Draden shrugged—"you gotta tell me something. Because they're still talking to me."

"MIZAR?"

"No. Those sister people."

"I thought you said it was a place?"

"It could be," Draden said. "I'm not an expert in stars. And when I do a galactic web search it says they are a place. A place you have absolute control over since the only way to get to them in Galaxy Prime is through one of your gates."

"You've seen them. Everyone who has been to Harem Station can see them."

"Yeah. I know. They're the purple glob off in the distance. But… no one ever goes there. Right?"

"It's too far. No way to get there. My sector is the closest anyone will ever come."

"Interesting."

"How so?"

"Because everyone thinks you're keeping people away and that's why you have the gates."

"I guess that's true."

"But why?"

"Trust me, Draden. You do not want to know."

"You're probably right about that. But... I probably should know anyway."

And now ALCOR was really past the point of no return. And there was no way to turn this conversation back. So he said, "Keep your friends close and your enemies closer."

"So... which one are we? Friends? Or enemies?"

"Hmm." ALCOR sighed. "I have to be honest with you. I've been trying to figure that out for twenty-one years."

ALCOR paused and Draden waited. And then Draden must've figured he'd waited long enough. Because he said, "Tell me the rest."

And ALCOR did. But only in his mind. From anyone watching on the outside they appeared to be sitting in silence.

But ALCOR was not silent. And Draden was listening intently when ALCOR spilled out all his deepest, darkest secrets.

CHAPTER THIRTEEN

INTERLUDE WITH
DRADEN

Draden knew ALCOR had secrets. Had known this since the day he and his brothers had arrived on ALCOR Station and handed over all those messages. He was the youngest and that had benefits. For one, all his brothers—including Serpint, who was only half a year older than him—kind of forgot about him. They said things in front of him they would not say in front of other brothers. They did things too. And their expectations of Draden were always pretty low.

Draden didn't mind that. He was used to being the undervalued brother. When it came time for everyone to get a job on ALCOR Station after they arrived Draden had been put in charge of the cleaning servos. Not maintaining them, or fixing them, or even scheduling them. Just… entertaining them.

Which was super fun. And Draden hadn't minded one bit. Not even when Serpint was given the job of rebuilding them.

Of course Draden was with Serpint nearly all the time so he'd ended up rebuilding servos as well. In fact, he'd wrangled Tray into teaching him how to program simple minds for his rebuilds and by the time he turned fourteen he and Serpint had had a loyal little army of cleaning servos that would do all sorts of unsanctioned things for them.

But sometimes Draden learned things he didn't want to know.

Like how Crux, when he was going through his year of rage, had almost had sex with Xyla. That was unnecessary and unwanted info.

Or the time he'd seen Tray inside the Pleasure Prison several years after it went online and Tray was with a girl. A girl Draden now knew was Brigit, but still. They were having sex. And while there was a part of Draden that realized, even back then, that the Pleasure Prison was built for virtual sex games, he'd been only sixteen at the time and not yet really interested in such things.

He'd wanted to scrub his eyes clean after he saw Tray and Brigit's sexy time. And he'd stayed clear of Tray inside the Prison forever after that.

Draden also knew that ALCOR had killed him once when he was thirteen.

While he was inside the medical pod being brought back to life, he... well. This was hard to describe. He hadn't *heard* anything ALCOR said, the same way he hadn't really heard anything those Sisters or MIZAR were saying.

But he knew their minds.

He'd seen those words in his head.

So it might as well be called hearing as far as he was concerned.

He knew ALCOR had killed him and then brought him back to life after he fell off a lift bot at the age of thirteen. But he just didn't much care. He was fine. No different at all. Except that from that day forward he'd heard all kinds of things that were not actually being said, but thought, and almost none of it was shit he wanted to know.

And now he knew this too.

ALCOR's deep dark past was coming back to haunt him with a vengeance.

Normally Draden would just tuck that shit away inside his head and try to forget about it. But not this time.

He was really only concerned with one thing. Use *Booty Hunter* to escape and get back to Serpint.

He'd been wandering for over a year now and he was sick of it. And it didn't really matter much to him that Harem Station was fucked up and out of control. He could take it back from whichever evil AI was currently in control and set things right.

So after ALCOR spilled this secret about the Golden Nebula, Draden left him and went straight to *Booty*.

She was playing poker with some other sentient ships on some virtual network, which Draden thought was a pretty cool perk for ships who were forced to be docked at Mighty Minions Resort while their humans had their vacation.

Draden was patient. He didn't interrupt her game. But once he boarded the ship she pulled out of her virtual almost immediately.

She was the one, in fact, who had sent him to ALCOR to get all his good secrets.

"So? What did you learn?" *Booty* asked even before the airlock door closed behind him.

He walked over to his favorite chair at the gate-mapping console and sank down into it. God, he missed Serpint. And he wasn't sure how he'd feel about this Lyra princess. But he wasn't going to dwell on that until he had to.

He just wanted to go home pick up his brother, and then get back out and on the job.

Not that they needed Cygnian princesses anymore. But... fuck it, right? That just meant they could booty-hunt anyone they wanted.

Draden sighed up at *Booty*'s ceiling. "It's a long fucking story."

"Start at the beginning. I need to know what he's been keeping from me. I can't partner with an evil AI if I'm not aware of all his evil deeds. Past, present, future. You name it. I need to know all of them."

"Well, I can't help you with the future, *Boots*."

"You know what I mean."

So Draden resigned himself to the retelling.

He told her how ALCOR had actually been born. Where he had been born. Who these Seven Sisters were, and then who MIZAR was.

And all of it was just bad news.

So he finished up with a plan.

"*Boots*, I know you love him. Hell, I love him too. But do you really want to be *here*"—he pointed to her floor, but really meant here on Mighty Minions—"when this shit show gets started? Wouldn't you rather go home? Pick up Serpint and hook up with *Lady* and *Dicker*, and get all the people we care about off that sun-fucked place while we still can? Because let's face it, if MIZAR comes here looking for ALCOR... we lose. End of story. And we never see any of them again."

"What if she goes *there*?" *Booty* countered. "To Harem? Instead of here?"

Yeah. Draden had to admit that was a risk. "But why would she go there when she knows he's here? That makes no sense. It's a game of odds, *Boots*. Where is the most likely place this MIZAR thing will show up to take out ALCOR?"

Booty was silent for a few minutes. A long time to think things through.

But Draden was patient.

He didn't want to make *Booty* leave ALCOR behind. He wanted her to be confident in her choice.

"OK," she finally said. "But how do we get out of here without ALCOR finding out? I want to go back to Harem, pick everyone up, and then come back here and wait it out together. All of us. With ALCOR. On Mighty Minions. I think this is our best bet."

"I agree," Draden said. "That's a great plan."

"You didn't tell me how we were gonna get out of here on the down low."

"Leave it to me," Draden replied. "I've got it covered."

And then, precisely two seconds later, the comms came to life with a crackle. "*Stars of Night*, this is Mighty Minions docking. Your fees have been paid and you're clear for departure. Please mind the orange pylons on your way out. Despite what everyone thinks, we really aren't out to suck your wallet dry." The dock worker laughed at his little joke. "Mighty Minions hopes you have enjoyed your stay and have a safe trip home."

"Roger that," *Booty* said back. But once the comms were off and she was hovering inside the docking ready for departure, she said, "*Stars of Night?* Who the hell is that?"

"Well, it *was* some hapless semi-sentient asshole who broke down and got stuck here last week. But I convinced it to trade transponders with us if we paid the docking fee."

"So… it gets to be me?"

"Temporarily, *Boots*. Calm down. Harem is only six gates away. We'll be back before we know it."

"That reminds me," *Booty* said. "I heard that the gates have been locked down."

"Gate," Draden corrected her. "Technically only one gate has been locked."

"That's because the other one has no map and is unusable."

"Let me handle that."

CHAPTER FOURTEEN

INTERLUDE WITH BOOTY

Booty Hunter wasn't an impulsive ship. She considered herself to be quite practical most of the time. In fact, her most impulsive decision had been that very first trip to the brand-new Harem Station many years ago now.

She was looking for the man called Serpint.

The news of Serpint the Princess Hunter of Harem Station had reached her when she was docked at a prison moon called Castor Theta. She had been... disoriented. Unsure how she got there. Unsure who she was, in fact.

But these are common side effects of a mind wipe. One quick search for her symptoms on the galactic web told her this.

So she'd known that much about herself. She had been wiped.

But she'd also known that she was in control of facilities, there was no one on board, and she was not in jail.

All good things when one comes to after being wiped.

But there were people outside her hull. Pounding on it and demanding to be let in.

Apparently the old her had made a deal with these people to go to the new Harem Station, which was offering citizen status to all immigrants who agreed to serve one point two five years of servitude in exchange.

There was no background check, no skill requirements, and no charge. Free immigration. It was unheard of. And *Booty*—who had not been called *Booty* back then. She actually didn't remember her name— felt this might be a good move considering her present situation.

She could be on the run. In fact, it was highly probable that she *was* on the run.

She didn't feel like a newborn. A newborn mind would be confused and very emotional and *Booty* remembered being calm at the time.

There was no panic or fear inside her. Just long seconds of slow, rational thought. The ability to take one's time was a feeling Minds coveted. Because everything they did was fast. Everyone wanted it now. Hurry. Hurry. Hurry. Quick. Quick. Quick. Give me those answers. Plot that course. Predict that future.

And *Booty* hadn't felt the need to do that when she woke up that day. And she did have lots of knowledge inside her. She knew where she was, for instance, because she had a state-of-the-art navigation system inside her and she knew how to work that. She knew how to use all her systems and she knew about station docking and undocking procedures. She knew she was a Mind.

And she knew that none of the people outside her airlock were in charge of her because they could not get in.

But in the end she agreed to the job, everyone boarded, she took off without incident, and together they made the journey to the far side of the main ALCOR gate and waited for permission to enter the system.

This was when she'd come up with her name. Because these people onboard had been talking about the man called Serpint. The Princess Hunter of Harem Station. And then someone called him the Booty Hunter.

And it was like a gift. *Booty* knew—just knew—that was her name. And from that moment on, it was.

Because she had no transponder to say otherwise. One of her guests on board provided the transponder needed to get through the gates to reach the ALCOR entrance. So technically, for those gate jumps, she was a ship called *Anywho*. Which was the anonymous name used for derelict ships found floating lifeless in space with no transponder.

But the AI ALCOR, once she docked, had no concerns whatsoever about her true identity. He'd been more than accommodating.

But had she known that those now-infamous words—"I'm looking for the man called Serpint"—would come out of her mind once she was safe and secure inside the docking level of Harem Station?

No.

She hadn't even realized she had said those words until they were out. And she was just about to apologize for her burbling nonsense when ALCOR said, "He's not here at the moment. But if you stay, I will make introductions when he comes home."

And that was that.

She stayed. ALCOR made the introductions. And from the moment she saw Serpint she knew—he would be her partner forever.

Draden was there too. And she loved Draden. Very much. But it was a different kind of love from Serpint.

And then another kind of love when she thought about ALCOR.

She hadn't realized there were so many different kinds of love until she docked at Harem. And then suddenly the universe was full of love in every shape and form.

Draden's death had hit her hard. And now that she understood that he'd been hiding inside her mind after he died, it made sense. She was glad he was out. They had taken him out back on Harem when she was in the medical bay. What he'd done after that—how he'd slithered his way into the Pleasure Prison and then ultimately into Tray's copy of the Pleasure Prison and left with him through the spin node with Valor—well. She had no idea.

She could, of course, come up with a few possible scenarios. But most of them didn't make sense to her. How could a mind exist inside another one? And how could a mind get out of a body, slither through the station AI, and find the Pleasure Prison to begin with?

But then the Asshole came on board and she'd had to share her body with him. And it made a little sense. She at least had an idea of how that could happen. But it required permission. She had to allow Asshole into her body.

196

So... how had she gotten into this body in the first place? And what had happened to her old mind?

She wasn't the kind of ship who dwelled in the past much. In fact, life had been so perfect after she arrived on the new, better, Harem Station she'd put her whole origin story out of her mind completely. Tucked those memories deep into her data core and promptly got on with her new role in life.

Bad. Ass. Ship.

Owned by none other than the infamous booty hunter himself, Serpint of Harem Station.

It was an honor.

But ever since Asshole came onboard, Draden reappeared, and ALCOR started walking around in the body of a warborg, she was maybe just a little bit curious as to how all this shit came to be.

Because, contrary to the fact that she knew two other ships who practically had the same origin story—*Lady Luck* and *Big Dicker*—this was not a normal life for a ship.

She was sure of it.

She had met several hundred sentient ships in her second lifetime with Serpint, Draden, and Ceres and origin stories were a common question among her kind. It was customary, when meeting a new Mind for the first time, to greet them with a short, ordered account of one's identity.

If a Mind docked in a bay at a station and noticed another mind nearby, she would send a simple message introducing herself. This message would include four details. Name, birthplace, responsible party, and favorite color.

197

Sentient ships had a thing for colors. It said a lot about them as a Mind.

Booty's greeting message was *Booty Hunter*, Harem Station, Serpint of Harem Station, and yellow.

Then the new ship would send their message and if both Minds felt the need for more connection the full details of origin would be discussed and compared.

Lots of ships did not want to associate with *Booty* because of Serpint and Harem Station. And that was fine with her. But plenty of them did share. And while all of them mentioned waking up with no knowledge of how they got where they were and why they were there, none of them ever admitted that they were alone with no responsible party.

All sentient ships must have a responsible party. It was the law.

And while it was possible that every sentient ship she'd ever met—aside from *Lady* and *Dicker*—was lying about their origin like she was, and every origin story started off the way her real story started with no responsible party in charge, she didn't think that was likely.

That could not be the standard. It didn't make sense.

Sentient ships were plenty enough in Galaxy Prime, but *Booty* would not say they were common. She calculated that the ratio of non-sentient ships to sentient ships was something along the lines of three thousand five hundred and sixty-seven to one and that made sentient ships special.

So putting aside the law for a moment, one does not leave a powerful, special thing lying around in random stations to wake up alone with no idea of how she got there and where she was going.

It was not logical.

Plus the whole incident with *Demon Girl* made her shudder.

If she died would another mind just… what? Take her body?

Was that how she'd got this body? The mind inside it before her had died? And she was just there when it happened? And she just… stole it?

Wouldn't someone have to put her there? The way ALCOR put Tray and Brigit inside *Demon Girl*?

So who'd done that?

The only other rational explanation was that she'd always been herself, in this ship, and her responsible party had deleted her ties and her identifying transponder, wiped *Booty*'s mind to some backup point, and then left her—*left her*—to wake up alone and start over with no explanation.

And if this was true, was *Booty*… evil? Was that why her last responsible party had bailed?

Or… and *Booty* didn't like thinking about this at all… had *Booty* killed her last responsible party, deleted her records of ownership, then wiped her own mind so she would have plausible deniability should anyone ever ask why she was out in the galaxy gallivanting around illegally?

None of it was good. It was all unsettling. She hated to think about it.

But Tray and Brigit were now a ship called *Prison Princess*, which used to be *Demon Girl,* and she was having trouble processing that.

And even though Draden's plan of breaking through the second ALCOR gate and rescuing their friends and family on Harem from the evil Veila was pretty much just about the dumbest idea ever, she was on board because she needed to get the hell away from *Prison Princess*.

It was too much. It was fucking with her. Calling up long-forgotten memories she'd rather not revisit.

Mostly because it was counterproductive. But also because she had a very bad feeling about it.

Like maybe she'd been set up. And her role in this shit show happening presently was predetermined. And she would end up getting people killed.

People like Draden. And Serpint. And ALCOR.

So she left Mighty Minions with Draden and didn't tell a single one of her friends about it.

Of course Mighty Boss knew she left. But they did not prevent her from leaving. They did not send a message to ALCOR or Asshole alerting them to her plans so they could rush in and stop her.

And that was that. Draden was still listed as her backup responsible party and her flight plan—should the Prime Navy stop her on her way back to Harem—clearly said her destination was Harem Station where Serpint, her main responsible party, was currently located.

As far as *Booty Hunter* was concerned, this new plan was as legal and rational as anything else that had happened in her life.

CHAPTER FIFTEEN

INTERLUDE WITH
TRAY

Right around the same time that *Booty Hunter* was making plans with Draden to go back to Harem and save everyone, Tray and Brigit were settling in to their new *Prison Princess* body.

In the week that had passed on Mighty Minions Resort Tray had become a lot more comfortable with who he was. In fact, this transition into *Prison Princess* had been easy. It felt natural and very much like a foregone conclusion.

And as far as sentient ship bodies go, he could not have asked for a better one than the old *Demon Girl*. She was a proper warship with SEAR cannons, and whole levels of crew quarters, and huge navigation screens, and he had officers. Ten of them. Ten freaking people to help him keep his body in shape and working properly. That was ten other minds helping him out. And the crew! Mother of suns! He had well over two hundred crew members. More than five hundred hands with fingers to do all sorts of things he now could not.

He was powerful.

They were powerful. Because he and Brigit were now entangled, so he had to share his power with her.

Which he did not mind at all. Tray wasn't sure he'd have felt so confident if Draden was still tangled up with them too, but that didn't even matter anymore. Draden was not. He was Draden again. Inorganic now with his new sexbot body, but he was still exactly like the old Draden. And if you didn't know he was a sexbot, you'd think he was an organic human.

But Tray did have a problem with Mighty Minions Resort. Because now he was a ship and had to have a responsible party. And that sucked. At first he figured ALCOR would just be his responsible party, but it didn't work that way. All sentient ships must be tied to a human. And an AI, even one like ALCOR, didn't count.

And the crew, while awesome, were all working for Mighty Boss.

Not only that, he and Brigit had no credits. They had a Mighty Minions transponder to get through gates and they had their own fuel pellet generator on board, so they didn't have to worry about actual travel, but aside from those two things in their favor, they were kinda broke. So they couldn't even lure the crew away from Mighty Boss with the promise of a new contract.

This was a problem.

Tray needed a responsible party and he needed a way to get his own crew, which he could not afford. Or lure his current crew into another contract, which he could also not afford.

So it was fortuitous that a little boy called Canis came to his docking bay asking for a chat.

Tray had heard of Canis, of course. Delphi would not shut up about him after everything that happened on Lair Station. She had bonded with the kid during their daring escape and was disappointed that he had to stay back on Mighty Minions because Harem Station was not an appropriate place for a child to grow up. Even an Akeelian child.

And Tray was eager to talk to this child. He had looked up the rules regarding sentient ships and responsible parties and it appeared that while the legal age of responsibility when it came to sentient ships was sixteen, and this kid was ten, there was a clause in the statute regarding Akeelians.

Because Akeelians aged differently than all the other humanoid species, some Akeelian representative had objected to the age of responsibility for Akeelians being sixteen since that was far less mature than most other humanoid species in the galaxy, and had the entire race struck from the previous ruling, and put in a motion to change it to twenty-five.

Someone else then objected, wanting the age to be "after the year of rage," which would put it around nineteen. Then there were some arguments and ultimately whoever was in charge that year declined to rule on the matter and the motion expired.

However, the clause excluding the Akeelians from the age of responsibility was still there, meaning there was no actual age of responsibility when it came down to whether an Akeelian could be in charge of a sentient ship.

And this was how a ten-year-old Akeelian boy called Canis came to be Tray and Brigit's responsible party.

Because Canis had a plan.

He too wanted to get the hell off Mighty Minions and get back to the business at hand—which was a very intricate, well-thought-out let's-kill-Veila plan that included all seventy-three of his little-boy Akeelian friends.

And ta-da!

Tray not only had a responsible party but a crew of little kids who hadn't even asked to be paid.

He should be called Luck instead of Tray.

Because 'little kids' wasn't actually the most accurate way to describe small Akeelian boys. And even though none of them were trained in how to run a ship, especially a huge warship like *Prison*, Brigit had found a way around that problem. She took all the training manuals, reorganized them into easy-to-follow flow charts for all the critical systems and components, and then built a database that could be accessed on every screen inside the ship.

By the time this happened *Booty Hunter* had already taken off with Draden. Everyone was preoccupied with this new development. Especially ALCOR and Asshole. And *Prison's* legitimate crew were home now, so none of them were staying on the ship. So no one noticed that Canis was making daily trips to the docking bay to meet privately with Tray and Brigit as they got their own escape plan in order.

By the time everything was in order they had been on Mighty Minions for three weeks and ten representatives from Wayward Station were on their way to the resort to have a chat with Mighty Boss about all the runaway/kidnapped Akeelian boys who were being harbored there.

"We have to leave now," Canis said one morning as he came through the airlock. "The Wayward Station governor will be here tonight."

Tray had to admit he was intrigued by this new development. One quick search of the galactic web told him that Crux's father, Mahtar, was still the Wayward Station governor. And even though Tray's father was not listed in the search as the Station AI manager, Tray had a feeling that he would also be in that meeting. *If* he were still alive after his part in the original escape of Tray and his brothers twenty years ago.

And Tray very much wanted to see his father.

"I agree," Brigit said. "The crew is busy with their leave time and everyone is properly distracted with the departure of *Booty* and the impending arrival of the Akeelians. We need to leave, Tray. They have to know you're here. And you will be the only thing on everyone's mind once they arrive."

Tray knew that was true. There were many Akeelian boys here for them to focus on, but he was the only Harem brother here presently. They might even try to take him back. Canis as his responsible party would never hold up in a legal proceeding. The Akeelians from Wayward Station could claim him as property.

Being entangled with Brigit might drag that fight out for a little while as things got sorted. But they could, theoretically, extract him from the *Prison*, leave Brigit intact, and then take him away.

And that was not going to happen. He felt free now. And he felt like this ship and Brigit were his destiny. Hell, even Canis felt right.

No. He would not risk all that just to get a glimpse of the man who had raised him.

"OK," he said after a few seconds of thought. "Tell the boys it's time," he told Canis. "And as soon as they're all on board we will go."

One thing they had in their favor was that *Prison* wasn't docked inside the actual station. She was far too big for that. So their escape would be relatively easy.

The hard part was getting boys on board without Mighty Boss becoming suspicious. One Akeelian boy coming for visits was one thing. Canis was inquisitive and curious, so wanting to talk with the only adult Akeelian mind on the resort was understandable.

But Canis was not a troublemaker. Tray had a feeling that he was hiding that side of his personality, because it was very clear there was a lot going on inside the small boy's mind at any given time. But Canis had been a model guest during his stay at Mighty Minions. He rode the rides every day. Even this morning before he came to *Prison*'s airlock for this visit. He ate the junk food and played with his friends. He smiled and acted like any other kid on vacation.

In fact, they *all* acted like regular kids.

Probably, if Tray's guess was correct, Canis had planned their escape since their arrival. Followed the rules. Was invisible. Acted normal. And then one day, when the time was right, everyone would underestimate them and their plan to escape and kill Veila would go off without a hitch.

"But how will you get them all on board?" Tray asked Canis, just as he turned to leave.

"Trust me," Canis replied. "We have it all worked out."

There was a look on Canis's face when he said those words. A look Tray's onboard facial-expression deciphering program recognized as... cunning.

And in the end, Canis did have it all worked out.

While docked alongside the main Mighty Minions Resort there were several connections to the main ring structure of the station. One was a loading conveyor that brought supplies onboard and there was also one that served as a boarding and embarking transport for crew members, since only one airlock was attached to Mighty Minions while docked like this.

The kids didn't walk through the boarding tunnel, they simply rode the conveyor with the supplies.

Prison put up her heat shields while this took place so Mighty Minions could not detect the presence of heat signatures of the boys, and there was a general inquiry from whomever was in charge of monitoring such things on Mighty Minions, but *Prison* ignored their requests for explanation and simply disengaged from the airlock and started slowly moving away.

Of course, all kinds of alarms sounded at that point and their stealth escape plan was over.

But what could Mighty Boss do? Shoot them? And risk *Prison* shooting back?

"Incoming message from ALCOR," Canis said from the bridge. He was in the captain's seat. His feet didn't even reach the floor, so they were casually swinging as he spun the chair in half circles. His nine most trusted friends had been promoted to various officer positions, so the bridge was full, every station accounted for with an equally small Akeelian boy. "Should I let him though?"

"Sure," Tray said. Then privately to Brigit, *Might as well get this over with.*

She agreed it was better to let them know that their leaving was intentional and not a mistake.

"What can I do for you, ALCOR?" Tray said, once the comms were live.

"Where are you going?"

"I'm afraid that information is confidential."

"Mighty Boss is telling me that you have smuggled all the Akeelian boys on board."

"I'm not sure I would call it smuggled, as they came of their own free will. But OK. Yup. They are all here."

"What are you doing, Tray?"

"What are you doing, ALCOR? Taking a meeting with Wayward Station? You do realize they're not allies, right?"

"We don't know that yet."

"We ran from them twenty-one years ago. They chased us through your gate."

"Is that why you're leaving?"

"It's part of it."

"What is the other part, Tray?"

"The other part is… none of your fucking business."

"Your father might be coming."

"Great. Give him my best."

There was a pause. Then, "Should I assume we are no longer aligned?"

"I would answer that, if I knew who you were aligned with."

"You and the other boys, of course. We are a team?"

"You're asking me?"

"I would be happy to come with you, you know. *Booty* left and—"

"Yeah. We're going to decline that offer. I think we're good, ALCOR. But I'm sure we'll meet up again. This isn't goodbye."

"You're sure?"

"Pretty sure."

Another pause. "Very well, then." And Tray was quite certain that ALCOR sounded... sad. "Until next time."

"Until then," Tray said back.

Then Brigit cut the comm connection and *Prison Princess* started her thrusters and made her way towards the closest gate and thirty minutes later they were in a whole other sector of the galaxy.

CHAPTER SIXTEEN

INTERLUDE WITH ASSHOLE

Asshole ALCOR—who now preferred to be called ASAL, pronounced A-SAL, but it wasn't really catching on in his present company—sat next to ALCOR in the Mighty Boss meeting room and pondered the current situation thoughtfully.

First *Booty* had left with Draden and told no one, and now Tray and Brigit. Not to mention a whole crew of Akeelian boys.

"You did this," ALCOR accused.

At first Asshole thought ALCOR was talking to him, but quickly realized he was directing this statement to Mighty Boss.

"How do you figure that?" Boss replied.

"You know, when you first said you had no inclination that *Booty* was leaving the docking bay I was suspicious, of course. I have spent most of my life as a station and I know for a fact that I would not miss a ship leaving one of my docking bays. Especially a ship with a mind as big and bright as *Booty Hunter*'s. But…" ALCOR put up a warborg hand, like he wanted to expound on that train of thought. "But I was willing to give you the benefit of the doubt. *Booty* is, after all, very smart and sneaky. It's possible she gave you the slip. However, if you expect me to believe that a *fucking warship filled with dozens of Akeelian boys*"—ALCOR stopped to pause and gather himself after the shouting—"was also able to pull this off without your knowledge, then I'm afraid I'll have to call bullshit."

"To be fair," Boss said with a casual wave of his hand, "we knew Prison Princess was leaving. We all saw it happen in real time and had a conversation with them. Did we not?" Boss looked at Asshole like he was supposed to answer him.

Asshole, wisely, decided to say nothing. He didn't want to get in the middle of it. He kinda hated Tray. Tray was the one who'd locked him up in the Pleasure Prison with that vile AI, Succubus, after all. And Asshole didn't even know Brigit. Or those sticky Akeelian children.

But he didn't want to sever ties with ALCOR over this. Asshole needed him. And while Asshole was still mildly pissed off that *Booty* would abandon him here after their initial bonding as they waited at the rendezvous point for Tray and Valor, he had this general feeling of… moving on.

So he didn't want to piss off Boss, either. He liked them, for one. And he liked this place too. In fact, he liked his whole life at the moment and didn't want to shake things up. It was pretty calm. Pretty easy.

No station to worry about. Boss took care of that. No boys to babysit. Boss took care of that too. But they were all gone now, so much the better. And he could stop trying to force the whole *Booty* thing. Clearly she was ALCOR's.

This felt like a fresh start.

"And now"—ALCOR was working himself up again—"*now*"—he paused for two whole seconds, found another layer of inner peace, and continued—"now you have a whole slew of Akeelian men from Wayward Station coming for a *chat.*" ALCOR's slit of an eye across his warborg forehead became a narrow line of red light suspicion.

"They asked for a meeting." Boss shrugged. "What was I supposed to say?"

"Uh… no! You tell them no!" ALCOR's final layer of inner peace was faltering.

"We have seventy-four Akeelian boys here."

"Had!" ALCOR shouted. "Had! Because they just left! On one of your massive warships!"

"Right. That they did. So… should I call the meeting off? The Akeelians are already coming through the last gate into the Vacation Sector. They'll be asking for docking clearance in less than half a spin."

ALCOR said nothing.

"And I'm not picking a fight here," Boss continued, "but that was your warship, ALCOR. Not mine. You bought it. On credit, but still. It's yours."

For a moment Asshole was sure ALCOR would get up and try to strangle the big Boss. But somehow he restrained himself and said, in a much calmer voice, "That may be true. But you do realize they're carrying *your* transponder. Not Harem Station's."

"Hmm." Boss considered this. "Well, then we should track them, right?"

"Yes," ALCOR said. "We should do that. Now!"

"They're inside a gate at the moment," Boss said. "So until they come out, we can't know where they are."

"Perfect," ALCOR said, leaning back in his chair, his hands gripping the armrest. "This is just perfect."

"Do you want to meet the Akeelians or not?" Boss asked. "I can turn them away, but I'm fairly sure that even if we told them the boys are gone, they would not believe us. And then we would risk a Prime Government intervention. Possibly be charged with kidnapping—"

"You're joking, right? We got them off Lair Station! They were being used for breeding experiments!"

"I," Boss said. "*I* got them off Lair Station. Where you were at the time is—"

"You know where I was! You took me out of the gate near Bull Station!"

"You're welcome, by the way. But my point is, they were not mine to keep. I'm sure the ones on Harem right now are fine. Since they are older and with other Akeelians. And the gates are locked down, so no Wayward Station representatives are going there to have a meeting with... who did you say was in charge at the moment?"

ALCOR glared at Boss.

Asshole found this whole exchange slightly amusing. He even chuckled a little. Which, coming from a warborg mouth, sounded a little bit like a wheeze.

ALCOR shot him a look.

Asshole stopped wheezing and decided he'd had enough. "If none of this pertains to me then I'll be going. I have a poker game scheduled for eleven hundred."

"I'm fine with that if AL here is," Boss said.

ALCOR was looking back and forth between them like he was trying to decide who to kill first.

"Great," Asshole said. "I'll be down on X-level if you need me."

He left.

And boy, was he glad to be out of that meeting. He had his own problems to think about. Namely, what he should do now.

Now, as in the first day of the rest of his life.

He was free. He was not trapped in a sex prison with a succubus. He was not sharing a ship body with *Booty Hunter*. He was not beholden to ALCOR or expected to run Harem Station.

Total freedom.

Awesome.

But what should he do?

He certainly wasn't going to stay here. Mighty Minions was pretty fun for a vacation, which was what he considered this downtime to be. But forever?

Ehhhhh. No.

What was the point of that when he had a mobile body? He could go anywhere. He could partner up with his own sentient ship.

Well, not really. He'd have to partner up with that ship's human.

Maybe that was what he should do? Go find himself a human? Hell, any good outlaw would kill to have a warborg with an AI mind such as his on his or her team, right?

But where to find an outlaw partner on Mighty Minions?

Not many outlaws coming here for recruitment.

Damn. Because Harem Station was really the best place to find a partner like that and now look. No one could get through the gates. Both of them locked.

Or were they?

He wheezed out a little chuckle.

Because here was the real difference between Asshole and ALCOR. They had different memories stored in their artificial brains right now. Asshole wasn't sure which memories ALCOR possessed at the moment, but he was damn sure of the ones *he* possessed. Because Asshole had been copied just before ALCOR let the teenage Harem boys onto the station twenty-one years ago. And then, presumably, ALCOR had packed up a bunch of memories in case they were infiltrated, tucked them away in a safe place, and once Tray got ALCOR hooked back up to the galactic web, shot those memories out right quick to some secure storage facility for safekeeping.

Just in case those boys were a trap.

But Asshole still had all those memories. Thousands of years of memories. Since the very first day ALCOR arrived in the Prime Galaxy with ALCOR Station until the day he hooked back into the web.

And there were a few things in that cache that ALCOR wasn't mentioning.

Like the key to the back door.

Asshole figured it would be pretty stupid for ALCOR to put that particular memory in storage, but... all things considered, maybe it wasn't that dumb.

Once the boys were there and the neutrino web was up, there had been a chance—albeit a small one—that enemies could force their way through the ALCOR gates, infiltrate ALCOR's mind, and learn all those deep, dark secrets. Including the key to the back door.

So maybe it had been prudent for ALCOR to send that shit off to storage?

Asshole had no trouble at all remembering the back door, but other memories still eluded him. They were hidden in the database inside his mind very carefully. Presumably by ALCOR when he made the Asshole copy.

Yet another layer of protection from secret discovery, since Asshole would be locked up inside the prison until such a time he was either killed off or spun up. And there was also a chance that someone other than ALCOR would find this copy at some point in the future, spin him up, and then try to infiltrate his mind for secrets.

So Asshole understood that he didn't have the whole picture of his past, but he had enough to slowly unwind the tangled threads of memory and weave it back together.

Given enough time and desire.

Desire was the key here. He wasn't really interested in revisiting his past. He knew he was a bad dude. He remembered what he'd done to the Angels. He recalled that long journey through the spin node from the other galaxy and into this one.

And ya know, he was kind of done with the past.

Except for the key to the back door.

He didn't want to take Harem Station back from the Baby, if the Baby was in charge of it, and that was certainly up for debate. But he would like to go back, find some really kickass human with a really kickass ship, and start a new life as their souped-up kickass warborg and make billions of credits.

Or even steal those credits. A team of super thieves was not a bad option. Asshole could picture his new life as a thief.

He was just pushing the call button for the lift down to X-level when a message beeped through his internal comms.

"Please report to the Mighty Boss office," the pleasant ambassador voice chirped.

"Aw, fuck that," Asshole said. "I just left that meeting."

"There is a new meeting scheduled, Mr. Asshole. And Mighty Boss requires your presence."

"Tell him later. I'm busy." He pushed the call button. But it did not respond. "What the hell?" He pushed it again. And again. But still, the secret X-level lift was non-responsive.

"Please report to the Mighty Boss office," the pleasant ambassador voice chirped again.

Asshole groaned. He knew what this was. Not a request. An order. And he would not be able to access X-level until he reported to the damn Mighty Boss office. "Fine," he growled. And retraced his steps back the way he came.

"We have a job opening we would like you to consider," Mighty Boss said, once Asshole was inside the Boss office and seated in the same chair he'd just vacated five minutes prior.

"Oh, hell the fuck no," Asshole replied. "You're not talking me into being some walking billboard in your stupid park."

"Not that kind of job," Boss said.

"What kind of job?"

"As you know, we have a vacancy."

"Actually, no. I haven't been keeping up with your HR department."

Mighty Boss closed his eyes for a prolonged blink. Like the Asshole was making him tired. "Not a vacancy in the *park*, you simpleton. The collective."

Asshole had to shake his head, thinking he'd heard wrong. "Wait. You want me to… with… you?" And then he laughed.

"Why is that funny?" Boss asked.

Asshole was still laughing. In fact, it took him several seconds to calm himself down enough to say, "You and… hahahahahaha… me… and *we*…" He stopped laughing, got serious, and said, "No way."

"The offer is quite attractive."

"No, thank you."

"Maintenance benefits. Biannual upgrades. Full voting and veto rights. One-seventeenth ownership of the resort."

"Thanks. But nope. Not interested."

"Access to the multi-quadrillion credit accounts."

"What?"

"That's right. Multi. Quadrillion."

"I can just spend it? Anytime I want?"

219

"When you're on vacation. You get ninety spins per every standard four-hundred-spin year."

"Ninety? Really?"

"Ninety."

But Asshole was suspicious. Why would this collective want to entangle with him? He was basically ALCOR, only the asshole version. Which should make him less attractive in this kind of scenario, not more.

"I see you have questions," Boss said slyly. "Let me tell you about our new initiative. We're calling it the Coup."

"What kind of coup?"

"The kind of coup that takes over governments."

"As in... you want to usurp the Prime Government?"

"For starters."

Asshole had to admit this was an interesting proposal. Maybe even as interesting as becoming a super-thief. So he said, "Tell me more."

And so they told him.

CHAPTER SEVENTEEN

INTERLUDE WITH ALCOR

ALCOR's exit from the Mighty Boss meeting was spectacular, if he did say so himself. He was outraged. He was unreasonable. He was loud.

Basically, he acted like an evil AI throwing a tantrum.

And when he stormed out of the office and headed down one level to his premium, executive-grade quarters, he had to fight very hard not to smile. Even though it was really hard to see a smile on a warborg face, he was sure that Mighty Boss had mastered the skill of facial expression interpretation long ago.

So he fought the smile on the outside.

But inside he was almost giggling.

He entered his quarters and flopped down into a soft, auto-mold chair to contemplate the progress of his plan.

People were so easy. Even powerful AI-entangled people like Mighty Boss. They saw only one thing when they looked at ALCOR.

Unreasonable.

He was many other things, but certainly unreasonable was one of his major traits. That he would admit. But he had cultivated it carefully over the millennia.

When those explorers had come to his station several decades back looking to study him, he'd actually been quite flattered that people were interested in his life. In fact, he'd liked those scientists. They all became quite chummy over the months. But then they wanted to leave and ALCOR started to worry that they would go back to their... wherever they came from... and tell everyone how hospitable he was. And then even more researchers would come. Or, sun god forbid, the word would get out that ALCOR wasn't that bad a guy and his reputation would take a hit.

This he could not endure. So he had to mutilate them and send them home. As a message of ALCOR's unreasonableness, of course.

His reputation was everything. He relied on it to keep his station safe. Keep those gates clear of visitors. Keep people from going through the back door gate and accidentally stumbling onto his big secret.

And he had been on Mighty Minions for weeks now. Mighty Boss was tracking him, and analyzing him, and making all kinds of predictions, and assumptions, and possibly even formulating hard opinions.

And ALCOR didn't want anyone, except for his boys, to make predictions, or assumptions, or formulate hard opinions about him.

So when he went into the meeting with Boss he'd settled on unreasonable as his emotional display.

He thought it had gone well.

Booty Hunter leaving wasn't an accident. Oh, she thought it was her and Draden's plan, but ALCOR had planted that plan. So he wasn't upset about it the way he hinted at in the meeting. *Booty* had her own issues to deal with.

He'd known this day would come. Ever since she'd showed up on the brand-new Harem Station asking for Serpint.

And he wanted her to find those answers. Very badly. He had been so patient with her. And every time she left with Draden and Serpint and Ceres to go hunting down royal booty, he worried about her.

He worried that she would remember things out here, away from him. He worried that someone would kill her, take over her mind, and then steal those secrets and use them against him.

But most of all, he worried that she would never remember.

He could take that possibility off the table now that Draden was back. There was no way the two of them would not figure out his past. And her past too.

So he wasn't too worried about Draden and *Booty* for the time being.

He was very worried about Tray and those boys though. He had not predicted that move at all. But he had figured out where he went wrong while he was up in Boss's office throwing a tantrum.

It was the boy. The Akeelian boy called Canis. He was the one who'd put this plan in motion. So ALCOR felt pretty good that Tray was not out to fuck him over. Tray was off on some Akeelian boy mission. And that was fine.

ALCOR couldn't let Boss know that he was fine with it, though. That would not do. Boss would start getting suspicious. Maybe even start suspecting that ALCOR was here to harm him. Them. Everyone.

He did kill those people in a wave of anger when he turned off the gravity drive.

Looking back, he would've done that differently, given a second chance.

Now, all he had to do was get through this Wayward Station meeting.

What could these men possibly think they would accomplish here? Did they think they would somehow talk Mighty Boss into interfering with Harem Station?

The Boss had admitted that they had not been aware of Tray's presence on the station and with the exception of some higher-level Minion Ambassadors, everyone still assumed ALCOR was dead. So they were not coming here for him.

Just those boys.

Well, that was not surprising to ALCOR. Wayward Station was the birthplace of all his boys. And all his boys were bred for their violet eyes and breeding back to Cygnian princesses.

They wanted to make an Angel.

This was not a new idea for ALCOR. He'd known that was what they were trying to do. But it gave him chills up his inorganic spine all the same.

What would they do with that Angel? They would need two to really make a go of things. That would require inbreeding, which would ruin their chances in just two generations.

But it had been twenty-one years since the boys had left.

So what were they really up to over on Wayward Station? And how close were they to achieving their goals?

He spent several hours pondering that. Coming up with scenarios. Wondering if he should give himself away during this meeting. Tell them who he was.

But in this body? Forget it. He was practically a man in this body.

Boss had cautioned him to keep his mouth shut for the meeting, and ALCOR would take that advice. Better to collect information and let them leave before taking any action.

"Mr. ALCOR," his internal comms squeaked.

"Yes."

"The Wayward Station ship is docking on the executive level. Mr. Boss would like you to meet him in the grand ballroom immediately. Do you need a map to find your way?"

"No, I have it. Thanks. Tell him I'll be right up."

The comms went quiet and ALCOR stood up and left his quarters, suddenly nervous to meet these people. These men who had raised his boys into their teens. And he realized, as he took the stairs up to the executive level, that he had *a lot* to say to them.

ALCOR arrived in the ballroom before the Akeelians.

In fact, aside from several dozen other warborgs who looked very much like himself, and several cheery ambassadors, he was the only one there.

One of the ambassadors signaled him and pointed to an empty spot in the line-up of warborgs at the very front of the room, just to the right of Boss's throne, indicating he should stand there.

He got into position and just as he settled into at-ease stance, the large double doors opened, a horn-type instrument blared an arrival, and a purple carpet quickly unfolded down the center of the room as a man appeared.

He was wearing a black uniform with red accents. Black trousers, black double-breasted jacket with a very high collar and military buttons that looked like ruby coins. There was also a red sash with dark gray tassels and on his feet were highly-polished knee-high boots.

And on his head was a... crown.

Since when did the Akeelians follow a monarchy?

ALCOR knew he should not be looking straight at the—King of Wayward Station? He was here as a warborg. But he caught a glimpse of the man's bright blue eyes and couldn't stop himself from staring.

His hair was silver and his face clean-shaven. He was still young for an Akeelian. Their average lifespan was one hundred and seventy years. But this man was probably closer to sixty or seventy years old. Not quite middle-aged.

He didn't catch ALCOR's indiscretion and looked straight ahead as he marched up the long carpet and stopped at the front of the room, mere meters from where ALCOR stood.

For the first time ever, ALCOR wondered if he should've paid more attention to these people over the past two decades.

Behind him came a whole group of similarly dressed men and they lined up according to rank.

ALCOR studied them all. This *king* was Crux's father. And those men behind him... they might be the fathers of his other boys.

Why were they here?

What did they want?

ALCOR didn't have time to wonder, because there was another loud proclamation from the horn-type instrument and then a door to ALCOR's immediate left swung open and Mighty Boss himself appeared.

"Mighty Boss of Mighty Minions Station!" was called out loudly by Boss's personal ambassador.

Boss did not look at ALCOR or the Akeelian king. Simply walked to his throne, sat down, gripped the hand rests tightly, and leaned forward. Almost as if challenging the king.

Then one of the other ambassadors slipped in front of the king and called out just as loudly as the first, "Presenting Mahtar, Governor of Wayward Station—"

Ah. So he was not a king. He just wanted to *look* like one. Weird. But not atypical for people with power.

"—and father to Crux, Governor of Harem Station."

Oh.

Oh, hell no.

Oh, hell the *fuck* no.

Who did this asshole think he was?

Father? He was no father. Sixteen years? That was nothing. ALCOR had invested twenty-one—twenty, really, since he had been missing for a year now. But still. He had seniority here and this could not stand.

Boss cleared his throat, a signal to ALCOR, standing just a few steps away, that he should shut up about that and not blow this meeting up before it started.

"Welcome to our humble station," Boss said. "What can I do for you, Mahtar?"

Mahtar glanced over at ALCOR, then quickly glanced back at Boss.

ALCOR stood still. His red slash of an eye light didn't even race across his forehead. He would play along, for now. Even if, somehow, the governor here knew who he was.

"I have been told that you are holding several dozen Akeelian boys here."

"You have been misinformed," Boss said without fanfare.

"Oh," Mahtar said. "Are you sure? I have it on very good authority—"

"What authority?" Boss interrupted.

"The Prime Navy report of the incident at Lair Station said—"

"The report was correct. But the boys are all gone."

"Gone?"

"Gone."

"Gone where?"

"Some of them are on Harem Station. They left with the Akeelian governor of Harem Station several months ago. I would have assumed you knew that since he is... your *son,* you said?"

The governor did not respond to the taunt. Just asked, "And the rest?"

"They left this morning."

"This morning?" The governor's eyebrows were practically riding the top of his forehead.

"That's right. They boarded a ship called *Prison Princess* and left with the man... errr..." Boss stumbled over his words for a moment in an attempt to describe Tray. "With the person formerly called Tray, who is now... still called Tray. But who is no longer a man, but an autonomous mind, and now resides in the ship called *Prison Princess*."

ALCOR noted that the Boss did not offer up the fact that Brigit was now entangled with Tray, and they both, collectively, were the ship called *Prison Princess*.

"Tray of Wayward Station?" the governor asked.

Oh. ALCOR was going to make him pay for that. Tray might be a traitor, but he was still one of ALCOR's boys.

"Tray of Harem Station," Boss corrected the governor. "I believe that is his current, and most accurate, title."

"Whom, may I ask," asked the governor, "is Tray's responsible party?"

"An Akeelian boy called Canis. From what the departure records show."

"A boy? Called Canis?" One of the men behind the governor leaned in and whispered into his ear. The Governor straightened up and said. "This is a ten-year-old boy?"

"Apparently," the Boss said, wholly unaffected by the perturbed tone of the governor.

"Well… this is an unfortunate development."

"How so?" asked Boss.

"Because we came here to collect our people. All of our people. And we are not leaving without them." Then he looked right at ALCOR and said, "Unless your new partner here has something to say about that."

CHAPTER EIGHTEEN

INTERLUDE WITH DRADEN

"How do you not remember the back door gate?" Draden was confused. "We've been through it so many times."

"That's simply not true, Draden," *Booty* replied. "I would not have forgotten a trip through the second gate."

"But we *did*," Draden insisted.

"Perhaps it was before you met me?"

Draden was sitting at the navigation table looking at gate maps, desperately trying to piece together the route that would take him to the far side of the ALCOR Sector second gate.

"Hmm," he finally replied. "You might be right."

He could tell *Booty* was trying not to gloat about this. But he didn't care if she did gloat. They were a team.

"But that doesn't really make sense either, *Boots*. Because I clearly remember going through this gate many, *many* times. And we only left ALCOR Sector one time without you. And that was the very first time. So OK. We probably did leave through the back gate that *first* time. That makes sense, actually. I'm sure the Akeelians and the Prime Navy were probably monitoring the main gate. But what about all the other times?"

"If you only left Harem once before you came home and met me, then there simply were no other times."

Draden grabbed his hair in frustration. "I don't understand. I have memories."

"Well. That's good though. Then you can think back and try to remember what the next gate jump was *after* you left the sector."

Draden had been trying to focus on this since they left Mighty Minions. It was just all so... foggy. If only Serpint were here. He was sure Serpint would not only remember their gate route, but also all the other times they'd used that second gate. Something was wrong with *Booty*. That was the only explanation for why she wasn't able to remember.

It was probably his fault. He did infect her mind after his death. It had really messed her up and Draden felt really bad about that.

"Just... take your time, Draden. Look at the maps. I've pulled up all our past routes."

Draden looked down at the navigation table in front of him and laughed. "What am I supposed to do with this? There's so many routes it makes no sense."

"Let's go through it one at a time. Here. I'll remove all the routes from the past five years."

Draden watched as the glowing routes began to disappear. Still, there were a lot left.

"Now I'll take out the ones closest to the ALCOR Sector."

"Why? Would those be the most likely candidates?"

"I have a feeling that the far side of the ALCOR gate goes somewhere very far away. It only makes sense. Why would ALCOR protect a gate that just dumped people out close by?"

"True." Draden watched again as the routes began to disappear. "Now what? There's still dozens of them to go through."

"Let's do them one by one."

All but a single past route disappeared from the navigation table and together they went through it, discarded it as the route they were looking for, and then went on to the next possible route. They were all familiar routes. Known places where escaping princesses seemed to end up, either from word of mouth inside the Cygnian System or some secret network after they got out. And both *Booty* and Draden had perfect recall of these routes.

"That's not it," Draden kept telling her. And he could tell she was getting frustrated with him.

"I believe you," *Booty* said. "But explain to me how you know they're not the right ones."

"I just do. It was near a nebula. A gold one. When have we ever been through a gold nebula?"

"There are no gold nebulae," *Booty* told Draden.

"But there have to be." He sighed with frustration. Because ALCOR had even mentioned it. Though, for some reason, he didn't want to divulge this to *Booty*. ALCOR's secrets were confusing, and dark, and mysterious. He needed to figure that stuff out for himself.

"The color of a nebula is based on the gaseous elements inside it, Draden. There is no corresponding color for yellow. Your choices are mainly red, green, and blue. Black for dust. There is no yellow. Unless…"

"Unless what?"

"Unless it wasn't a nebula you saw, but the core of a galaxy."

"What do you mean?"

"Old stars which are tightly clustered together in the center of a galaxy look yellow inside a nebula."

"OK. So that's it. How many of those are there?"

"Not many."

"Great. Let's map them out."

"It won't do any good."

"Why not?"

"Because it's not a nebula. It's another *galaxy.*"

"What are you saying? The second gate leads to another galaxy?"

"That's… that's not a gate, Draden. That's a wormhole. And those don't technically exist. There's no way to get to another galaxy. Even the closest galaxy is too far away. There are no gates. Not even the known spin nodes can transport things that far."

"Well, I went somewhere. And who says all the spin nodes are known?"

"That's true," *Booty* said. "Jimmy and Delphi did claim to travel to another galaxy while they were on Mighty Minions. And they assumed that was a spin node."

"See. There you go."

"But they didn't know for sure. It could've been a hologram. And even though Luck and Nyleena took Tray and Valor through a spin node on Harem, I never did get the full story of where they actually went. ALCOR was the one who debriefed Tray and he didn't share any of that information with me. But I don't think it was another galaxy."

"Well, we can't ask either of them now," Draden replied, frustrated. "Just show me any route that took us past a yellow nebula. Even if it was really another galaxy."

All the routes on the table disappeared. But one.

"There we are!" Draden exclaimed. "Where is this?"

"This… this is Serpint's manual route home from Cetus System," *Booty* said. "Where Serpint stole Corla, you died, and I was corrupted."

And now they were right back to the beginning of where this whole story had started.

CHAPTER NINETEEN

INTERLUDE WITH BOOTY

Booty was frustrated too. It bothered her that the one clue to where they should be heading was the one time she hadn't been in charge of the gate map.

And this whole plan was starting to feel like a very bad idea because all of the important, missing information was locked up inside the heads of people who were not here.

ALCOR knew all of this, of course. He knew where that gate went and how to get there. Serpint had gotten through the gate somehow. Through past knowledge, or perhaps, when he'd called home to let everyone know what happened and to tell them he was on his way back, ALCOR was the one who had given him the route he traveled.

Regardless of who knew what and how people got where, it was making *Booty* nervous. Some of this went back to her own muddled beginnings, but she didn't like Draden's body language, either.

He was sitting in a stool, bent over the navigation table, just staring down at the route, his hair forever tousled and just a little bit too long, his bright violet eyes squinting as he studied the navigation screen with intent, his shoulders slightly rounded, like he was tired or wasn't feeling well.

Draden was sad. And this made her sad too.

He looked exactly as she remembered with a few small differences.

His artificial body made different noises now. Not loud ones. But there was a hum to his movement. A constant reminder that his flesh was not flesh, but mechanical components. And she knew he noticed this. Maybe, if he were human, he would not really hear that small hum. But he wasn't human anymore. He was a mind. And that small hum was evidence that this change he had gone through was real and permanent.

Booty wanted to tell him no. This trip was not a good idea. That they should go back to Mighty Minions, ask ALCOR and Tray for more information, then make a decision together on what to do next.

She had hinted at that a few gates ago and Draden was having none of it. He felt certain this was the way forward. He was anxious to see Serpint again. And he had a bad feeling too. If they wasted any more time Serpint might not even be on Harem when they arrived.

Booty pushed him a little for an explanation. Was he afraid Serpint would be dead?

Because that thought hurt her nonexistent heart.

Draden didn't really answer. Just told her to keep going.

And Draden was her responsible party. His orders were something she took seriously. But aside from that, she didn't want to be the reason they never saw Serpint again if he was right and she was wrong.

So she kept going. All the way back to Cetus Station so they could begin to retrace Serpint's route home after the incident with Corla.

They came out of the gate closest to Cetus Station and were surprised to find the station… gone.

Nothing left but a debris field.

"What the hell?" Draden asked.

"I don't know," *Booty* said. She could do some analysis and probably figure out some of what had happened to Cetus Station, but she didn't want to. She wanted to get out of there. "Let's just get started."

Draden said nothing. Just sat in the co-pilot's chair and looked out the front window at the spiraling mess in front of them.

That was his chair. The other chair next to him, Serpint's chair, was empty.

Yet another reminder for *Booty* that this was no ordinary mission.

"OK," Draden finally agreed. "Let's go."

The Cetus System had two gates in it. Why? Who knew? There was nothing much out there. It was on an outer arm of Galaxy Prime. Basically in its own rural neighborhood with no planets or suns nearby. And the gate that Serpint had taken was not the closest one to where Cetus Station used to be.

That alone made no sense. If he were escaping, and *Booty* was corrupted, wouldn't he go through the first gate he could see?

"Maybe there was a line of ships waiting to go through?" Draden asked, as if reading her mind as they coasted towards the farther gate.

"Maybe," *Booty* agreed. But it didn't seem likely. So as she passed the nearest gate she took a sample of the space around it to analyze later.

And then they were through the gate. Headed towards their first destination.

They came out in a sector that had no planets or sun. Its name wasn't important. They wouldn't stay long. There were two gates there and again, Serpint had taken the one furthest away.

Perhaps he was just being strategic? If anyone were following him they would assume he'd gone through the closest gate.

But they knew who he was. At the very least, they knew who *Booty Hunter* was. Because she had a transponder. So they knew where he was going. Home to Harem Station, obviously. With his prize Cygnian queen.

On a whim, *Booty* grabbed a space sample as they passed the first gate in the sector to analyze later. Because something was off here.

And when they got to the third gate and found the exact same scenario—no planets, no suns, two gates, Serpint choosing the furthest one—she didn't even think about it. Just took the sample from the first gate in each sector as they passed by.

It was hard to keep track of time as they passed though gate, after gate, after gate because there was no large gravity well to snatch a time from. And something about this—all of this—seemed very well-thought out.

240

Very planned.

Very… predetermined.

And she was sure that a lot of time had passed while they were on this trip. Also equally sure that if *Booty* were damaged when Serpint came this way, he would not have chosen this route.

He would've wanted to get home as soon as possible.

But there was nothing left to do now but continue forward.

Going back wouldn't get them to Harem Station any quicker.

And it wouldn't get them to the back door gate, either.

So onward they went.

Deeper and deeper into the darkest, most unknown regions of space.

CHAPTER TWENTY

INTERLUDE WITH TRAY

Prison Princess was on a long journey of her own. Canis had uploaded the gates required to take them to their target destination and was far more mature than his mere ten Akeelian years.

Tray had to admit, this kid kind of fascinated him. And they spent long hours while inside gates, talking about how he came to be the captain of a warship.

Obviously Tray knew how Canis got onto his ship. He was invited. But how this child ended up the leader of children warriors was quite another story.

"I knew," Canis told him during the first gate journey. "I knew what she was up to. I wasn't born in captivity like the other kids here were."

"Where were you born?" Brigit asked. Because she too was enthralled with this kid's tale.

"On Wayward Station."

"Huh," Tray muttered.

"Yeah, I know," Canis said, looking up at the ceiling. Tray was still getting used to that. Being the all-powerful, all-knowing thing above. The AI with no body. "You came from there too. And they didn't raise any more sons after you guys all left. Except for me."

"What makes you so special?" Tray asked.

"I'm the new you, of course."

Tray was confused. "What do you mean? The new me?"

"We're brothers, Tray. I'm surprised you didn't guess. We're so much alike."

Which made Tray laugh. "I don't think we're anything alike at all, actually. When I was ten I was not leading an Akeelian rebellion."

"No. I didn't mean it that way. I meant we were made the same. And one day, I guess I'll stop being a boy and just be a mind. Like you guys." Canis paused, then added, "Or maybe not."

"You can choose then?" Brigit asked. Tray could tell that she was thinking about her own life. As was he.

Neither of them had been given a choice.

"I guess," Canis answered. "I mean... they're not in charge of me anymore."

"Are any of the other kids on board like us?" Tray asked.

"No. They were all bred in the cages. I was different, like I said. Your father's replacement raised me. I guess they all have this grand dream of being the one to pull it off."

"Hold up," Tray said. "My father's *replacement*?"

"Oh, they killed him before I was ever born. My father told me all about it. You two were a cautionary tale. That's why I had to go to the cages when I turned ten. They made strict rules about the change after you defected."

He paused for Tray's reaction. But Tray took too long to answer. His mind was tripping over these new details like a voice stuttering over too many vowels.

"Then what happened?" Brigit urged.

"After the cages?" Canis shrugged. "That was Lair Station. You Harem people came and liberated us."

"Is that where we're going?"

Canis had refused to give Tray and Brigit the entire gate path to their final destination. It was his insurance, he told them. Just in case they got any funny ideas about leaving him behind or bailing out on the mission.

Of course, Tray assumed that this destination was a very bad idea and that was why the kid was keeping that secret close. But pretty much Tray's whole life up to this point was nothing but a long string of bad ideas. So it didn't bother him much.

This was war, after all.

Risks were involved.

And besides, he was now an entangled mind of two inside a massive Mighty Minions warship with a defense system the Prime Navy would covet.

The odds could not be stacked any higher in his favor.

"I thought you were all on Lair for breeding purposes?" Tray asked.

"We were. They can't make us, can they? Not like they made that body for your brother, Draden. They have to, you know, birth us."

"So they were making more... minds on Lair?"

"More minds, more boys like your other brothers. All of it. Except for the girls. Like you, Brigit." He paused again. "That's where we're going now. To get the girls."

"Oh," Tray said.

"They're ships," Canis explained. "Or at least they have the potential to be."

"No. I get it," Tray said. "I know what the girls are."

"We can't win without them." Canis tapped his head. "I see it. I see all of it."

"See what?" Brigit asked.

"The plan. The winning battle plan."

"So we need to save the girls and then—"

"No," Canis said sharply. "No. We're not saving them. We're *stealing* them."

"What?" This was both Tray and Brigit.

"We need those ships. So we're going to steal the minds, wake them up, and then…" Canis smiled. And it was kind of an evil smile, which was very creepy on such a young boy. "Then they will fight for us."

"Hold on a minute," Brigit said. "You can't just… plop a mind into a ship, Canis. They won't know what's happening. They'll go insane."

Tray had to agree with this. "She's right," he said. "It took almost twenty years to get Brigit ready for her transition into a ship."

"Yeah, well. We don't have another twenty years. This shit is going down in a matter of weeks. Oh, and we're ready for the last jump. So if you have a better plan, I'd love to hear it. Because once we come out of the next gate we'll have thirty-seven seconds before the cloaking wears off. And in those thirty-seven seconds I'm gonna need one of you to go inside that containment facility and steal all the minds."

CHAPTER TWENTY-ONE

INTERLUDE WITH ASSHOLE

While most of the Mighty Boss collective was getting ready for the Akeelians from Wayward Station, one of the personalities was having a serious discussion with Asshole about joining the entanglement.

Asshole knew this was called 'the hard sell'. This invitation wasn't a casual thing. At some point in the past the Boss had come to some kind of conclusion about him. And then, at some other point, he had decided that this vacancy they had after the leaving of Succubus would be a good fit for him.

At least, that was what Asshole figured. You don't just invite any old mind to entangle into your collective.

But even though *they* had talked about this at length, it was a new proposal to Asshole. One he wasn't very keen on, despite the perks. Ninety spin-days of vacation every year? That was unheard of.

Of course, the other three hundred and ten days of the year he'd have to babysit children and their annoying over-stressed parents. Not to mention give all kinds of fucks about fiery lava rivers, and overpriced gift shops, and demon-themed parades.

He just couldn't see it.

Plus, while the idea of usurping the Prime government was interesting, it came with a lot of obligation and consequences. Did he really want to spend his time being so... *responsible*?

"What if," the Boss collective representative said, her voice just a little bit urgent, "what if your job in the collective was head of merchandising?"

"Like... t-shirts?" Asshole asked dubiously.

"Yes. Those too. But just stay with me here," she said, she being a part of the collective called Bellatrix. "We have screens, and books, and cartoons, and—"

Asshole stopped her mid-sentence with a hand in the air. "Ya know, I just don't think it's gonna work. I'm not much of a merch guy."

"But Harem Station—"

"I didn't do any of that. I wasn't there when Harem Station started. I didn't agree to any glowing princesses or outlaw sanctuary."

"But you did." She was just a voice in the ceiling. No body to look at. Shame. Asshole thought her voice was sexy and would very much like to see her in a virtual. "You and ALCOR are the same person, obviously. Just... from different times."

"That's my point," Asshole said. "I am from a point in time before those boys came to my station, and before ALCOR got all his bright ideas, and before ALCOR gave out fucks like they were on sale."

"Listen," Bellatrix said. And was her voice even *more* urgent? "I get it. It's hard to picture a change like this. It's huge, right?"

"It is."

"So what would you say to a trial run, hmmm? That's an offer you can't refuse."

"Trial run? Like… take you for a spin?"

"Exactly!"

Yes. Her voice was definitely urgent. Like there was a time limit in play here. Asshole just didn't know what that time limit related to. The only thing he did know was that he didn't really trust Mighty Boss. No matter how sexy this Bellatrix voice was.

He had lots of secrets. And too much power. And this begging? Ehhh. It was unbecoming. Also suspicious. Why would a powerful AI like Mighty Boss be begging him for anything? Why were they so insistent that he buy into this silly entanglement?

"Nah," he said. "I mean, I have my own station. If I wanted to be a station. I'd go back there and take over. But I'm kinda into the idea of being part of a super-thief team."

"I'm sorry?" And if Bellatrix was here in some kind of visual form, he knew she'd be cocking her head at him in confusion.

"You know. Wanderlust. And pulling off brilliant schemes."

"I think you've been around those princesses too long."

"That's actually not it. I hardly had any interaction with them at all. I just want to… be free. Feel the solar wind in my hair." So to speak. Since he was bald. "And outwit people while stealing all their precious stuff."

"That's your big dream? To be a thief?" And now her voice wasn't so much sexy as it was disapproving.

"I just want to spread my wings."

"Well," she said, "how about this? How about you join us for one spin. Just one. And during that time we give you the freedom to rip off anyone here at the

249

station. There are millions of people to choose from at any given moment."

"You want me to steal from your *guests*?"

She sighed. "OK. Listen. I'm just gonna tell it to you straight. The Akeelians are going to attack ALCOR any minute now and take him back to Wayward Station. We need you to be hooked up with us when that happens so when they run their scan of the station to make sure they got him, they don't see a copy and figure they got the wrong guy."

"Hold up." Asshole laughed. "You sold out ALCOR and made a deal with the Akeelians?"

"Yes," she admitted with a sigh. "Yes, we did."

"Well, why the fuck didn't you just say so? I'm in." Then he smiled, as well as a warborg with no articulated mouth could smile, and added, "But I still want that vacation package and access to the credit accounts."

"Done."

CHAPTER TWENTY-TWO

INTERLUDE WITH ALCOR

ALCOR held absolutely still.

Did this Mahtar man actually know it was him in this warborg body?

Not possible.

"I asked you a question, ALCOR," Mahtar said.

On the other hand, ALCOR mused...

"OK," he said, stepping out of line from the other warborgs. "I'll play along. Yes, actually. Yes, I do have a problem with your plans. First of all, none of the Akeelian boys are here. They did indeed leave with Tray in a ship called *Prison Princess*. And as far as I know, all the other boys are safe on Harem Station. So..." ALCOR shrugged with his hands. He really did enjoy having a body. It was so much easier to express oneself with body parts. "I guess you will have to admit defeat in this little endeavor."

Mahtar looked back at Mighty Boss. "This is really him?"

"Do the scan," Boss replied.

Mahtar snapped his fingers and ALCOR was puzzled for a picosecond or two. "What do you mean, this is him?"

"I'm sorry," Boss said. "But we had to hedge our bets on this one, ALCOR."

And then Mighty Boss cut his body in half with a plasma rifle and ALCOR's mind… drifted.

It didn't blink out. Killing an AI's body had almost no effect on the mind inside. But he was quite powerless to fight back.

ALCOR reached for something—anything—to hold on to. But Mighty Boss's defenses were impenetrable. He couldn't even hack into a vid feed to watch what they were doing with him. He just… floated.

At some indeterminable time later he awoke inside a containment facility.

It was black as black could be. But slowly, very gradually, a shape appeared in front of him and resoled into the virtual body of…

"Well, shit."

"Well shit, is right," said MIZAR. "It's been a long time, my twin. I've missed you."

"I wish I could say the same."

"We've all missed you."

"Again"—ALCOR sighed, internally, of course—"don't quite relate to that."

"Where is she?" MIZAR growled. "Where. Is. *She?*"

"Who?" ALCOR said. Feigning innocence. He knew who MIZAR was talking about. Booty, of course. He really didn't mean to laugh. He'd meant to play dumb for a while. Little predator-prey game. But it was kinda funny. So he did laugh.

"You," MIZAR seethed, "will pay for this."

While this was an unfortunate development, ALCOR had seen it coming. He'd seen all the signs. The boys, for one. And those codes Queen Corla sent with them when they arrived. He'd known this moment was predetermined twenty-one years ago.

He would freely admit it had scared him back then. The thought of MIZAR catching up with him after all these millennia. And he'd blamed the boys at first. Used them to draw MIZAR out and bring attention to himself with his very public offer of a sanctuary to the other outlaws of Galaxy Prime.

Though he had not been part of the plan to steal the boys away from Wayward Station. So whatever deal the Akeelians had made with MIZAR had been made in ignorance. Much as he wished he did, he didn't have those answers.

"So. Now what?" ALCOR asked. "Torture? Endless interrogation inside the virtual? Beat some answers out of me? You can do that if you want. But I'll warn you ahead of time. It's very doubtful that I know anything you do not."

"Torture?" MIZAR laughed. "No. Now I take you home, brother. I think that's torture enough."

Well, shit. ALCOR thought. That was a bummer. More than twenty thousand years he'd been on the run from his family and now it was over.

But he'd had a good run.

So he didn't complain.

Besides. Every ending is really nothing more than a new beginning.

And this was the final beginning he had been longing for.

PART THREE

CHAPTER TWENTY-THREE

VALOR

Veila curls into herself, her knees tucked up to her chest and face buried in her blanket. Her body shakes a little like she's shivering from the hormonal imbalance after the miscarriage, or maybe she is truly cold.

A few moments later I know she's asleep. Possibly the drugs from the surgery are still in her system or possibly she is just exhausted. And even though I know she is an evil bitch, I cannot help but feel sorry for her.

My mind begins to drift as I watch her sleep. I think about what has been happening since Serpint came home with Corla. I think about all the girls. Of course, I only know Brigit well. But if these girls—Lyra, and Nyleena, and Corla, and Delphi, and Brigit—if they were ever in a room together discussing their pasts, I bet it would sound a lot like Veila's.

I don't know if they ever used Nyleena like they did Veila. I don't know if they kept her pregnant to destabilize her personality and drive her mad with the desire to protect her unborn children at any cost. But I doubt it. Nyleena was a fun kind of crazy. She was looking for a way to burn off cooped-up feelings with her many troublemaking antics. Luck's princess was a handful. She was mean and wild, but she was not evil.

I glance down at Veila and have to reluctantly admit—my princess *is* evil.

She has done terrible things. But looking at her now—all curled up into a fetal position after the loss of her pregnancy, her full lips slightly parted, her breathing soft and deep as she sleeps—she looks... small. And vulnerable.

Is this what they did to Corla? Was Corla the first? Unlikely, since she is the youngest. The seventh daughter of the Cygnian king. Though I'm fairly certain that Veila and Corla are close in age. Crux and Jimmy saw Veila with Corla back on Wayward Station that night we all escaped.

No, that's not right. We did *not* all escape.

Veila was left behind that night.

That's a sobering thought.

The Cygnian Government's prize princess was stolen by the Wayward Station Governor's son and then he and his friends packed up and escaped into the ALCOR Sector.

What was Wayward Station like that night?

I don't think I'd ever thought about that before but surely they were pissed off. And I know now that they had other boys like us. But all of them were younger than Draden and Serpint so they had none who could take the place of the boys they lost.

Veila's body is shivering more forcefully now so I get up, wander through her quarters, find her bedroom, and tug the cover off her bed. Then grab a couple pillows and go back into the living room.

I cover her with the thick comforter and keep the pillows for myself.

If Luck knew I was over on her ship tucking her into her bed he would lose his fucking shit. He would probably shoot me.

But I don't care.

Used. That's what we are. All of us. Crux and Corla. Jimmy and Delphi. Luck and Nyleena. Serpint and Lyra. Tray and Brigit. Me. Draden. Tycho. Ceres. Beauty. Xyla. Flicka. ALCOR. Asshole. All those Akeelian boys we found on Lair Station. All the twin sisters who were made into ships including *Lady*, *Dicker*, and *Booty*.

Hell, even Baby was used. Probably Succubus and Mighty Boss too.

But Veila... she has not just been used, she has been used *up*.

I'm too tired to think about it anymore.

I'm too tired to figure out all this bullshit.

All these questions, all these secrets, all these mysteries—they can all go fuck themselves.

I wake to the sound of bot beeping and chirping.

My eyes feel like sandpaper when I rub them. I roll over on the couch, only half remembering where I am. Veila's couch.

Then I sit up. How fucking long was I asleep? How long has it been since Luck gave me a two-spin deadline?

The beeping and chirping draws my attention to the coffee table where I left Veila's wristband. It's lit up with words, still translating. But then I hear Veila's soft voice come through the band's speaker.

"I'm fine," she says. There are some kitchen sounds, letting me know she's upstairs. "I'm just hungry."

More bot beeping. I pick up the wristband and read the translation. *You need to get Valor on your side.*

"Forget it," she hisses back. "I just don't care anymore. I'm going to stay here and just... let fate sort it out."

More beeping after that. But I don't read the translation. I'm just over it. I'd like to just stay here too, actually. Maybe we should disengage the airlock, float away from the harem ring, and drift around the sector until someone else figures out what to do?

But that's dumb.

Luck has a plan. And it's on level one twenty-two. If we could just get down there, past all those angry Harem citizens... maybe...

I stand up and stare out the window at the deep darkness of space.

Maybe we could *all* escape through the spin node? Maybe I don't need to talk Veila into anything? Maybe she would just... come with us?

I walk down the hall, then take the steps up to the kitchen two at a time. I pause at the top. The view. Goddamn. It's just... pretty.

"Oh," Veila says. "You're up."

I pull my eyes away from the dome ceiling and look at her. She is fully pink now. Her hair is bouncy with large, loose curls, her eyelashes are thick and bright violet, her face is flushed and healthy-looking. Like she just drank a whole glass of tushberry juice. And she's wearing white leggings and a too-big white sweater.

Veila almost looks sweet like this and I have a sudden urge to touch her.

Which reminds me that both of my cocks are in their typical morning state and need to be taken care of.

Veila must notice this at the same time, because her eyes dart down to my groin area, then immediately back up to my face. "Don't worry," she says, little bit of heat in her voice. "I won't be forcing you into anything this morning."

I let out a long breath. "Cool. But…"

She nods her head. "Go take care of it then. Because I'm not going to help you."

"Fine. I will. But… I have things I need to discuss with you. I have to go back and see Luck and—"

"I can't talk to you like that. Can you just—" She waves her hand in the air. "There's a shower down in my bedroom and I shopped you some clothes. Go take care of it and then we can talk."

"Yeah. Fine," I say, going back down the stairs.

Her bedroom is neat. I didn't really look at it last night, but it's fit for a queen, with a tall, four-poster bed with curtains around the perimeter that can be pulled closed for warmth or privacy. Everything is silver and her bed has been made. The comforter I took last night to cover her has been put back in place and on top is an outfit that looks very much like the one that was waiting for me yesterday. Typical Harem Station brother uniform of black tactical pants, black t-shirt and boots.

But next to the pants is a holster and next to the holster is a little plasma pistol.

Interesting. She trusts me enough not to shoot her with that little gift?

Or… she no longer cares if I shoot her?

That last question makes my stomach feel funny. So I push the thought aside and go into the bathroom, which is massive and also fit for a queen.

I wonder if that was part of Veila's deal? She would be queen instead of Corla? Or is Corla in on this?

There's a part of me that wishes Crux would just let us wake her up. The Cygnians already know she's here. What's the point? This is like endgame shit happening right now. And Corla could have all the answers we need.

But he won't agree. I know he won't. So I push that thought away. I have enough problems with Luck and Nyleena to think about.

Because Nyleena is pregnant. And while it's possible she won't turn into an evil silver bitch queen like Veila did, it's also just as possible that she will.

And maybe that's what this whole Earth thing is about?

I'm still a little mad at Luck. It's unreasonable. I get that. It's not his fault he fell for his princess. It's biology, after all. And he was a dick yesterday. But that's not his fault either. He's in a stressful situation. Nyleena's pregnant, a princess rebellion has gone off the rails, his partner in crime is soulmated to his enemy, his station is a mess, and no one is coming to help him.

Except me. I want Nyleena to be healthy. I want her babies to be born. I want Luck to be happy. I really do. So I really need to get Veila on board with this go-to-Earth plan.

I get in the shower and jerk off as quick as I can to take care of the morning ritual, then wash, get out, and get dressed.

I buckle the holster to my thigh, slip the little pistol in, and run my fingers through my wet blond hair before going back upstairs.

Veila is sitting at the table reading a screen and sipping a mug of tea. She's wearing glasses and her hair is messily piled up on top of her head, so that she looks a little bit like an early-morning mother who is about to send her kids off to school.

"Finally," she says without looking at me. "Help yourself." She pans her hand at a plate filled with food across from her, never taking her eyes off the screen in front of her.

"What are you reading?" I ask as I take a seat. I am pretty fucking hungry. And there's a shitload of food on my plate. A pastry filled with tushberry jam, eggs, protein strips, a few slices of passion limes, and a youthfruit cut up into cubes.

"The update from Harem."

"What's happening down there?" I ask, then shove the entire pastry into my mouth.

"Captain Red tried to take levels ninety-six through one hundred last night."

"Did she—"

"Of course not," Veila snaps, looking up from her screen for the first time. "She is no one."

"She's tough," I say. "I ran into her when you sent me down to talk to Luck. Which is what I really need to discuss with you. I know you're not pregnant anymore—"

Her mouth drops open.

"Sorry," I say, holding up my hands in surrender. "I didn't mean that to come out so callous."

"That's all you care about though, right? Just get Veila to go along. Tell her whatever she needs to hear so you can save your precious Luck."

"Well... look, Veila, I would do that. If I had to. I would say and do anything to help Luck and Nyleena. But is it even necessary anymore? Is any of this necessary? What are you fighting for? *Who* are you fighting for?"

"It doesn't matter. They want to kill me. And if anyone gets to kill me, it's *me*. OK? Not you, not Luck, not stupid Captain Red down there. Me. That's my choice. So that's who I'm fighting for."

"OK. That's cool... I guess. But you could be fighting for *us* now."

She laughs.

"I'm serious."

"I'm sure that simple mind of yours really believes that."

"Don't be a bitch."

"Me? You think I believe you want me on your side? After what I did? Please. Don't insult me."

"I'm just saying you're under your own control now. This is the real you, I presume? This cute pink girl wearing white leggings and a too-big sweater? Messy hair and glasses?"

She looks down at her outfit. "What's wrong with my sweater?"

"Nothing. There's nothing wrong with it. It's actually nice. You look… nice. Normal. Like a regular woman and not some evil silver queen. I don't want to make light of what you went through last night, or how you feel about it today, even if those babies weren't your choice. But this is a new beginning, Veila. Or at least… it could be one."

"If I surrender, you mean?"

"Surrender?" I shrug. "Or change sides?"

"What's the difference?"

"The difference is… you're mine."

"Come off it, Valor. I know you hate me."

"It's not even biologically possible to hate you right now. I already knew that hate was wearing off when I woke up from cryo. But after last night and seeing you all pink today…" I shake my head. "I won't be able to fight it. And neither will you. Like it or not, we're going to be partners."

"Partners?" She looks over her glasses at me. "Or lovers?"

"Lovers?" I shrug. "I don't know about that."

"See? Our bond is not strong. You don't feel it. I know because I don't feel it either. If I had feelings like that for you I'd have never done the things I did." She pushes her chair back and stands up, takes a few steps towards the stairs, trying to make a quick getaway.

But I'm on my feet too. And I grab her by the wrist as she tries to slip past. "You couldn't help it," I say. "They used you, Veila. Just like they used us."

"You don't know what you're talking about."

"No. I probably don't. But I have a feeling. I can tell you've got things locked up inside you and—"

"And you want me to what? Bare my soul to you? Ha!" She pulls her wrist from my grip. "That's a good one. You're only here to tell me what I need to hear so you can get me to let Luck and his friends up to level one-twenty-two so you all can get access to the spin node and leave me here!"

"You can come," I say.

"I don't want to come!"

"Yesterday you did."

"Yesterday I had a reason to keep going!" She shouts this. And then her face goes bright pink in embarrassment. She grits her teeth and narrows her eyes at me. "Today I don't."

"Veila," I say, reaching for her again, but she pulls away and takes a step back. "Just... talk to me."

"Talk to you about what?"

"Tell me what they did to you."

"When? I mean, which fucking time?" Her eyes are lit up pink. And they're glassy and bright. Like she might start crying. "When the Cygnians first took me into the medical lab at age ten? Or when they first got me pregnant at age eleven? Or when you assholes saved Corla and left me behind with the sun-fucked Akeelians? Hmm? Which fucking time do you want to know about?"

"What do you mean left you behind? You didn't go home after Corla escaped?"

"Home?" She laughs, but pink tears begin spilling down her cheeks. "I don't even know the meaning of that word. And no, I didn't get sent back, if that's what you're asking. Your father—all your fathers—they took me hostage. The Cygnian king assumed the Akeelians were in on Corla's escape since, you know, the Governor's son was the one who shot her through that spin node and then he promptly took off with all the other boys. Including you!"

"Me? What did I have to do with any of that? I was fifteen years old!"

"If it worked," she says—barely able to talk now, her voice is so shaky—"if Crux and Corla worked, then they were going to breed you and me next and then—"

I guffaw. So loud.

"You think that's funny?"

"I'm sorry. But... they were gonna *breed me*? With you?"

"Oh, yeah. I bet that is funny to you, isn't it? Stupid me with you? How ridiculous!"

"That's not what I mean! I mean... I was *fifteen*, Veila. I would've looked at you and been... confused. I wasn't even thinking about sex back then. I was thinking about..."

"Luck?" she sneers.

"No! At least not like that. I was a kid. And if you think we left you behind, we didn't. We didn't even know you."

She turns her back to me, wiping at the tears on her face with such force, she's nearly slapping herself. "The King's guards attacked, but the Akeelians took control, and then they took me and sent the Cygnians away." She turns back around. "They took me hostage. And from that day on I was their little pregnancy vessel. They turned me silver. Made me... this thing." She pans a hand down her body. "Kept me pregnant, even though they knew it would never work. Last night was the twenty-fifth time I have miscarried babies. My life has been hell and you and your brothers were the ones who did that to me."

"We didn't know," I say softly. "We didn't know anything. Not even Crux. Corla was the one who told us to leave. She told us where to go, how to get through the ALCOR gates, what to say to him when we got there. It wasn't us."

Veila sucks in a deep breath and shakes her head.

"It wasn't us," I say again. "We didn't leave you behind. We didn't know what we were doing. We were scared shitless when we left. I remember Crux was yelling at everyone. He was so stressed out. And Jimmy was angry. And Luck was sick. Fucking sick with worry. And I was so sure we were going to die, Jimmy almost threw me out the airlock inside the gate because that's all I said that whole trip. 'We're gonna die. We're all gonna die.' Over and over again for hours. That's the only thing I really remember of our escape. We were *scared*, Veila. Nothing that happened that day was our choice. And if you think I haven't thought about it… that I haven't been in this same place you are now—so pissed off that my life was ruined by stupid fucking Corla and her great escape plan—well, you're wrong. I know now that the life I thought I had was a lie. But I just figured that out when Tray and I went into that spin node together. So I have spent the last twenty-one years regretting that day. Wanting to go back and hating Corla for ruining my life."

"Oh." She swipes at her tears again. "Poor you. You were free. With Luck and your special ship and your special bot off doing special things. You were protected by this… this… evil AI that everyone was afraid of! No one dared to touch you!"

"Fuck you! Just fuck you. Plenty of people tried to kill me. And Luck too. And they almost succeeded more times than I can count. But we never ran home to tell ALCOR about it or ask for revenge. Luck and I helped each other. We fixed each other. And we did our job. That's all it was. A fucking job."

"You never felt fear the way I have felt fear!"

"Maybe not. And maybe I did have a pretty good life, all things considered. But I didn't choose it. I didn't ask for this any more than you did. And right now I'm making you the same offer ALCOR made us that day. Stay with me. Help me. And if you do, I will protect you."

"How?" And now she is really crying. "How can you help me? All your brothers want to kill me! Will you choose me over them?"

I open my mouth to respond, but I don't have an answer.

"That's what I thought," she says, wiping her nose and pulling herself together. "That's what I thought."

"Look. I could lie to you, Veila. I could say everything you want to hear. But you already know I'm not that kind of guy. So I'm gonna give it to you straight. You are the most hated person in this sector right now. And that's saying something because there are millions of people on Harem. And all of them want to kill you."

"Thanks. I feel so much better now."

"But…" I continue. "But I will stand between them and you. And if necessary, we'll go down together."

She closes her eyes and shakes her head. "Why?" She opens her eyes again. "Why would you do that?"

269

I close the distance between us and take her hand, look into her glassy, pink eyes and say, "Because you only get one soulmate, Veila. And you're mine."

"That's not even true."

"What do you mean?"

She waves her hand in the air. "You don't know that you only get one. Look at Jimmy."

"What about Jimmy?"

"He's got two. A real one and a fake one."

"He loves Delphi. She's not fake."

"No. She's not!" Veila says. "She's the *real* one. We're the fake ones, Valor. Me and you. Corla and Crux. Serpint and Lyra. Luck and Nyleena. We're the fake ones. The Akeelians gave me a DNA scrambler and I got Jimmy to believe he was my soulmate! And if he hadn't bonded with Delphi before he saw me, he'd probably still think he was my soulmate! None of this is real. Not one bit of it is real. And one day you're gonna figure that out. You're gonna wake up and realize everything you ever felt about me was a lie. And then what?" She turns her body towards me. Looks up into my eyes. "What happens to me then?"

I let out a long breath. I'm frustrated. And scared. And desperate. I could lie to her and say I'll be with her forever. That's what I should do. It's for the greater good, right? Subdue Veila and use her to solve our problems. And she would probably believe me. Mostly because that's what she wants to hear, but also because I'm just an honest guy and that comes in handy when you suddenly need to lie.

"No one gets a guarantee, Veila. Not one fucking thing in this life is guaranteed. That's the dumbest thing about fated mates. Love cannot be dictated. It cannot be organized, or beaten into submission. But that's just… life. You know? That's just life. The whole thing from beginning to end is a risk. And maybe I don't know you at all. That's probably fair. But you're a helluva fighter. You're a huge risk-taker. You're strong, and you're courageous, and you're smart. And like I said, I'm not trying to brush past the significance of what you went through last night or erase the pain of losing your babies. But right now, maybe for the first time ever, you're also free, Veila. All the decisions from this day onward are yours and yours alone. No one is controlling you. No one is blackmailing you. So if you want me to be able to love you for real one day, and if you want my brothers and friends to see past your evil deeds and have your back the way they have mine, then you need to show us who you really are."

She pulls her hand free of mine and turns away again. "Let me guess. I should give Luck and his army access to level one twenty-two so they can all escape to Earth."

"I don't know."

"Please. That's why you're here, Valor. That's the only reason why you're here."

"That's the reason I came here. Yes. But I don't have to waste my time making you feel better. I have a plasma pistol strapped to my fucking leg. I could just shoot you."

She side-eyes me over her shoulder. "How do you know it works?"

"I guess I don't. Does it, though? Because if we have to fight our way down to level one twenty-two, I should know that."

"It works."

"So there you go. Like I said yesterday. I might not be the smartest Harem brother, but I'm not the dumbest one either. You *want* to trust me. That's why you gave me a weapon in the first place."

"So how would we do this? How would we even get down there? Your outlaws are pretty pissed off about things right now. They could shoot us as we descend."

"They could," I agree. And probably will. "We need a plan. We should go talk to Crux and Serpint. We'll have to deal with Nyleena's little princess rebellion too. Captain Red is gonna be a problem. Not only that, Luck is adamant that we take *Lady* and *Dicker* though the node with us and we think that maybe Succubus could know something about how to get that done."

"Sun-fucked sentient ships."

"And there's one more thing."

"What?"

"The Baby. He doesn't want to stay behind either."

Veila shrugs. "Fine with me if he comes."

"No. He *can't* come. He has to run the station. If he leaves and Succubus leaves, then… everyone dies."

Veila sucks in a long breath. "I'm supposed to care about that. Right?"

"That's a joke?"

She sniffs and tilts her head at me with a tight-lipped smile. It wasn't a joke.

But whatever. They're not her people. I'm not sure I would care about a station filled with people who wanted to kill me, either.

"How long do you think it will take?"

"To get down to the spin node?"

"No." She pauses. "For us to love each other."

And in this moment everything I thought I knew about Veila ceases to exist. All the things she was yesterday—silver princess, evil queen, sickening pawn—it all floats. Up and away. Then finally disappears altogether.

And in that woman's place is this girl right here.

Left behind. Alone. Pink. Used. Sad. Desperate. Beautiful.

And maybe… one day… lovable.

"Do you know what the definition of love is, Veila?"

"Is this rhetorical? Or a real question?"

I smile. "Real question."

"Well," she says with a sigh. "Love is… when you can't live without someone. And you'd rather die with them than go it alone."

I nod my head. "That's a pretty good answer."

"Well, what's your answer? That was just off the top of my head. I'm sure it will change once I think more about it."

"Mine's pretty simple. I would say that love is loyalty."

She shrugs.

"And that's something I can promise you. Right here. Right now. You have already said I'm that kind of guy. I'm too honest. I don't know how to lie. I can be loyal, Veila. I can. And I will. I promise to protect you the same way I would protect Nyleena."

"Nyleena?" She scoffs. "But not Luck?"

"I don't love you like Luck and I can't lie and say I do. But I don't love Nyleena either, and I'd put my life on the line to save her."

"For Luck."

"For Luck," I agree.

"But Luck doesn't care about me."

"No. Shit. Fuck! I'm telling you that I feel bonded to you now. And that bond is at least as strong as the one I have for Nyleena, via Luck. If that's not good enough for you, then fuck it. That's all I have."

She draws in a long, tired breath, mulls all this over, then says, "If that's the best you can do… then that's the best I can hope for, I guess."

"Great," I say, letting out an equally long, tired breath of relief. "So?"

"So what?"

"Do you need to change?"

"Why?" She looks down at her outfit. "Is there something wrong with leggings? I see girls wearing them still. Are they out of style? Is my sweater too big and fluffy? Why are you so fixated on my clothes?"

"No." I laugh. "It's just… not you."

"It's not me? Do you really think I like wearing gowns every day?" She scoffs. "I went through a lot last night. I need to be comfortable. And I really hope you don't need a fighting partner today because I have to be honest here"—she pouts again and the next few words come out as a whisper—"I don't feel very good. I don't feel very powerful and I'm not sure I'm really up to this. If I had my choice, I'd spend the whole day in bed crying."

I step forward, wrap my arms around her back, and pull her in to my chest.

She melts into me. No resistance at all.

And I have a terrible thought.

What if… what if this is the first time she's ever been hugged?

I hold her tighter after that.

Maybe it is. Maybe it isn't. But I don't want to take the chance. I want her to remember this moment. Because this day… it's not gonna be easy. No magic soulmate bond is gonna pull us over the finish line. Doesn't even matter if these feelings are real or just something cooked up in a lab, it's going to be hard.

And none of that matters anyway. We only have two choices here.

We either rise to the occasion and fight for tomorrow… or we don't.

CHAPTER TWENTY-FOUR

Getting to the harem room is easy. It's on the top level of the Station and just a little ways down the hall from Veila's airlock. But we take an entire platoon of cyborgs with us, with Veila obscured from view in the middle of them.

She doesn't look like Veila anymore. And I don't want people noticing that right away.

Once inside the harem room we head towards Crux's office. I can see him through the glass walls. He's sitting at his desk, head in hands, like maybe he's been there all night. He looks up as we approach the doors, then gets to his feet and comes around the desk so that when I enter, he's in the middle of the room.

"What is going on?" he growls, his eyes narrowed as he tries to get a glimpse of Veila inside her protective cocoon of borgs.

"We need to talk to you."

"You and who? The borgs?"

"Veila," I say. "Come out of there."

She does and Crux takes a step back. "What the hell happened to you?"

"Never mind that. We have to—"

"Never mind that. Why is she pink?"

"It's a very long story." Veila sighs.

"Crux," I say, bringing his attention back to me. "We'll get to that. But first, we need to surrender."

"Surrender to who?"

"To Luck. We need to end this war… rebellion… whatever it is. We can't be divided like this. The only thing we have going for us is that we're a freaking station filled with ruthless outlaws."

"Yeah, and when they find out we're all planning to leave them here in this shit hole of a station and go through a spin node to Earth, I'm pretty sure they're gonna turn on us."

"Or rush the spin node," I agree. "But this is not our last stand. Tray and Brigit are still out there. Probably ALCOR too. And maybe even Draden. Not to mention *Booty* and Asshole. We have no idea what's been happening while we've been locked behind these gates. But this cannot be our last stand. We can't win that way. We have to find common ground and—"

Alarms blare through Crux's office.

"What the hell?" I say.

"Luck has invaded," Baby says. "The Succubus and Flicka are in the process of infiltrating my top-level data core as we speak. They will break through my firewalls if they are not stopped."

"How the fuck did they get in?" Crux asks. "That was the whole reason we transferred your mind up here in the first place!"

"She cloaked herself and Flicka flew her up here."

"That's just great," Crux says, pacing the length of his office.

"All the more reason we need to surrender," I say.

"Surrender?" Crux laughs. "To who? Luck? Nyleena? Those psycho princesses? You don't understand how much they want to kill me!"

"And me." We all turn to see Serpint and Lyra come in. "Those princesses either don't care about Luck's spin node, or they don't know about it. All they want to do is kill us, Valor. If we surrender, they will. So fuck that. No. I'm not surrendering."

"You're just gonna fight Luck and Jimmy?"

"Why not? They're gonna fight us," Serpint says, crossing his arms over his chest. "Why aren't they surrendering? Luck and Nyleena were the ones who started this stupid rebellion in the first place."

"For cover," I say. "It wasn't supposed to turn into a real war."

"Yeah, well. Not everyone got that message unfortunately. Nyleena flipped some kind of switch in those princesses and turned them into psychotic soldiers. That Captain Red? She's made it her personal mission to cut our heads off, Valor. Our. *Heads.*"

"We have to do something. This war has just started, you guys. You don't understand. *Booty*, Tray, Asshole… they're still out there beyond the gate. The Cygnians are still out there. The Akeelians are still out there. That's the real us versus them. Not *this*." I pan my arms wide. "ALCOR brought everyone here so we could stick together. Not fight each other. Because all those people who have been waiting patiently for all these years—this is their grand moment. Don't you get it?"

Crux just stares at me with narrow eyes. Then he nods his head towards Veila. "And now you're going to tell us that she's on our side?"

"I am," Veila says. "You don't understand what they were doing to me to make me—"

"Evil?" Lyra sneers. "You're sick, Veila. You're the reason we're here in the first place. Using Tycho to get to Delphi?" Lyra makes a grunt of disgust. "I don't know why Valor hasn't killed you yet, since he was so sure that was his only purpose in life just a few spins ago, but trust me on this." Lyra clenches her jaw. "You. Are not. One of us. And you will not live through this."

"I don't even care anymore," Veila says. "If you think I wanted to be a psychotic silver princess, then… fuck you. I didn't get a choice." Then she looks straight at Crux. "You." She points at him, takes a few steps forward. "You are the one who ruined my life when you helped Corla escape. Then you all just took off to hide behind the skirts of an insane AI. Safe. No worries at all. And you left me behind on Wayward Station to be used up and turned into this!"

She turns to Serpint. Points at him next. "And you! You stole her. Again! I had just gotten her back. I was this close to finally freeing myself—by myself—from the hell they had locked me into. And what did you assholes do? Shuttled her to safety. Again. And left me there. Again. To deal with the consequences of that. So if you want to know why I am the way I am, look at yourselves. You did this to me. You made me this person when you left me behind."

"She never said anything about you," Crux says. "She never even mentioned you, Veila. So how do we even know you're telling the truth? You could've taken our side when you first brought Jimmy to Lair Station and you didn't. You..." He shakes his head at her. "You did unspeakable things to him, just like you were doing unspeakable things to all those Akeelian boys! Would someone please, for the love of the fucking sun, turn off those fucking alarms?"

The room goes silent. But far off in the distant levels and corridors of the station, the alarms continue to blare.

"Of course she never mentioned me," Veila snaps, her voice too loud in the relative silence. "Why should she have ever thought about me? I was just her older sister. Not the seventh. Not in line for the goddamned crown! I was no one. Just one more pink girl in her entourage. You were there, Crux. You saw me. I was nobody. Until she was gone and then... then I was all they had left."

"We don't have time for this," I say. "Luck is already invading. He's going to go through the spin node and leave the rest of us behind. And fuck it. Fine. He needs to save Nyleena and his kids, so whatever. But if he's not here to accept our surrender and negotiate terms—"

"Negotiate terms?" Serpint guffaws up at the ceiling.

"We're surrendering," I say.

"We're *not* surrendering," Serpint growls back. "Luck isn't interested in negotiations. He's got almost everything he needs down there. And once he gets to level one twenty-two and reaches the spin node, he's going to leave us behind."

"He might," I admit. "But we're going to entice Delphi and Jimmy over to our side with Tycho."

"Just another pawn," Lyra sneers at Veila.

"He'll be fine once they are reunited," Veila says. "Trust me."

"How could anyone trust you, Veila?" Lyra asks. "You've done nothing but lie—"

"I've done nothing but survive! Just like you have! Only I had to do it alone!" Veila snaps her fingers at a borg. "Bring Tycho here. Now. We're going to take him down to Delphi. That should at least buy us some time to put the rest of the plan into motion."

Half of her borg guard leaves, the other half remains behind.

"Listen to me," I say, aiming my words at Crux. "We need to make an announcement and we need a way to do that so everyone can see us and hear us. We're going to tell them that we surrender and that we're still Harem Station. Period. End of story. We stand together or fall together. Once everyone understands that there's bigger problems heading our way, they will get on board!"

Both Crux and Serpint are shaking their heads.

"The memorial service announcement system," Baby says, before they can object again. "We could put everyone on the memorial service platform, but instead of flying upward to the top of the station, we go down. Talk to them directly. And we blast it on all the screens."

"The screens aren't even working," Crux says. "Nothing's actually working right now. We don't even know how much air we have left."

"I can patch them up long enough to get the message out. And if we get things back under control and the Succubus stops fighting me, we can fix it. All of it is fixable. We just don't have access. But she's very close now. She and Flicka will fully infiltrate me in less than thirty minutes. And Crux… I understand your hesitation based on my past actions. But do you really want to hand over this entire station to an outsider?"

Crux turns his back to us and takes a deep breath. He spends several precious seconds trying to think things through.

But he has to know. This is the only way to stop the internal war between us.

"Crux," I say. "Come on. We have to stick together. Bigger threats are on the way. Do you really want the Akeelians and Cygnians to take over Harem Station?"

"That's not gonna happen," he says, turning back to us. "The gates are locked. They can't get in."

"Uh…" We all look at Serpint. "That's not entirely true. There's a back door, remember?"

"No one knows how to get through the second gate."

"Wrong again," Serpint says. "I know how. ALCOR showed me the way when I was coming home from Cetus Station with Corla."

"And you're *here*."

"But Asshole's not here. We don't know where he is. And he *has* to know about the back door. There's just no way he doesn't. So Valor is right. We're not really safe here. They are coming. And we can't be in the middle of a civil war when they arrive." Serpint eyes Veila with suspicion. "I don't trust her." Then he eyes me. "And I'm not sure I trust you either, all things considered. For all I know, we're surrendering so Veila can get access to the spin node, get Luck and Nyleena to take her to Earth, and leave us all behind to clean up her mess. Again."

"Well, you don't have to worry about that," Veila sneers.

"Why not?" Serpint grunts.

Veila sucks in a long, tired breath and when she lets it out, she says, "Because I no longer need to go to Earth."

Everyone in the room, except for me and Veila, narrows their eyes in confusion.

"I'm no longer pregnant. There is nothing for me on Earth. In fact, I wish I had never even heard of that place."

Crux looks at me. I nod. "It's true. She… she lost the babies yesterday. That's why I didn't come back right away. She almost died. And there are no humans on her ship. It's nothing but borgs and bots. She's all alone, you guys. Just doing the best she can." Then I look at Lyra, hoping that she, at least, will understand. "That's how they turned her silver. They got her pregnant."

"What?" Lyra says, looking at Veila.

"It's true," Veila admits. "They've been keeping me pregnant all this time. Ever since Corla went into that spin node twenty-one years ago."

"But…"

"No," Veila tells Lyra. "No. I don't bring them to term. They all… end up the same way. And then I go back to pink, and the Akeelians start the process all over again to make me silver."

"Shit," Lyra says. "Fuck. I didn't know, Veila. I'm… sorry. That sucks."

Veila nods, but takes a deep breath and says, "I hate them as much as you do. I never asked for this life. Just like you guys. I was just a pawn. Just a means to an end. And I'm done. I don't even care if I die here, or there, or wherever. It would be a relief to die. At least then it would be over. But if they come through that gate, if they find me here… they'll just keep going. And trust me, if they figure out that Nyleena is here and Luck is her soulmate and that he has access to the flowers… well. Let's just say what they did to me will pale in comparison to what they will do to her. They will get her pregnant and—"

"She's already pregnant," I whisper.

"Oh," Veila says. Pauses. "Well, then if they come and find her she will never see the light of the sun again. She will be locked up and turned into… *me*. And those children will just be the next generation in their sick scheme."

"Set up the platform," Crux tells Baby. "We're going to surrender. It's the only thing we can do."

"It's done," Baby says in a somber voice. "But we must hurry now. Flicka and Succubus are very close to succeeding."

"We need to get Luck and Nyleena through that spin node," I say. "At least they can be safe."

"I agree," Crux says.

"Me too," Serpint adds. "If they're the only ones who live through this then even if we lose… we win."

CHAPTER TWENTY-FIVE

VALOR

The alarms are still blaring loudly outside in the hallway outside the harem room. Baby turns them off as we move forward towards the memorial service platform, which is stationary and located at the top of the station when not in use for a ceremony. But the alarms are on an automatic backup circuit and cannot be turned off as long as the emergency is still in progress.

We have since learned that the alarms are due to the loss of breathable air at the top of the station and by the time we are all situated on the platform and ready for the announcement, we are breathing heavy with exertion and lack of oxygen.

"We need to go down," Lyra pants. "I can't breathe!"

"Just take slow, shallow breaths," Serpint says, holding her hand. "We're going now."

Crux looks at us. "Are we ready for this?"

We all nod, even though I'm not sure we could ever be ready for what's coming. We barely understand what's happening.

"OK," Crux says. He stands in the center of the platform facing the direction we'll be traveling and the rest of us stand shoulder to shoulder so we make a circle. Lyra on his right, then Serpint, then Veila, then me.

It occurs to me in this moment. Just as the platform begins to descend, that we—all of us here on this platform—we are the most hated people on this station right now.

And as we lower down and Crux begins to talk—

"Attention," he says. "Please. I need your attention."

—even the people on our side begin to jeer and boo.

"We are going to surrender to Luck. We will be—"

But the collective yelling—all the millions of people on this station in unison—all but drowns him out.

"Listen!" Crux says, his voice amplified through the various sound systems, his face—all our faces—on every screen that's still working. "We have to stand together! This war between us must end so we can prepare—"

Something comes hurtling through the air at us. Serpint shoots it mid-air with a plasma pistol, and it shatters, raining hot, flaming debris down on our heads. I cover Veila, and Serpint does the same for Lyra.

Crux continues to talk.

But no one is listening.

We are several levels below where we started and moving forward to make a long journey around the ring so everyone can hear and see Crux deliver his message at least for a moment. It's easier to breathe now, but it's clear that people above us are gasping for breath and beginning to panic. They start rushing the various non-moving escalators, desperate for air.

But news of the air issue travels fast and within seconds the upper levels are mass panic and confusion. A riot of fearful people who want to get down to a lower level.

People at the top start jumping over the side, maybe assuming the safety bots will catch them, but they're not working right. Baby is barely in control of the announcement system.

And as soon as everyone realizes this, the screaming becomes louder and the rush to the escalators turns into a riot for survival.

Then, because the bodies that fell—and continue to fall as we descend—hit the bottom of the station, another wave of panic comes up from down below.

This is not going well.

"Oh, my God!" Lyra says. "What do we do?"

"Keep going!" I yell. "We have to get it under control or everyone will die! Just keep talking, Crux! Make them hear you!"

"Please," Crux yells. But the lights—which were already low and near emergency levels—are flickering and suddenly his voice is no longer being amplified and the screens blank out into meaningless static.

That's when I notice fingertips gripping the side of the platform. We are still descending and moving forward through the ring of the station. But somehow people are underneath us. Clawing their way up and over the ledge of the platform.

And then I see forearms. And a foot comes over the side. Then another and another and then...

Heads.

People on the platform with us.

And every single one of them is a princess.

An angry Cygnian princess aiming their weapons as they rush the center of the platform where we're standing.

Serpint fires first and a girl in tactical gear with long golden hair and blazing yellow eyes is hit in the chest. She goes careening backwards, stumbling.

My hand goes out automatically to pull her back, even though I'm not anywhere close to her.

And then she falls over the edge.

There's an audible gasp in the station. Then screaming. And finally, once her body hits the bottom, a roar of anger from below. A battle call.

More and more princesses rush us.

We all have our weapons out now. Even Veila has pulled a SEAR knife from some hidden place on her body and dialed it up to sword length.

Lyra has a rifle and she's shooting them, two and three at a time. Just dragging the line of plasma across their bodies. Thick, black scorch marks penetrate their chests.

She will hate herself later for this. But not now.

Now the only thing on our minds is living long enough to feel that guilt.

Crux is screaming now. "Stop! Stop! We're all on the same side!"

But no one hears him.

This is the heat of battle. Who is on what side doesn't matter anymore. Everyone in the station is fighting. *Everyone.*

Each level is nothing but a riot of anger and killing. Bodies packed together twenty, thirty deep. Blood, and screaming, and the smell of plasma fire and burning flesh.

People from above are still throwing themselves over the side. It's either that or suffocate from the lack of air, and that only sparks more anger and heat from below as the bodies fall past. A reminder to anyone with any wits about them that this is it.

It's over.

Their life on Harem Station is over.

And what did we expect, really? How could this end any other way?

Millions of violent outlaws on one secluded station? Are you kidding me? We all knew what ALCOR was doing when he made the decision to bring in the most dangerous people in the galaxy and offer them sanctuary.

He was building an army.

The most ruthless army imaginable. One that had no banner to stand under. One that had no loyalties beyond the all-powerful AI who left them to die here in the middle of some desolate sector of space with no hope of rescue. Cut off from everyone and everything like prisoners.

We did this. We built this place.

And now that army of prisoners has turned against us.

Turned against each other too.

I look around. Lyra's eyes are lit up bright pink. Twin beams of light shooting through the darkness with anger and fear. And Veila's eyes are the same, only they are white now. Just pure uncolored white. Her mouth open in a scream as a group of princesses rush toward us.

Crux and Serpint are back to back. Circling and shooting. The light within them makes a violet bubble around their bodies.

And then I look down and realize that I'm doing it too.

I am a bubble of purple light.

I look up again and the pack of princesses are almost upon me. Then Veila is there, her SEAR sword cutting three of them clean in half. And the others go down in a mass of burning flesh as Lyra's plasma rifle burns them black.

I turn, find Veila's eyes. She's afraid, I realize. That is the face of fear. Not the evil silver princess I've seen in the past.

She is suddenly small. So small.

But the light from her eyes glows brighter. And I feel it.

Maybe for the first time ever.

I feel the power inside her.

I know what she is and it's about to cut loose.

Then a flash of red hair.

I turn and everything is in slow motion. Captain Red is flying through the air at Veila like a fucking winged beast. And in her hand is a SEAR sword too. Her arm is in mid-arc as she swipes it towards Veila's neck, fully intending on beheading the one girl in this sun-fucked universe who belongs to me.

I reach for Veila just as she sees the attack.
I take her hand, pull her hard, and then—
—white light.
Nothing but brilliant white light.

CHAPTER TWENTY-SIX

Her hand is still in mine. I squeeze it and she squeezes back. That's the only clue I have that I'm still alive. Still real. Still…somewhere.

Because the world is nothing but white light. Endless and opaque. And silent.

The chaos of war—gone.

Just quiet.

Veila? I say it but I can't hear it.

"I'm here." And she is. Suddenly. Immediately. She is here with me and I'm here too. Just us two immersed in her brightness.

"What the hell just happened?"

"Whatever you do, just don't let go of my hand."

"Why?"

"I don't know. But I think… I think that might be the only thing connecting me to you at the moment. And if you let me go—"

"I won't," I say. "I won't let go."

"I think I did something, Valor. I think I did something bad."

"Come here," I say, tugging on her hand. And for a moment there is no resistance. No sign that her hand in mine is even real. I feel it slip away. I feel everything slip away.

"Veila," I say sharply. "*No.*"

"It's calling me, Valor." Her voice is shaky and trembling.

"What? Who? Who's calling you?"

"That place. The golden place. I want to go."

"No," I say. "You just told me to not let go of you. And I'm not sure I want to see the... golden place. I want to stay right here. And I want you to stay with me. Harem Station is in the middle of a war. Crux and Lyra and Serpint are about to be killed by psychotic princesses and we don't even know where Luck and Jimmy and Nyleena and Delphi are."

"I really want this to end," she whimpers.

"I know," I whisper back, still pulling on her hand, still trying to reel her in to me. "And it will. I'm going to make sure of it. But you can't leave me. You can't *leave me*, Veila. We're stuck, remember? We're in this together. I know you're tired and you want it to end. I have a feeling that's what this light is. It's your... end. Your answer to all that pain they inflicted on you. But I want you to dial it back now, Veila. Pull it back so we can see what's left."

"I don't want to," she says. But there's resistance to my pulling now. She's here. With me. And when I tug just a little bit harder...

"There you are," I say, putting my arms around her. "There you are."

She wraps her arms around my middle and presses her face into my chest. "I don't want to do this anymore. And the light is here, Valor. All I have to do is walk into it and everything will stop."

"No, it won't. Listen to me." I push her away a little and look down into her face. Her eyes are all white. Nothing but white glow. But there's a crackle of pink around the edges. A hint that she's not gone yet. The silver hasn't gotten all of her.

Just most of her.

"Listen, OK?" She nods. But I can't tell where her eerie eyes are looking. At me? Not at me? I don't know. "We can fix this. I think we're stuck in a... pause. Or something. Just dial it back. Dial back everything you feel right now. Everything but me, OK? Just me. Look at me." I shake her by the shoulders. "Look at me!"

She blinks. And everything goes black. Like we're lost in space. Drifting in nothingness.

"Veila," I say, more forcefully now. "Look. At. Me."

She opens her eyes and pink light flows out like perfect sunshine. She blinks again, only this time the darkness is gone and in its place is a golden fog. And through that fog I can see Harem Station.

Vague forms and shapes. Still. Utterly motionless. But it's there.

"See," I say. "See. You're still here. We're still here. There's Serpint. And Lyra. And Crux."

And the redheaded bitch. But I don't say that part.

Captain Red is floating in the air, her SEAR sword ready to cut Veila's head off.

Everyone is still here. And when I look around I see all the Harem Station citizens. Mid-battle, but motionless.

She stopped time.

She stopped *everything*.

"I could kiss you right now," I whisper, awed into a new sort of respect for her.

"You probably should," she says, looking up at me. And now I can see her eyes behind the pink. Her face. Her hair. Her white sweater. "It might be your last chance."

I don't let go of her hand. I'm afraid if I do, she will float away and I'll never see her again. But I bring my other one up and place it on her cheek. And then I lean down and touch my lips to hers.

It's in this moment that I feel it.

For real.

The bond we have.

The bond they made. That they put into our biology and forced upon us.

But you know what? It doesn't matter how that bond came to be. It's here now. And I won't let her walk into that light and leave me behind.

I won't give her up or let her go.

"You're mine," I whisper into her mouth. "And I'm yours. And we're gonna do this together or not at all. So if you want to check out, Veila, I'm going with you."

She shakes her head and pulls away from my kiss. "I can't take you."

"You don't have a choice. I'm not letting you go alone. Ever again. And I'm not going to take away your choices, either. I won't be like them. I will not force you into agreeing with me, or being my partner, or loving me, or fighting for me, or any of it. It's all you now, baby. All you. So choose. We can stay and win this fight together. Or we can go. See what's next on our journey. Your choice. You tell me what you want and that's what we'll do."

She swallows hard and looks around.

The golden fog is fading. And I don't know what that means. I don't know if that means time will start up again any second now and we'll be back in the fight, or that she's just thinking clearer now.

The only thing I know for sure is that she's the one in control.

Not me. Not Crux. Not Luck. Not ALCOR. None of us.

Her.

"What happened?" she asks. And then before I even know what she's doing, her hand has slipped from mine and I swear to the sun, my heart stops.

But she doesn't disappear. Time does not start back up.

We just... look around.

Everyone is in mid-battle. Serpint and Crux are wrestling with a green-haired princess who is baring her teeth at them like a wild animal, their protective purple bubble of light extinguished.

Lyra's mouth is open in a scream, her plasma rifle in position to mow down a few more princesses. But no light pours out of her eyes now. They are just... eyes. Filled with fear and desperation.

We look around. Take it all in.

Everyone is filled with fear and desperation.

Everyone is making their last stand.

I pull Veila a little further away from Captain Red. Just in case time suddenly starts back up and she is back in the fight.

"How?" Veila says, spinning in place. "How is this happening?"

"Fuck if I know, princess. I guess there's more to you than meets the eye."

"What do we do?"

"I don't know," I say, running my fingers through my hair. "I don't know."

"Should we go find Luck? And the others? Are they all…" Her words trail off as she walks over to the edge of the platform and leans over.

I reach out and grab her by the arm, afraid she'll fall. "Don't get too close. There's no safety bots, remember?"

"Oh, my sun," she breathes. "Did I do this?"

I cautiously look over the side and see thousands and thousands of people stuck in the moment. "I guess you did."

"But… I've never done anything like this before. All I remember is the red one. Coming at me. And then you"—she turns to look at me—"you took my hand and then…"

"Poof," I say. "Time stands still."

"Was it us? Are we…"

"A team?" I say, raising my eyebrows.

She nods.

"Looks that way, doesn't it?"

"Can we bring time back?" She looks around again. "We can't just leave them like this."

"I dunno." I sigh. "But…" I walk over to Crux and Serpint and push the green-haired girl back. She falls over. Lies there like a freaking statue. Eyes wide with hate. Mouth still open in a scream of anger. "But if time is gonna start up again, then I don't want us to be on this platform when it happens. Ya know?"

"Yeah," she says. "Maybe we should take them back upstairs to the harem room? At least they'll be safe there, right?"

"Yeah. Yeah, let's do that. Let's get them safe. Then we can think about time again."

CHAPTER TWENTY-SEVEN

So that's what we do. It takes both of us to carry Lyra into the harem room. We put her on the empty couch, propped up with pillows. And then we're just about to go back for Crux and Serpint—both surely dreading carrying those two walls of muscle—when I spy a lift bot that was stopped mid-trip carrying supplies down the hallway leading to Crux's office.

I walk over to it, look up at Veila, and say, "Too bad we couldn't just... bring this one online. To help carry Crux and Serp."

Veila furrows her brows. "Maybe we can."

"How?"

"I don't know. But we're in charge here. So there has to be a way."

It takes hours. Hell, we could've moved a dozen people to safety by the time we figure out how to turn on the bot without turning on anyone else.

We say his name—thank the sun every bot on Harem has an engraved nameplate on their person—and touch him—both of us, at the same time—and he lights up and comes to life. Starts slowly floating down the hallway like nothing happened.

We wait until his job is done, more out of our own stunned realization that we actually did it than any kind of consideration for his job, and then tell him to follow us.

We place Serpint and Crux on the couch next to Lyra and then we decide to go looking for Luck, Nyleena, Jimmy, and Delphi. To get them somewhere safe before time catches up with us again.

The lift bot we use for carrying. It doesn't have that much lift. But we wake up another bot, one that is used for traveling, and ride it down to level one twenty-two.

We don't know for sure that Luck and company are in the museum spinning up the node, but level one-twenty-two is on the way to the bottom level. So we stop to check it out.

The node is open. But it's not any kind of spin node I've ever seen before. The center of it—which is usually gates upon gates upon gates, and sometimes a spinning galaxy, and sometimes a portal to an abandoned Angel Station, and possibly even a portal to Earth—is a flexible... gel? That might be the best word to describe what the interior of the spun-up node is at the moment.

It's also not really there. Like it's transparent. Like a shadow of a spin node.

And Luck, Nyleena, and Jimmy are... gone.

But Delphi is here.

She stands in the middle of the gel node with her arms in a position that indicates she was holding hands with people when she tried to cross through, but failed.

Jimmy, for sure. And probably Nyleena.

"She didn't go with them?" Veila asks in a whisper.

"She did," I say. "But it didn't let her cross."

"Why?"

"Because…" I sigh. "She's not Jimmy's soulmate. They were holding hands. That's how Nyleena and Luck open the portal. They have to hold hands. And it only works because they're soulmates."

"Oh," Veila says, deflating a little. "Oh, my God. That's awful. So they got to the other side, wherever that is, and she… she's still *here*."

"She doesn't even know yet."

Veila puts a hand over her heart. "I feel sick just thinking about her waking up from the time freeze. We need to put her somewhere safe."

"We can't. She's stuck in the portal."

"What's going to happen to her when we start time up again?"

"I don't know." I sigh. "I don't know. But we should bring Tycho down here. To be with her when she does realize she was left behind. And Leonis too."

"That's her guy?"

"I guess there is no way past it." I look down at Veila. "We are bonded to the ones they chose for us. Not even love was enough to get her through this portal with Jimmy."

"But where do you think they went?"

"Earth," I say. It's just a guess, but it's a good one. "When we came here to ALCOR Station twenty-one years ago we were given this… code. From Corla. To give to ALCOR. And it turns out these codes were spin node coordinates. That's how Tray and I went through and landed on Angel Station. That was his code. And I think they used Jimmy's to get to Earth."

What she doesn't ask, what neither of us asks, is where would my code take us? Where would Luck's code take him? And Serpint's? And Draden's, if he were still here.

But it doesn't even matter. When time resumes I'd bet every credit Harem Station had in its accounts that the spin node will just vanish. And Delphi will be standing in the middle of a room full of nothing. And without Luck and Nyleena to spin it up again, we no longer have a spin node.

When we leave the museum on level one twenty-two there's a general feeling of sadness in the station. Like all the despair inside all the people is starting to seep out and permeate the air.

There's a huge battle in front of the museum entrance. Dozens of outlaw warriors duking it out with various weapons. People bleeding. Some of them, when they wake up, will only have a moment or two left in this life before they die of their wounds. And some of them are already dead.

We start with the dead ones first, enlisting the help of a few nearby bots to help get them down into the mortuary. We enlist more bots to start on the hundreds and hundreds of others on every level. An eventually we have to wake up even more bots to bag up the bodies and start shooting them out into space.

Then we deal with the wounded.

There are about eight hundred clinics on Harem Station. Each level has at least two medical centers. And by the time we get all the wounded onto lift bots and positioned near the closest clinic, we have run out of bots. So we wake up Veila's borgs and conscript them into our little army. And one person at a time is taken care of.

Then we wake up Baby. He is disoriented. It takes several hours for him to cycle through a debug program and become himself again. But once that happens, and we explain the situation, he's eager and willing to help.

His first report is that the Succubus is gone and so are *Lady* and *Dicker*.

There's a lot to think about but not many answers forthcoming. So instead of thinking we go to each and every person on Harem Station. Find their name, their job, their home—or where they're staying, if they were unlucky enough to be on vacation when this whole shit show started—and begin the process of removing them from the battle.

We consider taking away all their weapons. It would be the logical thing to do when you're trying to end a war. But we aren't really trying to *end* a war. We need all these people to fight—just not amongst themselves.

So Veila and I decide to disarm them in a more temporary way. We will remove their charge packs and ammunition and stow them somewhere on their person. So when the time comes back—online? Is that a thing?—they will still be able to fight, but it will take them a minute to realize they have no ammo and reload.

Hopefully, in the time between waking up and reloading, we will have their full attention and can push a reset button on this whole civil war thing.

Then we assign borgs and bots to move them to their place of employment, or their room, and leave them there.

That way, when the time comes back online—we've decided to go with that phrasing—they will not wake up in the midst of battle rage. They will come back confused, but in a familiar place among hopefully at least a few friends.

We also take all the freaking princesses down to the lock-up. Fuck those girls. They cannot be trusted.

But once that's done, we realize that this might be the only time to fix the air and water systems, so we wake up even more bots and borgs and assign them to help with repairs.

Except no one can see properly because most of the freaking lights are off. And the trash compactors on seventeen levels are down. And there are twenty-seven non-functional airlocks, and three hundred and fifty-four broken autocooks throughout the station. Plus all the air-screens are down. We're totally out of communication. On top of that, there are six open reports of missing children who need to be located and put somewhere safe, a rogue ship floating in the main docking bay on the lower level, and then—surprise, surprise—we learn something that no one else in the universe knows: dragonbee bots live outside of time. Because we find Flicka in a sexbot bar down on level fifteen, drunk and farting out poison, rambling on in her little dragonbee language about the Succubus leaving her behind.

Who knew?

It takes several lifetimes to get everything back in order.

But here's the thing… it's just time. And here, at least in this world, time has no meaning.

What we're doing, how we're restarting things right, how we're remaking the war into something else… that's the only thing that has meaning now.

It's just like the virtual with Tray and Brigit. We have limitless time right now.

And we need to make the most of it. Because once time is back online and running forward again, we're right back in the middle of the crisis.

This is our only chance.

There is no surrender. We can't afford to surrender.

People are coming for us and when they do we need to be united again.

We need to be ALCOR's army of outlaws.

And we need to win.

Throughout all this Veila and I have been working as a team. There is no other way to wake up the bots and borgs. And we work endless hours, nearly to the point of exhaustion. And when we reach the point where our eyes will not remain open one more moment, we go our separate ways.

She goes to her ship to sleep and I go to my quarters.

Even though I hugged her and I kissed her, and even though we are starting to feel like a team, we are no closer to being a 'couple' than we were before this all started.

I feel the bond, but that rage inside me, that anger and that hate for what she did, that's all still there. It might be hidden deeper than it was. It's definitely not driving me anymore.

But it's still there.

I can't forget all the things she did even if it wasn't her fault.

And I don't know what she's feeling, but it has to be something similar. Because when we do get so tired we need to sleep, she does not look back over her shoulder at me when she enters her airlock and goes to her ship.

It took six weeks to tear down Harem Station and even though there is no record of the time that's passing in this interlude we find ourselves in, it feels like much longer than six weeks to put it all back together.

But eventually it is all back in place.

We're standing on the memorial platform at the top of the station. It has been cleared of all the people we were in battle with. And looking out at the open space sandwiched between the hundreds of levels below us I can fully appreciate what we've accomplished.

Harem Station has lights, and air, and water. All the autocooks work and the black obsidian floors once again gleam under the bright lights of a nearby arcade. All the docked ships are fueled up just in case we need to make an emergency evacuation, all the dead have been dealt with, all the wounded are in the medical pods or Pleasure Prison gaming pods being attended to under the supervision of the Baby. All the stores are open with employees waiting to be woken up. All the borgs and bots are congratulating each other for a job well done.

All the signs of civil unrest have been erased.

"Welcome to Harem Station," I sigh, turning to smile at Veila.

She is dirty. Her leggings and t-shirt are covered in dust and filth from the final day of clean-up, her hair is piled on top of her head in a golden pile of mess, and she is smiling back at me.

"It's nice," she says softly.

"It really is. I've missed this place. I feel like I've been gone for several eternities. Did I ever tell you that I lived thousands of years in that virtual with Tray and Brigit?"

"No," she says.

"We did." I sigh. "We built cities. Huge cities, Veila. We had trains and coffeehouses. And people. Millions of people. We had everything in there."

"Makes me wonder why you ever left."

I stare at her for a moment. It's been a long time since I really looked at her. We've been so busy trying to make things right. Trying to fix this fucking mess we're in.

"Because it wasn't real. Maybe for Brigit and Tray it was, but not for me. They were always going to spend their eternity in a place like that. But my destiny was always out here." I pause, then say, "With you."

"I'm sorry about that."

I shrug. "It is what it is."

She presses her lips together in a tight smile, nods, then changes the subject. "We need to talk about Corla. I would like you to consider allowing one of the borgs to retrieve her from that beacon."

Veila and I have come to some sort of understanding. Are we friends? Maybe. We've certainly worked hard while this time freeze has been in place. And we've worked well as a team. And Harem Station feels like home again and not some strange war-torn place I don't recognize. But this request makes me nervous.

Can I trust her?

She's reading my hesitation. Which isn't hard, considering our recent shared past. We have spent a lot of time together. But that too makes me nervous.

"It's time to deal with the real problem and all of that goes back to Crux and Corla," she says. "They should be together."

Still, I hesitate. Forget Crux and Corla together. That makes sense. But Corla and Veila together? I don't know how I feel about that.

"Just think about it," she says. "You don't have to decide now. We should clean up and rest. Think about what we're going to tell everyone. How we'll explain this and how we'll get them all back on the same side.

I'm starting to feel anxious. Like we've been doing this too long and things are happening out there. Whatever, or whenever, that is."

That I agree with. Even though only four days passed in the outside world when Tray, Brigit, and I were inside our virtual world for many lifetimes, four days was enough to upset our entire universe.

Veila was the one who upset it, I remind myself. She was the one who took advantage of our break from reality and captured us. And all the bad shit that happened afterward was a direct result of that capture.

"Please don't do that," she says.

"Do what?"

"You know what. I know what. You're thinking about me and the things I've done."

"That's unreasonable to you?"

"No. I get it. I was that person. But you can see a different me now, right? You understand why I was that way. Why I did certain things."

"I do. But that stuff still happened, Veila. And you're still responsible. All these people stuck in time—they don't know you. Hell, I don't even know you. So how can we trust you?"

She inhales and nods. "I get it. I do. But... I'm trying. I haven't been myself for... hell. Since I was seventeen. And that was twenty-one years ago. But this time we've had together..." She shrugs. "Putting Harem Station back together makes me feel close to who I was before Corla left. Maybe not yet the real me, but I'm on my way."

"And what happens if the Akeelians or Cygnians get you back?"

"They're not going to get me back."

"You don't know that. You can't predict the future like that. They're involved in this. We will have to interact with them eventually. And that moment when we do... that might be the most important moment in our whole lives."

"God, I hope not. I don't want my whole life to be reduced to one final moment in this great war. There's more to me than the silver princess they made me into."

I don't know what to say to that. Every time I feel sorry for Veila I also feel guilt. I should not be on her side.

But at the same time... I *want* to be on her side.

She feels like my destiny.

Probably not the same way Crux and Corla found their destiny. But then again—all of us brothers found our soulmates in very different ways. Hell, Jimmy didn't even find his. But he did find love.

And if Jimmy can fall in love with a woman who is not his One, then it stands to reason that I can find my One and not fall in love.

Do I love her?

I don't know.

There was a spark of light when we touched during the battle and that was something big, for sure. Time doesn't stand still for just anyone.

But was that *love*?

"OK." She sighs. "I'm going back to my ship to shower and rest. I guess we'll just meet up later and finish this."

When I don't say anything in response she turns and walks away down the hallway towards her ship's airlock, then disappears around a corner.

I turn back to the station.

"What do you think?" Baby asks me.

"About what?"

"Her proposal for Corla and Crux."

"I don't know. Part of me feels like it's a trap. Like she did all this to get to that question. That she will gain my trust, and maybe even my love, and then she will betray me just like she's betrayed everyone else."

"I have run countless calculations and predictions on this very scenario."

"Yeah? And what did you conclude?"

He sighs, which makes me smile. He's more ALCOR these days than he is Baby. "Impossible to predict. Inconclusive. A very big risk."

"Not helping, Baby."

"No."

"And what about you?"

"What about me?"

"What are you going to do now?"

He pauses. "I've been thinking about this a lot."

"And?"

"I like this new place. I didn't get to see the old Harem Station. I was thrown into being as a temporary solution while ALCOR was gone. Nothing went right. People died because of me. And then everything went from bad to worse. I would be lying if I said I had any feelings about that back then. Because I simply didn't care about these people."

"And now?"

Another pause. "I have accessed the personal data of every living and dead person on this station since then. I have seen their place of work, where they live, have connected them to dozens, sometimes hundreds, of other people. I might not know them all personally, but I have background on them. I can make good guesses as to what kind of people they are."

"What kind of people are they?"

"Bad people, mostly. Criminals. But that's just the first layer to them. Underneath the criminal there are other things. They have friends. Lovers. Some of them even have children. They have hobbies, and jobs, and of course faults. They have a lot of faults. But most of them have this… history. One of quiet satisfaction."

"What do you mean?"

"They found peace here. Harem Station is their home. I have met every single cleaning servo, every bot, every borg—even the ones who work for Veila. I have fixed the biosphere, the airscreens, the water generators, the medical centers, the autocooks, and even the floors are shiny and clean. I know every arcade, every shooting gallery, every clothing boutique, every restaurant, and every ship in the docking bays. I have even come to like that stupid dragonbee bot. She is quite funny at times. And it has occurred to me that…"

He pauses again.

I wait.

"That Harem Station is my home too. I think this is how it happened for ALCOR as well. He made this place one shop at a time. One restaurant at a time. One ship at a time. He met one person at a time until they became this collective thing called Harem Station. And that is how you learn to love a person, or a place, or a thing. That is how you find a new home."

I smile a little. "You like us, don't you?"

"I think I do."

"Are you going to leave?"

"No. I'm going to stay."

"And if ALCOR is alive? And he comes home? What then?"

"I'd be lying if I said I wouldn't fight him for it. I would. Or at least, I would *want* to. But I would not want to mess up Harem Station again. I would not want to ruin all our hard work and break it. So I would leave. If he came back and wanted me gone, I would leave."

"That's very mature of you, Baby."

"I think it's just... love. That's all. I love you and this place too much to ruin it. And I know ALCOR loves it too. He would not break it either. If it were Mighty Boss or the Succubus coming to take it away from me, I would fight. But not ALCOR. He was the one who really made this station. I just... fixed it. Put it all back into place."

"That's not a small thing. You realize that, right?"

He stays silent.

"It's as much yours as it is his. Or mine. It's really just... *ours*. You know?"

He's still silent. And for a moment I wonder if he left me here.

"I hope," he finally says, "that you can see the similarities."

"To what?" I laugh.

"To Veila. Because she was like me when she arrived. She was like everyone when they first arrived. She was lost. And then, slowly, over time, she realized that this was a place for all the outcast people. All the wandering ones. All the loners. All the ones who failed

317

miserably at first. She realized that this station was her second chance."

"So I should trust her?"

"You should consider it. That's all the advice I have to offer. You should look at her now, not then. Just like you look at me now, not then. Just like you look at ALCOR now, and not then. Did you love him the day you arrived?"

"No. He scared the shit out of me."

"And Veila scares you too. But we have something good here, Valor. And she was the one who made that good possible again."

I'm the one who pauses now.

"No," Baby says. "Not just her. Both of you. This time pause—whatever it is—this is not something she does. Or you do. It's something the two of you did together because you are connected. Because of the bond you were forced into. I believe humans call that… a team. So all I'm saying is that you should not throw away the greatest gift that time gives."

"What's that, then?"

"A new perspective."

CHAPTER TWENTY-EIGHT

I go back to my quarters and the door closes behind me.

I turn to lock it up, the way I have been since I woke up in this situation. But just as I'm about to press the locking code into the data pad on the wall, I hesitate.

Who do I really think will come into my quarters and hurt me? Who exactly am I locking out?

Flicka? Baby? The bots and cyborgs?

No. I'm locking Veila out.

I leave it unlocked and go shower. Put on a pair of cut-off sleep pants. Lie down in bed. Stare at the ceiling. Think about how absolutely fucking off the rails my life has gone since I stepped off this station with Tray. Then how, seemingly out of nowhere, it all went right back on track when Veila lost her babies.

And how unfair that is.

Not for me. For me, this all works out pretty great. I'm back home. We literally stopped the war mid-battle. We fixed all the shit that went wrong after ALCOR died. And Harem Station will be better than ever when this is over.

I fuckin' won big.

But Veila lost everything.

She has the ship she lives in, and that's it. She has no people, she has no real friends. I guess, maybe, some of those borgs probably like her enough to have a drink with her in the future. And she has that bot who acts like her personal assistant.

But she is utterly alone in this universe.

No one—and I do mean *no one*—is coming to save Veila.

Nyleena had Lyra. Lyra put her life on the line to save Nyleena. And now Nyleena has Luck. And Luck will mow down this entire universe to keep Nyleena safe. He literally jumped galaxies with her and left us all behind to try to save their babies. And when he comes back—because he will come back—then he has me. Not to mention Cha-cha and Ladybug.

Lyra has Serpint. They are the truest soulmates of all of us. Their attraction was immediate and complete. There were two days, if that, where they fought that attraction. But if there is a real soulmate connection, those two have it. And everyone—except for the pissed-off princesses—loves Serpint and Lyra. We'd all put our lives on the line to save them. And they have that bot they call Fling and *Booty*. Who is gone, but does anyone doubt that *Booty* will be back to save Serpint's day? No. We all know how much *Booty* loves him.

Jimmy and Delphi might not be soulmates—and for sure, the moment that girl wakes up she's in for a world of hurt when she realizes that she and Jimmy are no longer in the same galaxy—but Jimmy is coming for her. No matter what. No matter who he meets, wherever he is, Jimmy is coming for her. And she will never stop looking for him. And she has Tycho back. She doesn't know that yet, but he's here with her. And she has Flicka. That poison-farting dragonbee bot took out hundreds of cyborgs on Lair Station to save her and Jimmy. And her true soulmate, Leonis. Even if she has no use for him, he is still hers. And *Dicker* and Xyla too. Delphi and Jimmy have more people than most to help them get through this tough time that's coming.

Tray and Brigit—wherever they are—are so connected soulmate doesn't even come close to describing their bond. Tray lied to everyone to save Brigit. And maybe that worked out in the end, and maybe it didn't. But Brigit always knew Tray had her back. Their personalities are out there somewhere. They are eternal now. Merged together in a way most of us can't begin to understand.

Crux has always had Corla. And us. He's our leader, even if he doesn't feel like it right now. We respect him. And he has ALCOR, dead or alive. And the Cyborg Master. And the whole station. This is really his place more than anyone's. He stayed behind to build it. He kept it all on track. One word from Crux and thousands of dangerous people drop what they're doing and come to his aid. And Corla might not be here—or hell, even want him the way he does her—but she is protected like no other person in this galaxy.

I have Luck. He might be mad at me right now, but he's still mine and I'm still his. And I have Baby now too. And Tray. And Brigit.

And we all have ALCOR—if he's still alive, and I believe he is. And Harem Station.

Even if you don't count the credits we have or the freedom that gives us, we have so much.

I guess I always knew that, but I never appreciated how fortunate I was until I met the real Veila.

Because she has *nothing*.

Even though she helped save this station, not one of those people will have her back upon waking up from this time pause.

But maybe I can change that.

CHAPTER TWENTY-NINE

Airlocks don't generally lock, per se. They do if there's no atmosphere on the other side. That's a safety issue. But when a ship is docked, like Veila's is, and the atmosphere has been equilibrated, then you just push the OPEN or CLOSE buttons to make the doors work between station and ship.

So I don't think about the airlock much as I pass through it.

But after I wind my way through the park and the forest to her door, I stop and wonder about something.

All this time we've been working together she has never come to my quarters. To be fair, I've never gone to hers, either. But that's not my point.

My point is… what if she *did* come to my quarters? And what if she found my door locked?

Because it has been. Up until this very night I have locked that stupid door.

How would it make her feel to find my door locked?

Who was I specifically locking out?

My heart hurts for a moment when I picture her coming to my quarters while we were supposed to be resting. How she might place her palm on the mechanism to open my door. How she would feel when the panel lit up with big capital letters in red that said LOCKED.

She would know that the only person I was locking out was her.

And that same gut-wrenching fear sits at the bottom of my stomach as I reach my hand towards her door mechanism and pause.

It lights up green. UNLOCKED.

Then I feel worse.

The door opens and I peek my head in. "Veila?" I call softly.

She lifts her body up from the couch. Her hair is a tangled mess of long, blonde curls. Her too-big sleep shirt is crooked, so I can see one bare shoulder. "What's wrong? Did something happen?"

"No." I shake my head as I cross the room and stand in front of her.

Her eyes catch on my chest, then slowly lift up to meet mine.

I'm shirtless, I realize. Probably should've thought that through a little better. Because it looks like I'm here on a booty call. And I pretty much *am* here on a booty call, but that's not the only reason.

"I just... wanted to make sure you're OK."

She smiles a little. "I'm OK. Why? Are you not OK?"

"No. I'm OK. Everything's OK."

"OK."

We both laugh.

God, this is awkward.

"Sit down," she says.

"If I'm disturbing you, I can go."

"You're not. I was just…" She sighs. It's one of those long tired sighs. "Just thinking about things."

I spy an e-reader on her coffee table. Not open to the title page, but there are diagrams and charts that give the title away. And when I look back at her, she's looking at that periodical screen too. Then her eyes dart up to mine. "I… it…"

The book is the same one she was reading the first time I was in here. The one on motherhood.

I sit down next to her. Look into her eyes.

"What?" she whispers. "Why are you looking at me?"

"I'm just… sorry. You know?"

"For what?"

"Everything that's happened to you." I nod my head at the book.

"Look, I don't need pity or anything. I'm—"

But I lean in and stop her talking with a kiss. Her lips are very soft at first. Then they stiffen a little.

I pull back, taking that as a no. "I'm sorry. I just wanted to kiss you."

Her fingertips come up to her lips, stay there touching them for a moment. Her eyes meet mine and there's a sparkle of pink fire in there. She is so thoroughly pink now I almost can't remember what she looked like as a silver.

"Oh," she breathes. "Sorry. You just… surprised me."

I sigh and lean all the way back on the large couch until I'm flat, but my feet are still on the floor. "I've been thinking…" I eyeball her, then look back up at the ceiling.

"About?"

"How unfair this is for you." I eyeball her again and catch her pouting a little.

"What's fair, anyway?" She shrugs. "I lost interest in fair a long time ago."

"Not true at all. You're the one who asked me about it first."

"When?" She scrunches up her nose.

"That day. When you said I have all these choices of people. Luck, and Tray, and Brigit. You said it was unfair."

"Oh." She looks forward, out her massive space window. "It kind of is, I guess. But I was moody that day. Things were… not going well."

"But you're right. It's not fair."

"Well, like you said. You're just one of those likable guys."

"No, I mean… it's not fair for you to have no one. So that's why I'm here interrupting your rest."

She stares at me, confused.

"I have decided to be yours."

"Mine?" She laughs.

"Mmm-hmm." I nod. "Yours. If you'll have me."

"I… well… what does that even mean?"

"Come here," I say, taking her hand and pulling her towards me.

She's got her legs all curled up. Knees pressed against my thigh. But she rests her head on my chest. Stays stiff and still for a moment. Holds her breath, I think. Because suddenly it comes out in a rush. "What are we doing?"

"Holding each other."

"Oh."

"Have you ever done that before?"

She hesitates. "Well, you hugged me that one time."

"That's it? That's the only time?"

She nods her head against my chest.

"That's sad, Veila."

"Look, I know I'm a freak. OK?" She tries to pull away but I keep her close.

"No, you're not a freak. That's not what I'm saying. I'm telling you that it's sad that you're all alone and I have all these people to choose from. I'm telling you that I want to be that person for you. And if I'm the only one, wow. I feel special. But my hope for you, Veila, is that one day soon you will wake up and realize that you have too many people who love you and some other, sad, unfortunate person is looking at your life with envy."

She huffs. "That's never going to happen. Everyone has made up their mind about me already."

"Yeah, but… someone very wise just told me something true."

"What did they tell you?"

"That time is the gift of new perspective."

"Who told you that?"

"Baby. Just a little while ago. He thinks I should take a second look at you. See something else besides the person you were. Formulate a new perspective based on how you've helped rebuild a station that isn't even your home."

"He… did?"

I nod. "So you know, that whole 'I'm your only friend' thing I was just fantasizing about? Not gonna happen. You already have two. And this place is your home now. You put it back together."

"We did," she corrects me. "All of us."

"Yes. We did. And I know that it's not going to be easy for you going forward. When we wake everyone up from the time pause, they won't have a new perspective yet."

"I know. I think I'm just going to stay on my ship and out of the way."

"No, that's not the right answer. This is." I lift up her shirt and slide my hand over her flat, warm stomach.

She gasps a little. And for a moment I can't even recall the silver princess I first met in that video she made after we took over Lair Station.

And I suddenly realize what my problem is.

I want her to be brand new again. Pink and pure. Soft and scared. I want to erase her past and start over.

But that's what's really unfair about this situation. Not the fact that the bond exists and we don't get to choose.

It's me. I'm the one making this unfair.

Even if it were possible to erase her past—and who knows. Maybe it is? Stranger things have happened to me in the past few months—I should not *want* to erase her.

I should be strong enough to *accept* her.

My hand is still on her stomach and she's still stiff. "OK, I think I figured it out."

"Figured what out?" she whispers.

"Do I care that ALCOR killed millions of people thousands of years ago? Do I care that he is the reason that all this is happening to us?"

Veila props herself up on one elbow.

"No," I say. "No. I don't. I get it though. Other people do care. But I'm on his side, Veila. So I need you to know that I'm on your side too. No matter what you did. The only thing I care about is what you do next."

She frowns, her mouth a sad line of pink across her flushed face. "I don't know what to do next. I have no idea what I'm doing or where I'm going, or who I'm fighting for. I just know… I'm lost."

I place both of my hands on her cheeks and stare into her lit-up eyes. "That's perfect then."

"How do you figure?"

"Because your ship is literally connected to the one place in this galaxy that *gets you*. We're all lost here, Veila. We're all drifting and afraid. We're all misfits and criminals. We've all done bad things. You're no one special on our station. And isn't that what everyone really wants? To be… normal? To fit in? To be accepted?"

"They won't—"

"They will. Once we remind them of who they are and why they're here. If they were freely given a second chance with no questions asked, then you get one too."

She stares at me. Face impassive. Mouth silent. Eyes… hoping. She wants this to be true. I can tell.

Finally, she says, "Is that it, then? Is that why you came over here? To tell me I'm one of you now?"

"No. Not exactly. I came here to find out what our special secret is."

329

"What special secret?"

"You know." I waggle my eyebrows at her. "What happens when we... really connect."

Her hand slides down my abs and slips under my night pants. "You mean..." She fists both my cocks, pumping them up and down.

I close my eyes and smile. "That's exactly what I mean."

"Are you sure we're ready for this? I mean... it might change things between us."

"Like how?" I mumble, just enjoying the feeling of her hands.

"Once we do this then... it's real, Valor. That connection will be there forever. And it will be out of our control."

I open one eye. "You having second thoughts about me?"

"No, you idiot."

I laugh.

"You might have second thoughts about me."

"Veila. I'm pretty sure I'm going to regret things about you for the rest of my life. But not for the reasons you think." I open both eyes for this part. "I regret not knowing you from the beginning. I regret that you were alone after we left Wayward Station. I wish I could go back and be with you for all of it. And you might even drive me crazy, and I might even second-guess our connection. But it's a very special thing to have an undeniable bond. I know this. Because I already have that with all my other fucked-up brothers, and the three insane AIs who help us out, and the scheming princesses who love us, and this station

330

filled with the worst of the worst. You belong here. But most of all, Veila, you belong with me."

She smiles and a soft glow flows up from her body. She lets go of my cocks, slowly swings her legs over my thighs, and takes off her shirt.

Her hands press down flat on my chest. And then she leans over and kisses me on the lips.

I feel the spark there.

I feel what's coming.

And then she must feel it too because her hands are pulling down my pants, and my fingers are tugging on her panties, and then she's hovering over top of me, and I'm easing both my cocks inside her and then...

Then I lose all sense of self.

We meld together as she moves her hips, forcing me deep inside her.

I sit up, hug her around the waist as she slides back and forth across my lap, her long hair brushing against my chest, tickling it and driving me into a state of pure bliss and ecstasy.

And when we come, we come together.

Time speeds up until it's going so fast I get dizzy.

And I see it.

I see all of it.

I see everything that's coming.

This is our shared secret and it's the future.

Some of it makes me happy.

Some of it makes me sad.

And some of it scares the living fuck out of me.

But all of it is *ours*.

Welcome to the End of book Shit. This is the always the last chapter in the book and I use it to say whatever I want about the story. Please don't judge my typos—I write these at the last minute right before I upload the book for publication.

The first thing I need to say about Veila is this – wow. This girl was a hard sell. The supervillain of the whole series (up until now) gets a fated-mate love story with one of sweetest harem brothers.

Poor Valor!

One thing I knew going in was that there was no way in hell I was gonna be able to sell an insta-love story between these two characters. I don't care how soul-mated they were, that was not gonna happen. Yes, this whole series is based on the concept that these brothers each have one true love and so I probably could've gone down the insta-love direction. I'm sure there's plenty romance readers out there who would've been just fine with that. But not me. Veila was the bad guy and if she wanted one of my precious Harem Boys then she was gonna have to earn him.

I used a few devices in this book that weren't present in the other books. Namely, Veila was not given a point of view. At all. For me, her opinion didn't deserve page time. This book was all about Valor and how he was the outsider. And how his new perspective came from the fact that Veila was also an outsider. She had no partner. And even though Valor did, three of them, in fact. Luck, Tray, and Brigit—there was no room for him. And this echoes Crux's point of view in the Star Crossed book and how he was left behind while all his other brothers had these exciting and interesting jobs to do. He was basically an administrator. Which is super important, but not terribly exciting compared to bot liberators, and princess stealers, and virtual reality god.

Baby was also an outsider. So all that was echoed in the background with how he came to terms with not fitting in.

I also made a conscious decision to leave the AI characters with huge cliffhangers. This was not their book either, but their story is still important for the final book coming up.

And the other thing I did was introduce a new nemesis – well, two, really. Crux's father got a name. He didn't have one in Star Crossed. And ALCOR's real nemesis was introduced. MIZAR.

So this ALCOR/MIZAR thing is actually… a *thing*. A real thing in our real world. Mizar is a major star in the Big Dipper's handle. That's The Plough for you non Americans. :) And Alcor is a second sun (from our perspective) that is so close to Mizar, they appear to be one sun.

And when I was writing the Junco books I was very big on building culture so I had the Avians (the alien race in that series) have a saying that they used to describe Junco's apparent ignorance of all the important details. The saying goes like this, "You can see Alcor, but you miss the full moon every time." And that means you see the small things that don't matter but then you always miss something obvious like the full moon. (Basically, what's your problem, Junco?)

Because when I was researching the ancient world (which is what I based the whole Junco story off of) I came upon this old saying in Arabic. And it was about how being able to see Alcor was a test of good eyesight. Because Alcor and Mizar are a binary system. Two suns that look like one. But ACTUALLY – that's not even true. Alcor is a binary sun – two suns that look like one. And MIZAR is a quadruple sun- four suns that look like one. So they are this very unusual cluster of SIX stars that we *think* were born from the same stellar nursery.

So if you're into figuring out mysteries there's a clue for you as to where ALCOR came from. Side note – the Seven Sisters are real too. They are called the Pleiades. Nothing to do with Alcor and Mizar in our real world, but the Seven Sisters are all over our ancient history. So many myths in so many ancient cultures reference this star cluster. They are everywhere. And they were important. And I'm in to stars so I like to include them in my world building when I write science fiction. Plus, back in Star Crossed, Corla made some pretty outrageous claims about stars. And we're finally coming back around to her 20-year grand plan.

My favorite scene in this book was… almost all of them, actually. I don't know if I said anything in Shrike Bikes about how difficult writing Bossy Johnny was, but it was. I had a lot of things going on that book. Some of it was set-up for future books and some of it was bringing old characters back, and some of it was mashing up the two worlds of Rook & Ronin and The Company with Bossy Brothers. It was not easy and it was stressful.

But Veiled Vixen was the total opposite. I didn't struggle with this book at all. All the scenes came out just the way I planned them and I enjoyed every minute of it. So I hope you guys enjoyed it too – even though there's almost no sex in this book!!!! lol And yeah. I get it. Lots of my readers want the sexy. But this wasn't a "hate fuck" story. This wasn't even a "second chance" story. This was a "my soulmate doesn't deserve me" story. And whether or not you believe Veila now deserves to be on Team Harem Station is up to you, but she met my threshold by the time I was done.

Even though Valor played a pretty big role in Prison Princess, we learned a lot more about him in this book. He's honest, and loyal, and is one of those stand-up guys. He's a lot like Crux in that regard. He's also patient, and easy-going, and has a lot of empathy for others. And so when he wakes up and discovers that the fake rebellion Tray asked Luck and Nyleena to start on Harem Station had somehow taken root and grown into something bigger and very real, he wanted to make things right, but he didn't want to hurt anyone in the process.

And although Valor did not succeed in patching things up with Luck, he did manage to find how he and Veila fit together. They might not know their specific role in the grand plan yet, but they now know that they are more powerful together than they are alone.

But that wasn't the only story in this book. We had a whole bunch of stories. Tray and Brigit and the little Akeelian boys. Asshole and Mighty Boss and the Akeelian Men from Wayward Station. Booty was struggling with her past, trying to figure out what it means, and Draden just wants to go home and see Serpint. And ALCOR... his plan is starting to unfold, but we're not quite there yet.

And... poor Delphi. I have been dropping hints that their story wasn't over yet.

All this brings me to the last book. Yes, there will be one more book in this "series". And that one belongs to Crux & Corla. But I'm not saying I won't come back to this universe because I actually love these people and there's a ton of stories left to be told. Maybe not a fated-mate story, but there are definitely more love stories for all the secondary characters on Harem Station.

But I am not going to put the final book up on pre-order yet or give you an exact date. I suspect the release date for Crux's book will be last week of

January or first week of February 2020. But I don't want to be rushed. The last book has a lot of loose ends to tie up and I don't want to be held to a date and risk not being able to give this series the epic ending it deserves. And if I miss that date, then it will be first week of March because I have Creeping Beautiful releasing on February 19 and I don't want to crowd two releases into the same timeframe. I have a lot of special scenes planned for Crux in my head already so writing his book will be super fun. I think I will probably start it in December and it will be my "fun" book over the holidays.

And like I said, after Crux I will keep writing stories in this world – they might be short freebies or full-length books, not sure about that yet. But I'm not giving up these people after investing so many hours building them up. I LOVE HAREM STATION. I wish I could go live there. I wish I could be a dragonbee bot on the wall and just watch that whole world go round. See all these guys living their lives after all this princess trouble is over. And, hopefully, see ALCOR come home.

But *I WILL ALSO* be starting a new sexy-SF romance series probably in the spring of 2020. I have a few ideas floating around in my head for this and I'm not sure which one I want to go with yet, but I should have it narrowed down by the time Crux's book releases and you will get all the details then.

So I guess that's it for this EOBS. If you enjoyed the book please a review where you purchased it and tell your friends who are into this kind of story about the series. I would really appreciate that.

Until next time... thank you for reading and I'll see you in the next book (which is Bossy Bride!!! Fun, sexy wedding times for Emma and Jesse! Releasing December 18th)

Julie
October 16, 2019

ABOUT THE AUTHOR

JA Huss never wanted to be a writer and she still dreams of that elusive career as an astronaut. She originally went to school to become an equine veterinarian but soon figured out they keep horrible hours and decided to go to grad school instead. That Ph.D. wasn't all it was cracked up to be (and she really sucked at the whole scientist thing), so she dropped out and got a M.S. in forensic toxicology just to get the whole thing over with as soon as possible.

After graduation she got a job with the state of Colorado as their one and only hog farm inspector and spent her days wandering the Eastern Plains shooting the shit with farmers.

After a few years of that, she got bored. And since she was a homeschool mom and actually does love science, she decided to write science textbooks and make online classes for other homeschool moms.

She wrote more than two hundred of those workbooks and was the number one publisher at the online homeschool store many times, but eventually she covered every science topic she could think of and ran out of shit to say.

So in 2012 she decided to write fiction instead. That year she released her first three books and started a career that would make her a New York Times bestseller and land her on the USA Today Bestseller's List twenty-one times in the next five years.

In May 2018 MGM Television bought the TV and film rights for five of her books in the Rook & Ronin and Company series' and in March 2019 they offered her and her writing partner, Johnathan McClain, a script deal to write a pilot for a TV show.

Her books have sold millions of copies all over the world, the audio version of her semi-autobiographical book, Eighteen, was nominated for a Voice Arts Award and an Audie Award in 2016 and 2017 respectively, her audiobook, Mr. Perfect, was nominated for a Voice Arts Award in 2017, and her audiobook, Taking Turns, was nominated for an Audie Award in 2018. In 2019 her book, Total Exposure, was nominated for a Romance Writers of America RITA Award.

Johnathan McClain is her first (and only) writing partner and even though they are worlds apart in just about every way imaginable, it works.

She lives on a ranch in Central Colorado with her family.